STOLEN BABY

BOOKS BY L.G. DAVIS

THE LIES WE TELL SERIES

The New Nanny

The Nanny's Child

BROKEN VOWS SERIES

The Woman at My Wedding

The Missing Bridesmaid

Liar Liar

Perfect Parents

My Husband's Secret

The Missing Widow

The Stolen Breath

Don't Blink

The Midnight Wife

The Janitor's Wife

STOLEN BABY

L.G. DAVIS

bookouture

Published by Bookouture in 2025

An imprint of Storyfire Ltd.
Carmelite House
50 Victoria Embankment
London EC4Y 0DZ

www.bookouture.com

The authorised representative in the EEA is Hachette Ireland
8 Castlecourt Centre
Dublin 15 D15 XTP3
Ireland
(email: info@hbgi.ie)

ISBN: 978-1-83618-203-0
eBook ISBN: 978-1-83618-202-3

PROLOGUE

I'm hanging in mid-air, my legs dangling against the rough edge of the cliff. I can feel the grit beginning to crumble as the ocean below me roars and spits.

One of my shoes slips from my foot, tumbling down into the void. I grind my teeth as terror overwhelms me, my desperation surging. Are these my final moments?

Tears blur my vision, my voice barely a whisper lost in the wind. "Please," I beg, "please help me."

But my plea is met only with cold, hard silence.

How did it come to this? The person I trust most, someone I always believed to be gentle, kind, and loving, stands motionless above me on solid ground. Looking at me as my fingers slip, they shake their head slowly, a look of sadness in their eyes.

My arm muscles tense with all the strength I have left. I can't hold on for much longer. They could still save me, if only they would forgive me.

"I made a mistake," I gasp desperately. "The baby... I'm so sorry. Please don't let me fall."

Above me, a raven caws, its black wings spread wide against the dimming blue of the evening sky.

I don't want to die. I desperately want to live, to be with my daughter, to make the most of every precious day of this little life we all have. To protect her. To keep her safe.

But my hands are losing their battle and the wind whips at my back, urging me to let go, to surrender to the darkness.

ONE
NORA

A dull ache pulses from deep within my chest as I stare at the crackling fireplace. I reach up and, with a quick, almost unconscious motion, pluck a strand of hair from my head and feel a sharp, fleeting sting.

It's been two weeks since my sweet baby girl Danielle died, and my grief is still overwhelming. I try to find something to distract myself and take in the living room, with its tall bookcases and a section dedicated to the children's books I illustrated. There is a large bay window that overlooks our garden, leading into the woods, and I can hear birds softly greeting the dusk.

I glance at a photo on the wall, of the three of us on a family vacation in Miami when my daughter Isobel was eleven, the same year I became Mrs. Nora Swanson. I can almost hear Isobel's laughter, see her running along the beach, her hair flying in the wind. It feels so long ago. When Tom joined our lives, I was foolish enough to believe that the hard times were over. I was no longer a single mom, and the future looked so bright. Until the first miscarriage, then the next, then Danielle.

The door creaks open, revealing Isobel, her long, chestnut

hair falling in loose waves around her face. "Hello, Mom." She smiles as she comes in and sets a tray down on the coffee table. She has brought me a bowl of lentil soup, steam rising upward in delicate tendrils.

Isobel studies my face, her brown eyes showing weariness far beyond her nineteen years. She reminds me so much of her father with curly hair and eyes the color of hazelnuts. Looking at us, it's like watching two seasons coexist side by side—her, the colorful, fiery autumn, and me, the icy, barren winter. I have angular cheek bones, my hair is so light that it's almost white, my eyes a pale, frosty blue. Even my skin is pale no matter how long I lay in the sun. Isobel, however, tans beautifully, her skin turning a lovely honey gold in summer.

She's such a sweet girl, my daughter, and as I watch her, memories flood back to me. Of the two of us all alone in a homeless shelter after my mother died and left me young and pregnant with no money to speak of and all her debt. For years, I had to scrape by on low-paying jobs and government support in order to feed my baby, a baby I didn't think I'd raise on my own.

I had been so sure that Anthony, Isobel's father, and I would spend the rest of our lives together. Until he disappeared, the night I told him I was pregnant.

Fortunately, Isobel hardly asks about him, and when she does, I tell her the truth.

Some of it, anyway.

I thank Isobel and inhale the comforting scent of garlic, cumin and lemon, and she sits beside me, close enough that I can feel the warmth radiating from her skin. "I was thinking, Mom, that we could go out together sometime. You haven't left the house for too long." She takes my hand. "Tom mentioned that there's this clifftop over Gray Peak Beach that offers a beautiful view of the sea. We could go on a gentle hike or drive up there to get you some fresh air."

I used to love hiking, but right now I can't bear the thought of stepping out of the house. I can already see the pitying looks of the locals in our small town of Ellery Creek, Maine, after my third lost pregnancy in two years. I know they'll find out eventually, but I haven't been ready to share the news yet. Those close to us think that the doctor ordered bedrest and that's why I haven't been out for a while.

My mother died when I was sixteen, and my dad a year before that in a car accident. Tom's parents, who left him this house, adopted him late in life and died before he finished college. The few other family members we both have are scattered across the country. So it's really just a secret confined to our little family home. A secret on top of many others.

Having Isobel at sixteen and being judged for it by everyone in this town was the hardest thing I ever faced, and that fear of judgment never really left me.

Isobel leaves me to eat, and a little while later I head upstairs to ask if she wants a cup of tea. But behind her bedroom door, I hear the telltale signs. Muffled retching and sobs, with Isobel's en suite bathroom tap not loud enough to drown them out. A sharp pang of dread hits me. It has been four years since my daughter fought against bulimia and I had hoped never to hear those sounds again.

"Isobel?" My throat feels thick and heavy.

"Mom?" Isobel says when she finally opens the door, her arm wrapped around her middle over her baggy sweater. Guilt claws at me. She must be overwhelmed, not just by the loss of the baby but everything else too—breaking up with her boyfriend around the same time she fell out with her best friend, Lauren, and leaving the apartment she shared with her to move back home a few months ago.

I should have tried harder, even though for the last two weeks, I've been drowning.

I reach out and wrap my arms around her stiff body, pulling

her close in a hug, but our embrace is awkward, our bodies not fitting together like they used to.

"Are you okay?" I ask finally.

"I'm fine, Mom. Just exhausted," she murmurs against my shoulder.

She pulls away before I do. "I'll head to bed now," she says softly.

"Goodnight, Izzy," I whisper to her retreating back.

I make a mental note to add to my to-do list that I need to try and have a proper conversation with her.

I'm usually a loner, but I used to have a close friend, Mary, who lived a few houses down the street. Then she got married and moved to Georgia with her new husband about a year ago, and we haven't really kept in touch much. She was always so helpful with Isobel's fight against her eating disorder in the past. I miss her, and I wonder if she ever thinks about me. But for now, I will have to figure this out on my own. I can't even talk to my husband Tom about it, at least not this evening.

Tom has been up in the attic "sorting things out" since he got home from work, and I'm sure it's because he's actually grieving up there, in his own private space, perhaps sorting through boxes of things we'd put aside for our baby. He is strong, but I don't want to give him even more burdens to carry right now.

Soon he comes down to the kitchen where I'm drinking my tea, and I approach him, hugging him from behind as he ladles himself some of Isobel's soup. My husband is a handsome man and has a certain charm about him that still makes my knees weak. He cares for his appearance and wears his jet-black hair cropped short, his beard meticulously trimmed.

He turns around and wraps an arm around me, pulling me close. His lips brush against my cheek: "I love you. I know you feel lost right now. But I want to give you something to remind you you're not alone."

Out of his jeans pocket, he pulls out a silver compass bracelet. I recognize it—something from our honeymoon in the Canadian Rockies. I misplaced it months ago. He must have found it in the attic.

"Remember when we were hiking and you got lost?" Tom slides the bracelet onto my wrist. "It took me over an hour to find you."

"I was terrified. I thought I'd never find my way back."

"But I found you," Tom says gently. "And then I bought you this. I'll never let you get lost in your grief. I promise, Nora."

Tears well up in my eyes. "You've always known how to find me."

"And I always will."

Our fingers entwine, and we stand there, lost in memories of happier times.

I met Tom, the current Ellery Creek High School principal, at a local community center where I took Isobel for free meals and after-school programs. He was a math teacher at the time and also worked as a volunteer. A tall man with a warm smile and a dimple on his chin, he approached us and after a long conversation, he offered to help me find a job, and a friendship started that quickly turned into something more.

We married a year later in a small ceremony at the local courthouse, with two witnesses and Isobel standing by our side. Tom's love enveloped us, easing the pain of the past and filling our lives with hope.

He quickly became the father figure Isobel never had, always there for school plays and parent–teacher meetings. He loved Isobel as if she were his own daughter, and eventually, my heart healed some and I allowed myself to fall in love with him as well. He was the stability we both needed, the missing piece in our little family puzzle.

I was happy until we decided we wanted to have a child, and after the first miscarriage, my deep desire began to consume me. After the second miscarriage, Tom and I looked into other options. I wanted to adopt, but Tom was set on having a biological child. This led to many arguments as he suggested taking out loans in order to afford a surrogate, while I strongly opposed going into debt, given my experience of struggling financially.

Needless to say, the latest loss hit me really hard. At thirty-five, my biological clock is ticking.

"Remember the way Danielle kicked?" I allow a small smile to touch my lips. "Like she was already dancing to a song only she could hear."

"If she were here, I'd sing to her every night." His voice trembles.

"You would have been amazing with her." I pull in a deep breath and exhale slowly. "She would have been so loved."

The room suddenly feels smaller, as if the walls are pressing closer. I can't help thinking that it's my fault that she didn't make it into this world. That maybe my lies and the secrets I've been keeping poisoned the babies I lost.

My thoughts drift to the article I keep in a small pocket in my purse, an article I've kept since I was sixteen. I will never stop carrying the guilt around with me; I will never let myself forget, no matter how much I wish I could.

But I did what I had to do to protect my daughter.

TWO

A week after I heard Isobel throwing up in her bathroom, I'm back on the couch on another quiet evening, my book untouched beside me. The doorbell rang a few minutes ago and I'm waiting for Tom to go and answer it, but he doesn't.

Then I hear another sound.

A baby, crying.

A rush of urgency hits me as I toss aside the cozy blanket, its knitted strands getting caught on my fingers, the novel I was about to start reading tumbling to the floor. I stride across the wooden floor with my bare feet, feeling the sharp contrast against the still warm couch.

My steps quicken as the sound seems to grow louder. I hurry down the hallway and it feels never-ending. Those wails are urgent now, unmistakable. It's definitely a baby in distress and every cell in my body is compelled to answer its cry.

"Tom!" I call out, my voice cracking. But he doesn't answer.

He came home from work fifteen minutes ago, and it sounds like he's taking a shower. A day spent among sweaty teenagers can leave anyone needing a good scrub.

I don't bother calling Isobel because I know she's not home.

She spent the whole day at the college today, but she called a few minutes ago to say she will be home soon. I wish she would stop worrying about me and instead focus on her studies, so she does not jeopardize her scholarship, but she rushes home every chance she gets.

My hand hovers over the doorknob. Nobody has knocked, nobody has rung the doorbell since that first time.

I spend my days in and out of sleep and constantly dream of crying babies. It would be easy for me to think I'm still asleep, but this sounds so real.

Turning the doorknob, I take a deep breath, bracing myself. The hinges protest with a soft creak as I push the door open and I'm met by the warm glow of sunset that floods the porch.

But then I look down and what I see stops me in my tracks—a basket with a baby inside it, covered in a pink blanket and a small baby bottle next to it.

No one else is here.

The baby's cries have died down, leaving an eerie stillness behind, and a shiver runs down my spine. But then the baby cries again, each wail tugging at my heartstrings.

I move closer, drawn to the basket as if pulled by a thread. "Shh, shh, it's okay," I whisper. The child, so tiny it must be no more than a few hours old, looks so fragile.

"Hey, little one," I murmur softly, lifting the baby with utmost care, feeling the warmth of its body against mine. As the cries subside into soft whimpers, a surge of protectiveness washes over me, fierce and unyielding. It may sound crazy, but it feels as though the baby is destined to be in my arms.

"Hush, little one. It's okay." My lips brush against the baby's soft hair, and I inhale the scent of new life. Again I feel it. There's a profound connection here and it's visceral, a gut-deep certainty that this baby is meant for me, meant for us. As if this baby is my Danielle in another body, a piece of my heart returning to me.

There is a note nestled in the folds of the blanket. My hands shake as I reach for it, unfolding it slowly as I cradle the baby in my arms, looking around me to see if anyone is watching.

The smudged words on the note were clearly scrawled urgently and it sends prickles along my skin: "Her name is Daisy. Please keep her safe."

I drop the note back into the basket, clutching the baby to my chest as I lift the basket in my other hand and carry them inside.

Once the front door is closed, this improbable, impossible situation washes over me and I'm left standing there, frozen.

"Tom!" I call again several times, louder and more desperate this time. The word hangs trembling in the air and I clutch the tiny baby closer.

When Tom finally appears at the top of the stairs and sees me with the baby in my arms, his mouth drops open as he comes down toward us.

"What in the world..." He looks like he is about to pass out, his voice trailing off as he reaches the final step. "Nora, what... Where did—" His voice fades away.

Just as I'm about to respond, a whimper from the baby interrupts the charged silence between us.

My throat tightens as I put down the basket and reach for the note, pressing it into his hand. Tom reads the spidery words, concern and confusion crossing over his face. Then his attention flits between the note and me, before settling on the baby cradled in my arms.

"I don't understand, what does this mean?" he asks, glancing at the piece of paper.

"Someone left this baby... for us." Every fiber of my being is screaming that this child is the baby we lost returned to us, a gift that I need to embrace and protect at all costs.

"But... what? That can't be true." His voice wavers as he scans the room, perhaps hoping to see someone else appear out of nowhere to explain. "I don't get it. Who would do that?"

"I don't know," I say as I make my way to the living room with the baby in my arms and Tom behind me.

My legs are about to give out, so I lower myself onto the couch, holding Daisy in my arms, while Tom sinks into the leather armchair across from me.

As soon as I sit down, the baby begins to squirm and search for a source of food. Her tiny hands grab at my shirt, determined to find what she needs. My heart swells with love and protectiveness as I witness this small creature seeking nourishment and comfort from me as though I were her mother.

Tom runs his fingers through his hair. "Nora, you can't possibly believe that someone would just abandon a baby on our doorstep without any explanation or motive. It's crazy!" His voice reflects both disbelief and agitation.

"But they did. You read the note." I hold on to Daisy tighter, my voice full of emotion. "Tom," I begin, my voice shaking like the light dancing on the walls, "whoever left this baby, and whatever the reason, this is an innocent child. She needs us."

He doesn't respond right away; focused on the baby, his leg bounces with nervous energy.

"Tom?" I urge again.

Finally, he speaks, his tone low and steady. "Honey, we have to think about this carefully."

"Think? What's there to think about?" The longing in my voice lingers in the air. "I think... she's meant to be here. Can't you feel it too? This baby could be our second chance. Of all the other houses in this neighborhood, she was left at our doorstep. It can't just be a coincidence, Tom. There has to be a reason."

He nods slowly, and something in his expression shifts, then he reaches out, gently stroking the baby's cheek with a tenderness that mirrors my own.

He clears his throat and stares at the baby again, his face

softening. He wants it to be true as much as I do. "It's possible," he responds. "But there are complications, legal and moral. What if someone comes searching for her?"

I bite my bottom lip, somehow feeling both scared and excited. The consequences could be big—legal issues, societal judgment, and the unknown past of this baby girl who has entered our lives. But the strong desire to protect her overpowers any doubts I may have.

"Baby, I can't ignore this feeling that she belongs with me... with us." My voice trembles. "But I wonder who her parents are."

Tom puts his hand on mine across the baby, giving it a gentle squeeze. Then he frowns and gets up from his chair, picks up my novel from the floor and places it on the coffee table. "I'm not sure about this, Nora."

"But why? We're not doing anything wrong. Someone left her on our doorstep. They *wanted* us to have her. Look, what if she's in danger and whoever brought her here thinks she's safe with us?" The baby starts whimpering again and I hold her a little tighter. "I have an idea. How about we just keep her for a few days? We could see how it goes and if anyone comes looking for her, we can reconsider then."

Tom is conflicted, the struggle evident on his face, but after a tense silence, he agrees. "Okay, Nora, we'll keep her for now."

I let out a shaky breath, my heart soaring. This may be madness, but it's also the clearest I've been since everything fell apart.

I don't know what lies ahead or what this decision will bring. But as I glance at the baby in my arms, her eyes understanding our secret connection, I know that some things are worth the risk.

I've been depressed for so long and nothing has been able to bring me out of it until now. This is the most alive Tom has seen me in weeks, otherwise he might have put up more of a struggle.

I guess he's afraid if he takes this baby away from me, I'll sink even deeper into that pit of sorrow. And he's right.

Before we can say anything else, headlights from a car shine into our dim living room.

"Isobel," I say and go to the window, watching her getting out of her pink Mini Cooper, her expression unreadable in the dim light.

I turn to Tom, who's fidgeting with his hands. "What are we going to do? What if she doesn't understand?"

"She lives here, Nora. There's no way of keeping this a secret from her."

I hold my breath until, a few minutes later, Isobel enters, her eyes widening at the sight of the baby in my arms.

She looks completely exhausted and rumpled as her hand moves up and down her right arm.

Standing frozen in the doorway, she looks from the baby to Tom and then finally brings her attention to me. The tension in the room is palpable as we wait for her reaction.

After what feels like an eternity, she takes a hesitant step forward, her expression softening as she looks at the baby. "Mom, wha... What's going on?"

"Hey, honey," I say, trying to sound calm. "Look who we found on our doorstep. Someone left her there."

Isobel walks closer, almost tentatively, as if she might disturb the baby with her movements. She looks at the baby and her lips move a little, like she's trying to smile but can't quite do it.

"The poor little thing. Who would leave a baby like this?" She shakes her head slowly. "What are you going to do?"

"Someone who must have been completely desperate. A note was left, asking us to take care of her. Her name is Daisy. We've decided to keep her for a few days to see if anyone comes looking for her."

"Daisy..." There's a tremor in her voice and for a moment

I'm finding it hard to breathe. What if she insists on us contacting the authorities? They'll take Daisy away. And right now, nothing on earth could be more unbearable to me than that.

Tom looks just as nervous as I am as he stands by the mantle, clenching and unclenching his hands.

"Isobel?" I nudge.

"Sorry." Her head shakes slightly again, as if she's trying to clear her thoughts. "It's just a lot to take in, you know?" To my surprise, when Daisy starts crying louder again, Isobel reaches out her arms. "Can I hold her?"

"Sure." I give the baby to her, even though it's a wrench to let her go. She cradles the small bundle in her arms, softly greets and rocks her, causing the crying to stop almost instantly.

"Hi there, little one," she whispers. "Welcome to our home."

THREE

I startle awake in the middle of the night and quickly sit up. For a second, I wonder whether I dreamt everything about Daisy. But then, I hear faint sounds coming from the nursery down the hall. I rush to the room that was supposed to be Danielle's. When I push the door open, I find Isobel sitting in the rocking chair, softly singing a lullaby to Daisy, who's peacefully sleeping in her arms.

The room is warm and cozy, decorated in soft pastel colors. The large white crib stands in the center next to a rocking chair with two soft cushions. A rug with a playful pattern covers the hardwood floor, and a white day bed is tucked against the far wall, a stack of cream and white pillows piled high at one end.

Last night, Isobel offered to be the first to assist with Daisy, just as she would have done with Danielle while I recovered from the birth. I resisted at first—I didn't want to be parted from Daisy, not even for the night—but Isobel seemed happy and energized at the thought, and it was good to see a light back in her eyes again.

We have an extra bed in the nursery, for whoever takes on the night shift when the early newborn nights are long and broken by feeds. If Isobel prefers to sleep in her own room, she can simply wheel the baby crib there. And if Daisy sleeps well and doesn't keep me and Tom awake, we also have a co-sleeper attached to our bed. It's amazing to have two wonderful people to help with Daisy; I remember all too well how exhausting it was to do it all on my own when Isobel was born.

Isobel looks up at me in surprise as I walk in. Daisy fits perfectly in the crook of her arm, as if she was always meant to be there. But as she stands up carefully, I see a tear glistening on her cheek.

"Are you okay, sweetheart?" I whisper.

She hesitates, then looks away. "I was just thinking of Danielle, the little sister I'll never get to meet."

"I know," I say, and stifling my pain, I take Daisy into my arms, feeling her warmth and the gentle rise and fall of her chest as she breathes in her sleep. I hold her close, and her little hand clutches my shirt, while Isobel watches us, a smile playing on her lips.

In that moment I realize the unbearable weight of my sadness has melted away, replaced by a sense of peace I haven't felt for so long.

"I think she is happy here." Isobel reaches out to stroke Daisy's cheek. "It will be so hard to let her go in a few days, Mom."

I don't want to think about it; I can't. I tighten my grip on Daisy, as if by sheer willpower alone I can keep her with us forever.

I know why Isobel didn't insist we take Daisy to the police. She saw it just like Tom and I did. This little baby is a miracle; she brings the possibility of a fresh start for all of us. A gift of hope from the universe. We were all so ready to have a baby, our hearts full of love, our home prepared, and she came to us.

"Tom and I think we should keep her inside for at least a

week," I say. "To see if someone shows up for her; maybe we don't have to get the authorities involved."

"And if not? What if no one comes?"

"We'll keep her. She was brought to us for a reason. Someone wanted us to have her. You saw the note."

"But how will we explain it to everyone, to the neighbors?"

"Well, I haven't left the house in ages. The last time anyone saw me outside, I was pregnant. No one knows yet that I've lost —that it didn't work out."

Isobel pushes a hand through her hair. "So you'll pretend she's your baby?"

I nod, and frown at her. "You haven't told Lauren about Danielle, or anyone else, have you?"

"I didn't. You asked me not to." She pauses. "Anyway, Lauren and I don't talk anymore."

Neither of us speaks for a while. Carrying secrets is not an easy task; nobody knows that better than me.

"I should get back to bed," Isobel says finally, yawning. "Can you take over from here? But if she cries again, I'll be happy to do the next feed as well."

"No, Izzy, you get some rest, you need to take care of yourself. I've got this."

"I really don't mind, Mom," she says quickly and slips out of the room before I have a chance to protest further.

I stand up and lower Daisy, who's still sleeping peacefully, back in her crib.

For a few heartbeats, I watch the little miracle that has brought light back into our lives. While she can never replace Danielle, the new love I feel for her is as powerful and inevitable as the sunrise.

I know, without a doubt, that I simply can't bear to lose this little girl.

FOUR

Tom is frantic when he wakes me up the next morning, pacing back and forth in the room.

"Babe, what's wrong?" I ask and he stops moving around like a battery-operated toy and turns to me.

"Daisy's gone," he says.

"What do you mean she's gone?" My mouth feeling dry, I sit up in bed and panic grips my chest, squeezing the air out of my lungs. How could this happen? I was with Daisy until around 5 a.m. this morning when Isobel, who said she couldn't sleep, came back to take another shift. When I left to go back to our room, Daisy had just finished a feed and was sleeping again in her crib, while Isobel read a book in the bed by her side.

Tom's face is pale as he explains that he found her crib empty in the nursery just now.

"Where's Isobel? She slept in the room with her. She must have taken—"

"No, she has lectures today, she's not home. She must be in Amberfield by now. She was supposed to bring the baby to our room before leaving, remember? She wouldn't take Daisy to her classes."

Amberfield is less than an hour away from Ellery Creek, and Isobel used to stay there in a small apartment we bought for her, sharing it with her best friend, Lauren, a girl who was born and raised in this town. They've known each other since Isobel was twelve, but they had a fall out so huge that Isobel moved back in with us, preferring to commute instead for lectures, although it isn't every day as the college has a great platform for online studying.

I throw back the covers and rush out of bed. "Are you sure? Let me go look."

"Nora." Tom grabs hold of my hand. "Of course I'm sure. She's not there. I looked everywhere. And it's not as if she can move around herself and hide."

I run out of the room anyway, my bare feet pattering against the floors as I head toward the nursery. The door creaks open and I see it for myself—the empty crib. No sign of Daisy.

When I look back at the door, Tom is standing there, his face pale, then he crosses the room and walks toward me, putting both arms on my shoulders. "There's only one explanation," he says in a deep murmur. "Isobel must have taken her. What if she took her to the police station?"

"She wouldn't do that. She agreed with us, Tom. She was on board that we could keep her, at least for a while. I'll call her."

"I already tried. Her phone is switched off." His hands fall from my shoulders.

"Well, maybe she switched it back on now." My fingers tremble as I rush back to our room and dial Isobel's number from my phone, my anxiety amplifying with each ring. But Tom is right. I try again and again, but it goes straight to voicemail each time. Dropping the phone onto the bed, I cover my face with both hands and sink down next to it.

"What are we going to do if she really did take Daisy to the cops?"

"I don't know." Tom glances at his watch. "There's nothing we can do for now; we just have to stay calm. I need to get to work, keep going as normal, but I'll give Robert a call, see if he knows something."

Robert is Tom's friend; they play tennis together. He's also a detective with the local police department.

"Wait, you'll tell him what we were doing, what we were going to do? You can't do that."

"No, I'll just ask him if there have been any new interesting cases they're working on."

"Okay." I pause. "Tom, I keep wondering who Daisy's parents are. Will they get her back now, do you think?"

"Does it really matter who they are at this point, Nora? The fact is, whoever they are, they abandoned her. They don't want her. I very much doubt she will be returned to them."

"You're right." I massage the bridge of my nose. "What matters is that we want her. We want her so much, and we would give her everything."

Tom attempts a weak smile and kisses me on the forehead before he heads to the door, pausing before walking out. "We'll get her back, baby. I promise."

As soon as he leaves, I go back to the nursery, staring at the empty crib as if willing Daisy to magically appear. I drop into the rocking chair, trying to calm my troubled mind.

I've only known Daisy for a few hours, but it feels like an eternity. It is so cruel after everything I've been through. I held her in my arms, felt the overwhelming joy of motherhood, only for it to be snatched away so soon. Would Isobel really take her away just like that? Did she think she was doing the right thing? What will happen to Daisy now?

Suddenly the sound of a car pulling into the driveway startles me from my racing thoughts and I rush to the window, hoping beyond hope that it's Isobel's car, and thank God, it is.

My stomach twists as I sprint to the front door, flinging it open with shaking hands.

"Isobel, where's Daisy?" I blurt out as she steps out of the car.

Isobel's eyes flicker with something I can't read, and for the smallest moment I think she might be angry with me. But then she's calm, and her smile is gentle and unguarded.

"I took her out for a quick drive," she says casually. "She woke up early and she wouldn't stop crying, so I thought the movement of the car might soothe her."

I yank open the backdoor. Daisy is there, sleeping inside a car seat, another one of the things that would have belonged to Danielle. I immediately unbuckle her and scoop her into my arms. She stirs a little, but she doesn't wake up. Her tiny hands curl into fists, her rosy cheeks flushed with sleep. I hold her close, feeling her warmth seep into my bones, grounding me in this moment of chaos. Then I hurry back into the house, with Isobel closing the door slowly behind us.

"Why? Why did you do that, Isobel?" I snap at my daughter, my voice rising with each word. "Do you have any idea how worried we've been?"

Isobel's expression hardens, her proud jaw jutting out. "Oh, come on, Mom," she retorts, her tone bordering on defensive. "She's fine. I just wanted to help soothe her, and you and Tom were sleeping. I decided to miss my lectures today so I could help look after her, and I couldn't concentrate on anything now anyway, not with all of this going on. Can't you just be glad I'm helping out?"

I struggle to contain my frustration. Of course I'm relieved that Daisy is safe and sound. But I can't shake the worry that festers at my core.

"What if someone saw you? What if they start asking questions?"

"I thought we had a story ready?" she says. "That Daisy is your newborn baby. We're not hiding her, are we?"

I shake my head. "It's just that... Isobel, you can't just take her out without letting me know. You could at least have left me a note or sent a text or something."

"You're right. I'm sorry, Mom." She runs a hand through her hair. "I just didn't think it would be a problem. She was still awake driving in the car so we went for a quick stroll in the park and then we came straight home. I didn't think it would be a problem. I thought you'd know I had her."

I sigh, my anger melting away in the face of Isobel's sincerity. "Just let me know next time."

Isobel nods, and as I carry Daisy to the kitchen, I'm hit by a paranoid thought. Surely Isobel would have known better than to take Daisy without leaving so much as a note or a message? Was it really a mistake, or did she worry I would be reluctant to let Daisy be seen in public so soon? Now she's been seen in the neighborhood, there's no way back. We can't change our minds, give her up and pretend we hadn't kept her for days already. Not that we were going to, but perhaps Isobel wanted to make absolutely sure?

I know my daughter, and I can see she loves this baby just as much as I do.

I also know how clever and determined she is.

After I've called Tom to let him know that Daisy is here, Isobel and I sit at the table, eating breakfast with the baby safe and cozy in a sling around my chest.

With her rosy cheeks and a peaceful expression, she seems content as I sway her gently and kiss the top of her head. Her tiny hands occasionally curl into little fists as she stirs, her soft, warm breath tickling my skin.

She's awake and her wide but still unfocused eyes dart

around as if she's seeing all the pieces that make up the world for the first time. Occasionally, she lets out a gentle gurgle or a tiny sigh. A few weeks from now, she will be able to smile and laugh and I cannot wait to discover the things that bring her joy.

I sigh as I take in the space around me, appreciating everything anew as if I've just regained my sight. Unlike Tom, I'm not much of a cook even though I like watching cooking shows, but this kitchen always brings me a sense of calm. The antique copper pots and pans—passed down through Tom's family—hanging over the stove, the fresh herbs growing in pots on the windowsill, and the sweet scent of roses that wafts in from the garden outside make this space feel warm and welcoming. I love the way sunlight streams through the stained-glass window above the sink, touching the worn wooden countertops.

I'm utterly relaxed and content, until the shrill ring of the doorbell shatters the calm of my home.

"I'll get it." As the bell rings one more time, I carefully remove Daisy from the sling and place her in Isobel's arms before hurrying to the front door.

When I open it, my stomach drops at the sight of one of our neighbors, Martha Harris, standing on the doorstep, her arms laden with sunflowers. Martha is in her late forties with neat, graying hair. She used to work at one of the local bakeries until the owner died and it closed down a few years ago. Now, since she has not been able to find another job, she spends her days gossiping and tending to her garden, or watching the world go by from her porch. She keeps tabs on everyone around.

"Good morning, Nora!" she says, her voice bright and cheery. "I saw Isobel with your newborn earlier and couldn't resist stopping by to congratulate you!" she chirps, thrusting the flowers into my hands. She leans in and whispers, "Some people were worried you wouldn't be able to carry a baby to term this time either. Not me, though. I believe in miracles."

I struggle to find the right words. But before I can even open my mouth, Martha is already pushing past me.

"I really had no idea you had given birth! Why didn't you tell us? When did it happen? And where's the little one?" she asks, glancing in the direction of the stairs. "What's their name?"

"It all happened very fast. She's called Daisy, and I'm sorry, but right now she's sleeping. Thank you so much for the flowers, Martha. It's so sweet of you to stop by."

Martha's smile falters for a moment before she regains her composure. "Oh, of course! We wouldn't want to wake baby Daisy now, would we? Well, I'll just have to see her another time then. I can't wait to tell everyone on the street! This is such wonderful news, Nora."

"Actually, Martha"—I force a smile—"we would appreciate it if you didn't tell everyone she has arrived just yet because, well, we are still adjusting to everything. We would rather keep it quiet for now. We're not really ready to welcome visitors."

A flicker of disappointment crosses her face before she quickly plasters on a veneer of understanding.

"Of course, of course." She lets out a chuckle. "I completely understand. Your secret is safe with me. We women are good at keeping secrets, aren't we, Nora?"

FIVE

After Martha leaves, I decide to do some tidying up in our bedroom, but find myself distracted, staring at my collection of sneakers in the closet with Daisy cradled against my chest.

My beloved sneakers, all kinds of them, are lined up against the closet wall, each marking a moment in my life. Some are fancy with intricate patterns and thick soles, some old and worn out, the kind of shoes I'd thrown on when running errands, participating in one of the town's marathons, or going on an impromptu bike ride with Tom.

I bring my lips to Daisy's ear and whisper, "Can you see those blue ones with the stripes, Daisy? I wore them to my first date with Tom... your daddy. And those white leather ones with shiny studs and gold laces? They were for our wedding day."

That's right. I love sneakers so much that I wore them on my wedding day instead of fancy heels. I associate them with both comfort and empowerment; they're the only kind of "fashion" I care about.

As Daisy makes a gurgling sound, I take a deep breath and make myself look squarely at the bright-red pair that caught my eye and interrupted me in the middle of my tidying. They're new, untouched, and sitting pristine in the corner. Tom bought them for me the day after we found out I was pregnant with Danielle and I decided to save them for after her birth, perhaps to mark my first walk around the neighborhood with her.

I look down at Daisy, her eyes blinking up at me. "Your daddy made fun of me when we just met. He said when I wear sneakers, it seems like I'm always getting ready to run." At the time, I had laughed it off, but maybe he wasn't too far from the truth. My obsession with sneakers started after my mother died, the day that changed me forever.

I take one step toward the shoes and that's when I hear a soft creak behind me. Isobel is standing there, watching us. I didn't even notice her come in. Without a word, she walks over and picks up the new pair of sneakers, holding them out to me.

"Come for a walk with me," she says quietly, her voice low but insistent. "To that cliff I told you about. It's beautiful. You need to get out, Mom. You've been stuck in this house for too long."

I shake my head, already feeling my chest tighten. "I... I can't, Isobel. Daisy—"

"We'll take Daisy with us," she interrupts and her tone is firm but gentle. "You can't keep hiding from the world, Mom. You used to love walking, remember? And biking... all that outdoorsy stuff. You loved the fresh air. You need to break this cycle of being stuck indoors."

She places the sneakers in my hand.

"It'll be good for Daisy too," Isobel adds, glancing at her baby sister. "She needs fresh air and to experience different environments."

From the determined look on her face, I know she's not going to take no for an answer. With a heavy sigh, I look down at the sneakers, observing the intricate red stitchwork, my fingers toying with the laces. "All right. Give me a few minutes to change."

About forty minutes later, we're at the top of the cliff. The wind is relentless up here, sweeping through the sparse grass with a low, constant roar, and tugging at my hair and clothes.

It feels much colder than I expected for an April day, so I pull the edges of my light leather jacket tighter around me, even though I'm also wearing a navy fleece-lined sweater underneath.

Isobel is walking next to me, with Daisy strapped to her chest in the sling. She's wearing an olive-green parka, zipped up, and a knitted beanie to keep her hair from whipping around in the wind. Daisy is snug, bundled up in a tiny fleece onesie and a knitted hat with little bear ears. Her little hands are curled into fists, poking out from the sleeves, and her legs occasionally kick out, jabbing at Isobel's sides. She doesn't seem bothered by the cool wind, just quietly taking it all in. Every now and then, a soft coo or gurgle escapes her.

As we wander, we come across a bench nestled between rocks, offering some protection from the wind but still granting an unobstructed view of the sea. The ocean stretches out before us, powerful and untamable, with waves crashing against the rocky shore below. Above, the sky is a muted, steel gray, with clouds gathering in the distance, foreshadowing rain.

I sit down on the cold bench, feeling its chill seep through my jeans as I gaze at the horizon. Daisy kicks again and this time her little foot comes into contact with my side since I'm sitting quite close to Isobel. She's so new to the world, only just out of the womb, and her little movements remind me strongly of the sensations I had from Danielle as she grew inside me.

"Do you ever think about him?" Isobel asks suddenly, her voice almost lost to the wind.

I look at her, startled. "Who?"

"My father." Her eyes stay fixed on the horizon.

A cold knot tightens in my stomach. For years, I've skirted around the subject of Anthony. Isobel has never asked many questions, and I thought that meant she was content with the little I have told her.

"It's better to let the dead rest in peace," I say finally, my voice tight.

Isobel stiffens, then slowly, she turns to face me. "What? He's dead? You never told me that. You said... you said he just left."

I flinch. Damn it. What have I just done? As I think of what to say next, I instinctively reach for a piece of hair on my scalp and pull it out, flinching at the sharp sting.

"I'm sorry, I didn't mean it like that. It's just been so many years, Izzy. He could be dead, and I guess I've just come to think of him that way." I stand up abruptly, my legs shaky as I start walking again, desperate to avoid this conversation.

But Isobel won't let it go. She's on her feet in an instant, following me, her steps quick and purposeful. "What are you hiding from me?" she snaps, her voice rising above the wind. "You think I don't see it? The way you shut down whenever I ask about him? The way you avoid the topic like it's some secret? Why can't you just be open with me? I deserve to know the truth. It's my dad."

I stop in my tracks and whirl around to face her, my chest heaving with frustration. "Some things are better left in the past, Isobel. They aren't worth digging up."

"Maybe not for you," she retorts. "But I'm his daughter. I have a right to know who my father was. Everyone deserves to know who their parents are."

Her words hit me like a slap, and for a moment, I can't breathe.

Then I turn a little too fast and the next thing I know, I

stumble over a rock in the path, right on the cliff edge. Isobel screams, “Mom!” but she’s too late, I’m falling.

It all happens so fast.

SIX

I'm writing my daily morning list and sipping some water when I hear Daisy stir in the co-sleeper next to me. Even though she just woke up, her eyes are wide and bright and her lips are slightly curled in what looks like a smile. I know it's just a reflex at this stage, but it's enough to make me smile right back. Her hands wave gently in the air, her fingers curling and uncurling as if she's discovering the simple joy of movement.

Soon my thoughts go back to Isobel and our conversation yesterday, walking along the cliff. When I fell over, so dangerously close to the cliff edge, our difficult conversation ended abruptly. Isobel hurried toward me, and we hugged each other, Daisy sandwiched between us, adrenaline and relief releasing from our bodies in gasps and wild giggles.

But I know our conversation isn't really over, and if she finds out what I'm hiding, I will lose everything.

The fear that these precious moments with Daisy could also be snatched away makes me feel faint, as if the oxygen has drained from the room.

In an attempt to stop the downward spiral, I begin to sing

softly, a song my grandmother used to sing to me when I was little, replacing my name with Daisy's.

"Good morning, little Daisy, the day's come to play, with sunshine and laughter to brighten your way."

As soon as the words leave my lips, her eyes follow the sound of my voice and her lips part as if she wants to respond to my song.

Finishing the tune, I notice her squirming and I lift her out of the co-sleeper; she needs a diaper change. With her still gazing up at me with those trusting eyes, I carry her through to the nursery. As I lower her onto the changing table and kiss her nose, I begin to sing the same song again, telling myself to focus on the here and now, not my fears of the future.

Finally, we head down to the kitchen and I make her bottle before going back to the nursery to feed her there, because it's just so peaceful in that room.

Only when Daisy is all fed, do I move to the window and pull back the curtain. Outside, the world carries on. Martha is already up, chatting animatedly with Mrs. Lewis over the fence while Mr. Drews tends to his garden, his weathered hands expertly pruning his roses with a sense of calm I wish I could borrow. The sunlight filters through the leaves of the willow tree, casting dancing shadows on the grass below.

I should feel reassured by the scene outside, by the normalcy of it all, my quiet suburban street. But instead, a shiver runs down my spine. I'm sure by now Martha has broken her promise and spread the word. We have to introduce Daisy to everyone soon anyway, but what if Martha somehow discovers that Daisy is not mine? Did someone see her being left on my porch?

I have managed to keep one secret to myself all these years, but what if I fail to keep two? After all, it only takes one slip—like what happened yesterday on the cliff—one careless word, for the surface to crack and the truth to come tumbling out.

As Daisy stirs against my chest, I almost can't breathe, and when I hear a movement behind me, I turn my head so fast a sharp pain shoots through my neck.

Isobel is standing in the doorway, wearing a pair of pink satin pajamas with white polka dots, her hair a wild tangle of strands that escaped the confines of the messy top bun she likes to wear around the house.

"Mom? Are you okay?" She glances down at Daisy in my arms. She's exuding so much warmth and kindness today, so different from the girl that confronted me on the cliff yesterday. I'm just glad she dropped the questions about her father and my past, for now. The entire rest of the day yesterday, it was almost as though she had never even brought up the topic.

I force a weak smile onto my lips. "I'm fine, sweetheart." The lie comes easy, but I can see she doesn't believe a word I'm saying even though she nods.

"Are you sure? You don't look well." She takes a step closer and reaches out to touch my arm. "Did something happen?"

The warmth of her touch grounds me and I force myself to meet her eyes, to appear calm and collected.

"Nothing happened. I was just... I'm just tired. I didn't sleep well last night." I don't mention that replaying our conversation over and over kept me awake far into the night.

Isobel studies me for a moment longer and doesn't look convinced at all, but she doesn't press the issue. Instead, she gently takes Daisy from my arms.

"Here, let me hold her." Her voice is soothing as she cradles Daisy against her chest, then places her back in her crib, as skillfully as if she's done it many times before. Like Daisy was made for her arms.

She finally turns back to me, her brow furrowed. "Mom, you can't be fine. You're shaking."

I wrap my arms around myself, trying to quell the shivers.

"I'm worried, that's all. That someone might find out that Daisy isn't really my baby."

"Well, you don't have to worry about that." She glances in the direction of the window. "No one will know anything unless we tell them, remember? Everything's fine."

Everything's fine. All I can think as I tighten my arms around my body and continue to look out of the window nervously is that my OBGYN told me the same thing during my pregnancy with Danielle. The checkups showed a healthy baby, and I believed everything would be all right this time. But it was all a lie. Both the doctor and the machines were wrong.

In my world, "fine" is just something we say to make ourselves feel better. A mask we wear to hide what's really going on underneath.

"Yes, I know," I say, but I can't keep my hands still as I push back my sweat-dampened hair.

"Mom"—Isobel reaches for her phone, which is tucked into the pocket of her pajama top—"I'm calling Tom."

"No. Don't," I say quickly.

I really don't want him worrying about my state of mind. What if he thinks I'm not strong enough to handle this and decides to take Daisy to the authorities?

But Isobel doesn't hesitate. She dials the number, and I watch helplessly as she holds the phone to her ear, her voice steady as she speaks to her stepfather.

"Tom, Mom's not in a good way, I think she might be close to having a panic attack." Isobel listens for a few seconds, then holds out the phone to me. "He wants to talk to you."

I hesitate for a moment, then reach for the phone. "Tom?" I whisper, turning away from Isobel and walking back to the window.

"Hey, honey." His voice is steady and reassuring on the other end of the line. "Are you okay?"

"I'm fine." I wipe my wet cheeks and force a smile. "I was

just a little worried about Daisy, and what's going to happen to us all. But I'm okay now."

"Are you sure? You don't sound it. Should I come home at lunch?"

Lately Tom has been coming home sometimes at lunchtime to check up on me. But now Daisy is here, I want things to change. I have to prove to him that I can handle this.

"No, Tom, it's not necessary." I try to keep my voice steady. "I'm fine, really. Just needed a moment. You stay at work. Everything's under control here. And Isobel doesn't have lectures today, so she'll be home. I promise, we'll be okay."

There's a beat of silence on the other end of the line, and I hold my breath. "All right, if you're sure. But don't hesitate to call me if you need anything, okay? Anything at all."

"I will. Thank you, babe," I say softly, before ending the call and handing the phone back to Isobel.

I'm a little annoyed when Isobel sticks around as I spend time with Daisy, as if she's worried I might break down at any moment. But her presence is also comforting; I'm glad not to be alone and she has such a knack with Daisy, her face lighting up every time she holds her.

After a while, she insists that she should take Daisy so I can get some rest. At first, I hesitate but her gentle insistence wears me down, and I finally agree. I know it's important I get regular breaks and rest, as I'm determined to keep my mental health in check. And as she leaves the room with Daisy in her arms, I decide to do something I haven't done in a while.

I go to my study, ready to start drawing again. The walls are decorated with framed covers of books I illustrated, a gallery of my past accomplishments. I sit in the chair at the desk and run my fingers over an incomplete piece I started before Danielle died. It's a whimsical landscape scene featuring woodland creatures. I pick up a pencil, its familiar weight comforting, and with each stroke, I pour my fears and anxieties onto the page. I try not to think about it too much; I just let go and draw.

But after a short while, what I've produced depresses me; it's just a chaotic swirl of unsettling shades. Darkness and confusion spread across the page, a reflection of the tangled mess inside me. Frustrated, I tear at the paper, shredding it to pieces.

Then a new idea forms, like light breaking through clouds. Daisy. Her room needs something special, something that's just for her. Inspired, I clear the shredded remnants from the desk and pull out a fresh sheet of paper.

My hand moves before I fully realize what I'm doing, sketching the outline of a baby rabbit, its ears drooping and eyes wide with confusion. Lost and alone. The idea comes suddenly, gripping me, and I begin to shape the story through my lines and strokes. A little baby rabbit, wandering the woods, searching for her mother. But she is nowhere to be found, though she looks everywhere, beneath the trees, among the brambles... everywhere. I sketch the rabbit's soft fur, making it delicate and vulnerable to contrast against the roughness of the woods.

Then I add another figure, a larger rabbit—a mother, but not her mother. This one finds the lost baby rabbit and leads her into a warm, hidden burrow. The scene tugs at something inside me and the strokes of my pencil grow more deliberate now, more tender. The mother rabbit takes the little one in, cradles her, offering warmth and comfort.

I'm at peace as I draw, shaping the scene not out of fear or guilt this time, but out of love. The baby rabbit is cared for, nestled in the arms of her new mother. Each stroke of my pencil adds more depth to the story. The two rabbits playing, hopping around their cozy den, sunlight filtering through the trees.

I imagine Daisy staring up at these scenes from her crib, her bright little eyes soaking it all in. As I work, a smile spreads across my face, and I feel a rare sense of peace. But in my enthusiasm, I make a sudden, sweeping gesture and my hand knocks over a small jar of red paint. It crashes to the floor, splattering everywhere. The crimson liquid spreads out, pooling and staining the floor, and for a moment, it looks like blood.

My smile falters and I freeze as I stare at the red stains, the way they seep into the crevices of the wooden floor. Just like that, the secrets I've been hiding, the choices I've made, all come rushing back.

The joy I felt moments ago evaporates.

My secrets are doing everything they can to strangle me, and I'm more convinced now than ever that, one day, the truth will come out. Then I will lose everything. Isobel, Tom, and now Daisy too.

I lift my hands in front of my face and, in my mind's eye, I see them gripping the cold iron bars of a prison cell, the unforgiving metal biting into my skin.

SEVEN

The warm water caresses Daisy's delicate skin, droplets beading and mingling with the soft tufts of her dark hair. Trying not to think about the red ink I spilled last night, I cradle her tiny slippery form in my hands, amazed at how perfectly she fits there, as if she was always meant to be mine.

I gently pour water over her and when she releases a sweet little cough, it reminds me that she's due for her first newborn checkup at the doctor right about now. I'm not her mother on paper, so walking into a doctor's office at this point would be too risky. But what if she falls sick? What would we do then?

"That's not going to happen, right, little D? You are strong and healthy," I whisper into her ear. I inhale deeply and allow the fresh and soothing scent of lavender baby wash to clear my mind for just a little while. There is a deep and uncomplicated joy in this moment—the joy of tending to a newborn, the delightful sensation of skin against skin, the intimate bond between mother and child.

"Hey," I whisper, running a cloth gently over her belly. "It's just you and me, Daisy girl." Her eyes lock onto mine, deep pools reflecting a trust so complete it stirs something deep within me. From a distance, I hear cars whizzing by, a dog barking, and the muffled hum of a lawnmower. But in the soft cocoon of the bathroom, all that fades away into nothingness. It's just Daisy and me. I focus on each little toe, each finger, committing every detail to memory, just in case.

No, I will not think about that. She's here and that's not going to change.

"Mom?"

I startle at Isobel's voice, and swiveling around, I see her leaning against the doorframe, wearing scuffed, black jeans and her backpack slung over one shoulder. I'm reminded of when she was as little as Daisy and I would brush her damp curls back from her face after her bath, before tucking her into bed with a story.

"Isobel." I smile. "You're home early."

She shrugs, a curtain of brown hair falling forward. "My last class got canceled. Professor came down with something."

"Ah." I turn back to Daisy, willing my hands to be steady as they resume their gentle task. I feel Isobel watching me.

"Hello, Daisy girl." She drops her backpack to the floor and steps into the bathroom. Then she leans over the tub, brushing a kiss on Daisy's forehead, and for a moment, I expect her to retreat, to leave me to this soothing ritual. But instead, she lingers.

"Mom, you should really support her head more... like this." Her hand guides mine, correcting my hold. "And be careful around her eyes."

"Isobel, I know how to give my own baby a bath," I say, sharper than I intend. "I've done it before."

"Your baby," she repeats quietly, then shrugs. "Yeah, of course, Mom." She steps back, but still continues to hover in the doorway. The silence between us stretches, filled only by the soft sounds of water splashing against ceramic and Daisy's babbling.

I can feel Isobel's hesitation, as if she's expecting me to mess up somehow.

But I won't—not now. Not ever again. Daisy depends on me to stay steady and strong.

The memory of yesterday's panic attack claws at the edges of my consciousness. But that was just a blip, I won't let it knock my confidence as a mother to this little one.

"She slept through last night," I say to Isobel to get the conversation going again. "Five whole hours." Last night, while feeding and then reading to Daisy, I fell asleep and ended up sleeping in the nursery with her.

"Actually, no, she woke up once. I woke up to go to the bathroom when I heard her crying, so I took care of it. You were sleeping so deep you didn't hear her."

"Why didn't you wake me?"

Isobel shrugs, her face impassive. "You seemed tired last night. I wanted you to sleep."

"Isobel, I—" My voice catches. I want to reassure her, to swear that I am capable of taking care of Daisy on my own. But the words dissolve like bubbles in the bathwater. To be honest, I can understand her concern, after seeing me broken time and time again.

With my arms holding on to her small frame, Daisy remains relaxed and peaceful, but her small fingers flex every few seconds as she gets used to the warm water.

"Are you sure you don't need my help? I can dress her if you like."

"Isobel, I'm fine. I've got this. There's no need for you to hover."

She doesn't react to my snappy tone. "Just making sure everything's okay."

"Really, I'm fine," I insist, the warmth from the bathwater suddenly feeling suffocating. "You can stop treating me like I'm on the verge of shattering."

Isobel's face briefly betrays a flicker of hurt or frustration before she composes herself and nods. She doesn't say anything else as she turns on her heels and leaves. The bathroom door clicks as it closes behind her, leaving me alone with my sharp words lingering in the air.

I exhale slowly and focus again. "Sorry, Daisy. Mommy didn't mean to raise her voice."

I finally lift her from the bath, wrapping her in a plush, pink towel, her tiny, wet toes wriggling in the folds. Then I nestle her to me and pad softly through the hallway to the nursery where I lay her down on the changing table. Her eyes are drowsy now and it won't be long before she takes a nap.

When I'm done putting her in a diaper and a onesie with the slogan "I stay up all night and sleep all day" printed on the front, I step out of the nursery with her in my arms and approach Isobel's door. I pause for a moment, then knock softly, almost hoping she won't ask me to come in.

"Isobel? Can we talk?" The door is open a fraction, so I push it open slowly.

My daughter is sitting on her bed, reading a book in her lap. She doesn't look up as I enter, but I can sense the tension in her shoulders.

I remember when we first moved in with Tom. The pride in his eyes as he showed us the room he had prepared for her—pale-pink walls with delicate stencils of flowers, a four-poster bed fit for a princess, and a cream carpet that swallowed your feet whole. He had gone above and beyond to welcome us, to make his stepdaughter feel special and at home.

At that point, Isobel had already outgrown the color pink, but she had been so excited as she skipped into the room. To this day, she refuses to let us change anything in the room, holding on to one of the happiest days of her life. A lot of boxes are still yet to be unpacked from when she moved back home, after the fall-out with Lauren.

"I'm sorry, Izzy. I didn't mean to snap at you earlier. It's just... I'm still getting used to everything."

"Uh-huh." Her voice is flat, eyes still downcast.

"You don't have to worry. Daisy's safe with me." I glance down; her eyes have almost drifted shut. I need Isobel to believe what I'm saying, to see my strength, my capability. "I've done this before, remember?"

"Of course." She finally looks at me, her eyes skimming over my face before darting away. There's something unsaid swirling in their depths.

"Sweetheart," I continue, "I'll be careful. I know I haven't been well lately, but I would never let her down or allow her to get hurt."

Isobel waits for a moment before she closes the book in her lap with a soft thud. "Mom, sometimes people do terrible things without meaning to."

Her words settle onto my skin, cold and heavy, and I take a step back.

"What's that supposed to mean?"

She flicks her wrist. "Nothing, Mom. It's nothing."

"Isobel—" But she's already dismissing me, shutting me out and I retreat, holding Daisy tighter than before.

This isn't like her at all. My daughter is the most compassionate person I know, always quick to forgive and forget. But would she forgive me, if she knew everything?

Ignoring that nagging question, I enter my own bedroom and settle Daisy in her co-sleeper, then perch on the edge of our bed. The walls of our bedroom are painted a soothing shade of sage green. Large windows with sheer white curtains allow the natural sunlight to filter in, and at night, they offer a glimpse of the stars. Our bed, covered in a cozy quilted duvet in calming earth tones, is the focal point and it's accented by pillows of varying sizes and textures. Tucked in one corner is a reading nook where an armchair upholstered in deep forest green fabric stands next to a bookshelf stocked with my favorite novels and poetry collections.

Standing nearby is a tall floor lamp for late-night reading sessions. My gaze moves to the hand-knitted cream blanket created by Isobel in her last year of high school. Draped over the arm of the armchair, it adds a touch of warmth. The reading corner reminds me that I still haven't started reading the book on my nightstand. *Returning to Green Mountain* is a typical romantic comedy about a middle-aged woman who's fired from her job as a corporate lawyer in Manhattan and moves back home to her small, quirky hometown in Vermont where she ends up falling for the local carpenter. The book's predictability and familiarity would be comforting and would keep me from getting lost in my thoughts. I have to start it tomorrow.

I look down at Daisy, taking in the delicate features of her face, the gentle rise and fall of her chest with each breath. She's so fragile, so trusting.

Then the spacious room feels small suddenly and the air too thin. I can't catch my breath and my panic is overwhelming. I try to fight it but it's like being trapped in chains. I struggle to keep from shaking.

It's that question, the one that floated to the surface of my mind just now.

What if my daughter has already found out who I really am, what I did?

EIGHT

The rich smell of bacon and eggs invades my sleep before the clink of a plate on the nightstand fully rouses me awake. I blink against the morning light that spills through the curtains, disoriented for a heartbeat before Tom's face comes into focus, a soft smile playing at the corners of his mouth.

From the tray, he picks up a glass of lemon water and hands it to me. "Thought you could use a good start today." Even though his eyes are tired, they hold a warmth that melts away the remnants of my nightmares.

Taking a sip of the water, I glance at the empty co-sleeper. "Where's Daisy?"

"She's with Isobel in the nursery. I want you to sleep in and take it easy."

"Thank you." I put down the glass again and push myself up against the headboard, grateful for his concern. He knows me so well, and my life lately has been a brutal fight against fears, both real and imagined. And it's exhausting.

He leans in to press a quick kiss to my forehead before standing. "I've got to head out. Lots of meetings today. Eat up. I'll try not to be late home."

I nod, watching him stride out of the room.

I manage to eat a few bites of breakfast, then I set the tray aside and slip out of the warmth of the bed, padding across the floor to the bathroom. I miss Daisy and want nothing more than to go to her immediately, but I know I also need to take care of myself. The mirror greets me with the reflection of a woman who is evidently still hanging by a thread, her wispy shoulder-length hair falling limply around her face. I've always been on the pale side, but now my cheeks are almost translucent.

I decide to take a shower, only the second one this week. It's been days, no—weeks, since I've made any attempt to keep up appearances, and now I must assure Tom and Isobel, and myself, that I'm all right.

Stepping into the shower, I twist the handle to turn on the water. Slowly, steam starts to rise and fill the room, fogging up the large mirror that takes up most of the wall above the sink. The sound of the shower blocks out all other noise, and for a brief moment, I feel completely enclosed in my own little world.

As the water cascades down, I listen intently for the baby monitor that I brought with me into the bathroom to crackle. There's no video, it's sound only and right now the only thing I hear is water. Daisy and Isobel must be sleeping.

As I scrub and rinse myself off, I imagine the water cleansing away more than just the physical grime. I also wash away the guilt, the fear, and the secrets that cling to my skin. Moving on to my hair, I work the conditioning shampoo through the strands and memories flood back of how thick and lustrous it used to be, how Tom loved to run his fingers through it.

Feeling clean and refreshed, I turn the water off and step out of the shower onto the soft bathmat, and as I reach for the towel, a small smile spreads across my face. Despite everything, I'm still here, still fighting, still breathing. I will become strong again. Strong enough for Daisy, for Isobel, for Tom. For our precious little family, my world.

Towel wrapped snugly around me, I head out of the room to check on Daisy and Isobel.

But no one is there. Once again, the crib is empty.

I know Isobel was looking after Daisy, though. I shouldn't panic. She's probably just in her room or downstairs. But still I hurry to Isobel's room, pushing the door with more force than intended. It creaks open to reveal an untidy bed and scattered clothes, but no trace of her or Daisy.

Back in the hallway, I glance out of one of the windows. The driveway is empty. Isobel's Mini Cooper is gone, and I'm immediately furious. How could she do this to me again?

"Stay calm," I instruct myself and rush back to our bedroom to grab my phone from the nightstand. But she hasn't texted me, she hasn't tried to call. My fingers tremble as I dial her number.

"Mom?" Isobel's voice is casual, way too casual.

"Where are you?" My words are clipped, the annoyance surging like electricity through my veins. "Is Daisy with you?"

"Oh, yes, we just went to grab some stuff from the bakery. We'll be back soon. I got you your favorite donuts from Sweet Delights. The maple glazed ones." Isobel's nonchalance only fuels my rage. What is she playing at?

"Isobel, we talked about this—" I start, then pause as I hear Daisy coughing. "You can't keep taking her out without telling me. It's not okay. Why didn't you message me?"

"Really, Mom, you worry too much. We'll be home before you know it."

"Okay." I squeeze my nails into my palms. "What's done is done. Just... come home soon, please."

"Will do. See you soon." She hangs up, and I'm left holding the phone, the cold plastic coated in sweat.

. . .

"Mom, we're back," Isobel calls out breezily twenty minutes later.

I rush from the living room to the kitchen where I find her putting away the bakery items, while carrying Daisy with the other arm.

"Isobel, why did you do that? I told you not to take Daisy out again without telling me."

"I didn't want to disturb you. Tom said to let you rest. You need to stop panicking over nothing, it's not healthy."

I let out a breath and glance at the windows, seeing the willow tree outside swaying gently in the wind. "Just don't do it again, Isobel. Next time you want to take Daisy out, I need to know. I thought I made myself clear last time."

"Sure, Mom. I understand." She rolls her eyes, but hands me Daisy as a gesture of peace.

I settle her in her baby chair on the counter and start making her bottle.

As usual, Isobel hovers at the edge of my vision, watching every move I make.

"Is everything okay, Izzy?" I ask, trying to keep my tone light.

"Everything's fine, just making sure you have what you need," she replies quickly.

I turn my attention back to Daisy, her soft suckling sounds grounding me. Yet, Isobel's stare makes the back of my neck prickle.

"Isobel"—I clear my throat—"do you think I'm unfit as a mother?"

"No, Mom. Of course not. You're a great mom."

But a mother knows when her child is lying.

If only Isobel knew how far I went to protect her. I'd do the same for Daisy, because that's what mothers do. We'll do anything for our children.

NINE

I've just fed Daisy and I am sitting in the study, while she's lying on the floor on the same baby mat Isobel had used when she was this age. It's still in very good shape and the mobile toys hanging from the overhead arch are bright and cheerful as they were back then. The little monkey with its infectious grin, the jingling bell in the shape of a sunflower, and the butterfly with mirrored wings.

One day soon, when Daisy is able to reach up and grab them, I imagine she'll love them as much as Isobel did. Right now, though, she's simply gazing at them. I'm not even sure she can see them clearly. Aren't newborns only able to see a few inches away from their face? That's what I read somewhere, but the way Daisy's eyes seem to focus on the toys, I wonder.

It's only eight in the morning and Tom left just fifteen minutes ago, not long after Isobel. I'm finally getting back to some illustrations for a middle grade book I've neglected for weeks, when I hear the doorbell, then urgent knocking.

The study is just a few doors from the front door, so the sound is loud and clear and causes Daisy to flinch a little. If she weren't already awake, she would have been right now.

Perhaps Tom forgot something and is struggling to find his keys, as he often does. My husband is the most forgetful person I have ever met.

Picking up Daisy and cradling her in one arm, I make my way to the front door and peer through the peephole, also expecting to see the police.

I'm both relieved and annoyed when I see not only Martha but also Mrs. Lewis, from two doors down, their heads close together in hushed conversation.

I knew there was no way Martha would keep such exciting news to herself.

I consider ignoring their knocking, hoping they'll go away, but I know Martha too well to rely on that. With a resigned sigh, I open the door a crack, making sure that Daisy is out of sight. Thank God she's a quiet and content baby when she's fed and changed.

If the two women see her now, they will only want to stay longer. I know this was probably inevitable, but I'm not ready for all the visitors yet. I want to be able to control the news myself, to wait for our family to adjust. I'm also not ready for anyone to coo over her and study her features, wondering if she looks more like me or Tom.

"Good morning, Martha, Mrs. Lewis. What brings you by so early?" It's hard to be polite while inwardly cursing them, but I do my best.

Mrs. Lewis gives me a knowing smile. "Oh, Nora, I haven't seen you in ages. But when I heard the news from Martha here, I knew I had to come and see for myself." She glances in Martha's direction. "How wonderful to have a baby in the neighborhood again."

Martha catches my sharp gaze and I see that her cheeks are tinged with embarrassment.

"Nora, I know you said we shouldn't come to visit Daisy yet, but we couldn't resist," she stumbles over her words. "A new life, a fresh start, it's so exciting."

A fresh start, indeed. But my mouth goes dry, knowing that Martha must have already spread the news like wildfire throughout the entire neighborhood.

Even though my blood is boiling, I plaster on a smile. "Yes, it was quite unexpected. But we're overjoyed with our little one."

In that moment, Daisy starts whimpering softly and Martha leans in closer, trying to see if she can catch a glimpse of her.

"What a beautiful sound. Could we come in and see her?"

"I'm sorry, but now really isn't a good time. Maybe some other time."

Disappointment flashes across Martha and Mrs. Lewis' faces, but Martha quickly recovers, her smile returning.

"Oh, no worries. We wouldn't want to disturb the baby," she says sweetly. "But do let us know when we can come by. We'd love to see the little one and congratulate you properly."

"Of course, and thank you both for your well wishes." I proceed to close the door.

As Martha and Mrs. Lewis walk back down the path, I let out a sigh of relief, and once the coast is clear, I hurry back inside, locking the door.

Daisy and I head back to the study, but I move her into the sling around me as she has started to cry. After walking around the room singing to her, she finally falls asleep and I go back to my desk, struggling to get going with my illustrations as my mind whirls.

It will be a week tomorrow since Daisy turned up on our doorstep. So far, nobody has come looking for her. Nobody has reported us. Somebody deliberately left her in our care. We should have told the authorities nonetheless, but surely it would not be considered kidnapping?

With my thumb, I wipe away a small river of drool from the

corner of her mouth. Just as my nerves begin to calm down, my phone rings and it's Tom asking how Daisy and I are doing.

"We're okay." I let out a long breath. "Martha was here, and she brought Mrs. Lewis with her this time."

"She showed up again?" Tom sighs with frustration. "Doesn't she ever get the message?"

"Apparently not. I was tempted to show them the baby to stop them coming back. But I decided not to. I want us to keep her to ourselves for now. I just hope nobody comes for her, Tom. She belongs here." I pause for second. "Thank you."

"For what?"

"For letting me keep her." I know plenty of people would have freaked out and insisted we take her to the police, but not Tom.

"For a while now, I was so terrified that I was going to lose you, Nora, and Daisy brought you back to me. I haven't seen you so happy in a long time." From his end, I hear the distant sound of the school bell ringing. He waits until it stops before continuing. "And it's not just you. You know how desperate I've been for a baby. That little bean has stolen my heart as well, and it's all been so strange and so sudden, but I'm happy that we're doing this, giving her a home and parents who love her. Everyone deserves that. And we have so much love to give."

"I agree." I smile down at Daisy. "Did you talk to Robert?"

"Actually, I did. And he didn't mention anything about any missing babies. I'm sure he would have, it would be a huge deal."

Some of the tension in my shoulders melts away and I exhale heavily.

"Well then, if no one reported her missing, nobody else wants her. And we do. I don't think her biological parents will tell anyone what they did... leaving her on our doorstep."

"Yes," Tom says. "I agree, I think we just need to move past it and stop thinking about who it could have been, whether they'll change their mind and come back for her. I know it's hard, but it'll drive us insane and there's nothing we can do about it."

Since Daisy arrived, Tom has been tossing and turning almost every night; he's clearly filled with anxiety even though he's trying not to show it to me. He's been sharing the night-time feeds with me and Isobel, and I can clearly see the bond he has with Daisy already, his tender care and affection tinged with a hint of sorrow he doesn't want to show. I know he thinks of Danielle, and all the babies before her. But I have to believe those wounds will heal, in time.

"I really think everything is going to be all right, Tom."

"I hope so. Anyway, for now, let's just keep a low profile. Look, baby, I have to go. A staff meeting is waiting for me to attend."

"Okay, Mr. Principal," I say with a smile. He only got the position six months ago, and I couldn't be more proud.

As I hang up the phone, I glance down at my wrist and notice the silver compass bracelet Tom had slipped back on my wrist after finding it in the attic. It's supposed to make me feel grounded and less lost, and it did for a while. But now the metal catches the light, and the piece of jewelry transforms into a handcuff, tight and cold against my skin.

Struggling to breathe, I slide it off. I can't stand the feel of it on me anymore. Without it on, my wrist feels lighter, but my chest still feels tight.

I absentmindedly flip through sketches and try to focus while Daisy snores softly, and that's when I hear it. Sirens. Daisy doesn't wake up even when the sound gets louder by the second, but my pulse is beginning to race uncontrollably.

I think the vehicle is turning into our street.

TEN

The next day I am still reeling from the terror, even though the squad car drove past our house without stopping. I keep trying to remind myself that we have a note to prove that someone left Daisy, we didn't just take her. But then, of course, how could we prove we didn't write that note ourselves?

It's been seven days. Seven days since that tiny, wailing bundle was abandoned on our doorstep and changed my life forever. Since then I've avoided looking online to see if a baby has been reported missing, but it's always been at the back of my mind, and today more than ever.

I slip out of bed, scoop up Daisy and go to change her in the nursery. I'm just finishing up when Isobel comes in smiling, and takes her from my arms, kissing her on the forehead.

I press a kiss to Isobel's cheek and tuck a strand of hair behind her ear. "I'm going to make her bottle. Can you hold her for a bit?"

"Of course." Isobel clutches Daisy to her chest, her lips pressed to the top of her little head.

In the kitchen, as I reach for the formula in the cupboard

above the sink where I keep it, I pause, my hand hovering in the air. The cupboard is overflowing with unopened tins of formula, far more than I remember Isobel bringing home two days ago. There are also two brand-new baby bottles on the kitchen sink.

"Morning, honey," Tom says from behind me just as I reach for one of the tins. "I stocked up yesterday. Didn't want you worrying about running out or having to go out of the house, if you don't want to." He moves toward me, the light catching the fine lines etched around his eyes, lines that speak of fatigue and worry, and takes the can from me. "I'll make the bottle."

As I sit down at the kitchen table, he gets to work, measuring powder and warm water, and when he's done, he caps the bottle and hands it to me. "Here you go, and I'll make you some breakfast. You need to rest, Nora. You look exhausted. When Daisy falls asleep again, you should try to get some rest."

I nod and make my way back upstairs where I find Isobel nestled in the armchair with Daisy cradled against her chest, just like that first night. She's humming softly, a melody I remember from her own childhood.

"Hey, honey," I whisper as I step into the room. The air smells of baby powder and lavender.

Isobel's head snaps up, her expression shifting swiftly from one of calm to mild surprise.

"Mom, hi! I didn't hear you come in." She brushes a stray lock of hair from her face.

"Sorry, I didn't mean to startle you."

"She's all yours." She stands, a little too quickly, and places Daisy into my arms. Her finger lingers for a second on Daisy's cheek. "I need to get ready for class. I have several lectures today and I'm volunteering at the animal shelter afterwards."

"Okay." I give my daughter a kiss on the cheek. "I'll see you in the evening, then."

"I'm glad to see you're feeling better, Mom." Isobel's eyes

soften, and a smile tugs at her lips. "You've gone through such a hard time lately."

"I am, so much better. Thanks to our little miracle." I allow a small smile to dance on my lips.

I'm definitely feeling more energetic than I have been in a very long time. Food no longer sits like lead in my stomach, and I have found the strength to have more showers. I'm also getting more work done. Yesterday, an unexpected email arrived. An author in need of illustrations for an upcoming fantasy book asked if I would be interested in working for her. Soon, I'll take on more clients, but for now, I need to focus on Daisy and getting our lives back to normal. But I am looking forward to getting back into the swing of things—finding purpose again, keeping busy with work, and letting myself feel creative once more.

Isobel takes one last look at Daisy, then she turns away, walking to the door, but I call her name and she looks back.

"Sweetheart, we haven't really talked lately... about you. Everything has been about me or Daisy. How are you holding up?"

"Me?" Her laugh is brief and a little strained. "I'm fine. But school's been crazy."

"And Joe?" I venture. "Are you two still broken up?"

"Yeah." A shadow of sadness crosses her features and she forces it away with a smile. "He thinks I don't make enough time for him."

"Well, maybe he's right, sweetheart. You've been so busy taking care of me and have put your own life on hold."

"Mom, I—"

"Promise me, Isobel," I interrupt gently. "Now that I'm getting stronger, promise me you'll focus on yourself. Your dreams, your relationships. You can't live for me, it's your turn now. Find your happiness."

Isobel comes to kiss me on the cheek this time. When her

lips brush against my skin, they leave behind a fleeting warmth. "You're the best, Mom."

"Not really. I'm so sorry I was so absent for so long." I pause. "How are things with Lauren? Are you two on speaking terms again?"

Isobel shoves a hand through her hair and shrugs. "Haven't seen her much lately." She heads back to the door. "I should get going, Mom. Shower. College. Lots to do."

As she walks away, her hurried footsteps fade down the hallway into a distant whisper.

After Isobel and Tom have left for college and work, it's just me and Daisy again, and she's making soft coos from a blanket on the living room floor.

I'm on the floor with her, leaning on the coffee table that's scattered with sketches as I continue working on the artwork for her bedroom wall. But Daisy keeps distracting me with her cuteness.

Reaching out to tickle her belly and feet, my eyes land on my laptop perched close to the edge of the coffee table next to my glass of water. I'd been responding to emails a few minutes ago, but now I need the laptop for something completely different.

The screen blinks to life again, and I'm greeted by the familiar blue glow of the internet icon. I hesitate, my cursor hovering over it and then before I can second-guess myself, I click. The Ellery Creek paper's website materializes and I read the headlines and snippets of local news, both from Ellery and surrounding towns, searching for something—anything—that would indicate a baby is missing.

I just can't stop myself. I'm on edge as I scroll through the various articles, but I end up finding nothing.

Seven days have passed, yet the world seems oblivious to

the tiny life that found its way to our doorstep. There are no desperate pleas for information, no news of frantic search parties combing through the woods. Just recipes for pumpkin pie and trivial disputes at city council meetings. But somebody here in Ellery Creek must know about Daisy. Who her real parents are, and why she was left on our doorstep.

ELEVEN

By the time Tom wakes up this Saturday morning, I'm already up and dressed in jeans, a yellow sweater, and a pair of worn-out green and white sneakers that I ran a marathon in three years ago.

When Tom sees me, he's instantly wide awake. "Hey, are you... Wow, you're going out?"

"I'm going shopping to get some clothes for Daisy. She needs a few things that are specifically for her." So far, Daisy has been wearing Danielle's clothes and that has been useful, but seeing them leads to a sadness that can feel overwhelming at times.

Tom sits up and watches me with concern as I grab my purse. Slowly he pulls himself out of bed. "Are you sure you're ready for this, love?" His brow furrows with worry.

The truth is, I am nervous to step outside again, especially to go to an area crawling with people. But being trapped indoors is not the solution either. I have to start my new life and be the mother I know I can be. Capable, confident, and stable. So, I put on a brave smile and reply, "I'll be fine, Tom. It's just a quick trip, and I really want to do this."

I'm determined to show him, and especially Isobel, that I'm improving and becoming stronger with each passing day, that they don't have to worry about me anymore. I also want to experience the joy of shopping for my new baby.

I'm excited to buy Daisy a cute little outfit with rabbits on it, to match the artwork I've been creating for her nursery wall. I already picture her small body nestled in the soft cotton, while she looks up at me with her big, innocent eyes.

He nods slowly. "All right then, but please be careful. I can cancel tennis today and go with you, if you like."

I shake my head, feeling a sense of independence swelling within me. "I need to do this on my own. I'll be fine, I promise. Isobel offered to watch Daisy before running some errands in Amberfield. I'll be home before she heads off." I give him a reassuring smile before kissing him goodbye.

Before I step out of the front door, I glance through the windows overlooking the street. Most of our neighbors are milling about their front yards, enjoying the mild spring temperatures and tending to their own tasks or gossiping with one another. I take a deep breath, then push open the door and hurry to my car before anyone calls out to me. The air is filled with the fresh scent of blooming flowers and the occasional hint of wet earth from recent spring showers and I suck it all in before getting behind the wheel.

As I drive toward the shopping district, my hands grip the steering wheel tightly, my fingers stiff with anxiety. The familiar streets feel foreign to me after weeks of isolation. But I refuse to turn back.

Ellery Creek's downtown area is the heart of the town, a charming fusion of old and new.

The main street is beautiful with brick sidewalks, which are slightly damp from last night's rain, and vintage lampposts with intricate ironwork. The shops here offer a delightful mix of quaint boutiques, family-owned stores, and cozy cafés. Each storefront has its own unique character, brightly painted fronts and large inviting windows showing off their carefully chosen merchandise. The air is infused with freshly brewed coffee and pastries from the local bakeries.

Through my car window, I notice the familiar faces of people I know going about their morning routines. Mrs. Thompson, a recent widow who runs the flower shop, is setting out pots of vibrant blooms, her gray hair tucked neatly under a wide-brimmed hat. Mr. Malloy, the barber, stands outside his shop, sweeping the sidewalk and chatting with passersby.

Across the street, Mrs. Donahue is in front of her bakery, Sweet Delights, busy arranging freshly baked pies and cakes in the display window, while she tries to chase off children who press their noses against the glass, desperate for some treats.

As I drive to the baby boutique, I pass by the town square, a peaceful green space in the center of the bustling downtown area. The square is dominated by a grand gazebo, often used for concerts and community events on weekends. Today, it stands empty, but the surrounding benches are occupied by locals enjoying the morning sun.

This town hasn't changed much since I was a child. At the center of the square is a huge oak tree that has stood for centuries, its massive branches stretching wide and providing shade to the entire area. The Ellery Oak is a cherished symbol of our town, and its trunk is carved with the initials and hearts of countless couples over the years. Legend has it that sitting beneath this tree brings good luck. When we first started dating, Tom and I sat there a few times, just in case the legend is true.

Finally, I reach the baby boutique, Tiny Tots Treasures, a small, charming shop with a pastel blue facade and a wooden sign hanging above the door. The display window is filled with adorable outfits, tiny shoes, and soft toys, all beautifully arranged. I park the car and when I enter the shop, the bell tinkles softly, announcing my arrival.

I'm really doing this. I'm taking the first steps back into the world, reclaiming a part of myself that had been buried under layers of pain. The fluorescent lights overhead seem too bright, too harsh after weeks of dim, cozy lamplight at home, but the scents of baby powder and fabric softener envelop me and do their best to ease the tension in my chest. I wonder if they have some special air fresheners hidden around the store. I can just imagine the shop owners sitting at a table having a meeting about using homey scents that are associated with newborn babies.

Clutching my shopping list in my hand, I smile at the racks of tiny onesies and dresses. My fingers graze over soft fabrics and vibrant colors and as I browse through the aisles, I can feel the anxiety slowly melting away. Finally, I approach a display of outfits featuring white rabbits. One is a soft pastel pink with tiny bows, and the other a soothing mint green. These would look perfect on Daisy, I decide, and I carefully fold them over my arms.

I also grab a teddy bear with fur the color of buttercream and shiny black button eyes. Then I spot a shelf of baby bibs with a variety of designs: stars, moons, animals, and some with names embroidered across the fabric. I see names like Lily, Jack, Grace, Oliver, and Ava. But then my fingers pause as I come across one bib with the name "Amber" stitched delicately in elegant script.

My mother's name. Instantly there's a rush of memories and emotions, even after all these years.

The bib slips from my hand, and I stand frozen for a moment. I need to get out of here.

I hurry to the checkout counter. The middle-aged woman at the till, who has beautiful braids, smiles warmly as I approach. She rings up my purchases, each delicate item scanned and carefully folded before being placed in a glossy paper bag.

"Congratulations," she says softly. "These are going to look simply adorable on your little one."

"Thank you." As I turn away, ready to leave the shop, I freeze. Through the window, I catch a glimpse of a woman walking down the sidewalk, her figure obscured by the glare of the morning sun.

I know her. She's one of the nurses that took care of me when Danielle died. I'm good with faces and she has a distinct birthmark on her left cheek that gives her away. I can fool the neighbors, but that woman knows the truth. She knows that my baby didn't survive. She personally offered me her condolences. I'm so glad Daisy stayed back home with Isobel or how would I have been able to explain her to the nurse?

I wait until she disappears from view, then hurry out of the shop but a woman's voice calls out from behind me.

"Excuse me, Ma'am!"

"You forgot these," says the woman from the boutique, the bag clutched in her outstretched hand, filled with my purchases.

"Thank you." I force a smile as I take the bag from her outstretched hand.

"No harm done, dear," she says, patting my arm gently. "The early days as a new mom can make one quite forgetful. I have three kids of my own and I remember how exhausting it was."

I nod and murmur a quick goodbye before hurrying away.

When I arrive home, and after the mini fashion show with Daisy in our room, where I get Isobel's stamp of approval on my new purchases, I expect Isobel to dash off for her errands in Amberfield. But instead, she stays, watching me from the center of our bedroom, a quiet concern in her eyes.

"Are you all right, sweetie?" I ask, scooping up Daisy from

my side of the bed. She's back in the plain onesie I found her dressed in. As she curls into my arms, the familiar warmth of her tiny body begins to soften the knot of anxiety that's been tightening in my chest since I left the shop.

"I should be asking you that question, Mom. You walked in looking pale as a sheet. What happened?"

"Nothing." I avoid her gaze, focusing instead on running a hand over Daisy's fine hair. She blinks at me, those slow, sleepy blinks that are so rare but always manage to calm me. "I just... I guess I'm not used to being out. It felt strange, a little uncomfortable."

Isobel steps forward, pulling us both into a hug, and when she steps back, she's still holding my hand. "Tom's tennis was canceled because his partner sprained his ankle. He's on his way home to take you out on a date. Just the two of you."

"We can't, who's going to watch Daisy? You're leaving for Amberf—"

"Not anymore." She reaches for Daisy, patting her back gently. A loud burp escapes, making us both chuckle. "I'll stay with her. What I had to do can wait."

"Okay, thank you. Did Tom say where we're going?"

Isobel's smile widens. "I suggested you cash in that voucher I gave you for your anniversary."

"Oh, the boat ride!" My eyes widen, the memory slowly surfacing. With everything that's happened recently, I had completely forgotten about the gift. Isobel had been so thoughtful, knowing how much I loved going out on the water.

My paternal grandfather used to take me on fishing trips every Sunday after church. He had a heart attack and passed away when I was twelve, four months after his wife suffered the same fate, but those memories stayed with me. Peaceful afternoons on the lake, surrounded by nothing but the water and the sky. Since then, the only other time I'd been on a boat was when Tom proposed to me.

Tom arrives ten minutes later with a bouquet of white tulips —my favorite— which I accept along with his kiss. Soon after, we are in the car, heading for the ocean. But as the clifftops come into view, a painful knot begins to form in my stomach. It's this feeling I get when something terrible is about to happen, and honestly, I'm invariably right.

TWELVE

We take winding steps from the cliff down to the harbor. The boating place is quaint and peaceful, tucked behind a line of tall reeds that sway gently in the breeze. There's an old wooden hut with a collection of small rowboats and kayaks in faded paint.

Today the ocean stretches wide and calm, the water glassy beneath the light of the sun. The only sounds here are the occasional call of seagulls and the soft lap of the waves.

Tom leads me to our rowboat, and as we approach, I notice something familiar. A picnic basket is sitting in the boat, similar to the one we had on the day he proposed.

"Did you arrange that?" I ask, raising an eyebrow at him.

His grin is as boyish as ever. "Maybe. Thought you'd like a surprise."

"Oh Tom, that's so sweet. I love it."

We step into the boat, and I feel the gentle sway as he pushes us off from the shore, the oars dipping into the water with a steady, rhythmic splash. The air smells faintly of algae and wood, the scent mingling with the fresh breeze that tugs at my hair.

As we glide farther from shore, the world feels quieter, more distant. I can feel my shoulders loosening, the tension slowly unwinding.

"I'm having so much fun, but I miss Daisy," I admit. "I can't stop thinking about her."

Tom glances over with a knowing smile. "Sweetheart, you need to relax. This is our time."

I nod and try to let myself settle into the moment, watching the water ripple around us as Tom continues to row farther out to sea.

After a while, he stops and pulls out the picnic basket. Inside are carefully selected snacks—freshly baked bread, soft cheeses, grapes that glisten like tiny jewels, and a bottle of sparkling water.

The warm and yeasty smell of the bread instantly pulls me in. As Tom slices it open, the scent grows stronger, filling the air between us. I take a piece and the crust crackles beneath my fingers before I bite into it. The food, the way the ocean unfurls toward the horizon, the gentle sway of the boat—it all feels perfect.

"I never told you this," I begin, swallowing a bite of bread, "but when I was eight or nine, I was convinced I'd grow up to be a fisherman."

Tom stops mid-chew and raises an eyebrow. "A fisherman? Really?"

"Well, fisherwoman to be accurate." A nostalgic smile tugs at my lips. "My grandfather used to take me out every Sunday. I loved it so much. I remember telling him I didn't need school anymore because I already knew what I wanted to be. Grandad said I could be anything."

Tom pops a grape into his mouth and leans in, intrigued. "So, what happened?"

"He made me a certificate. Called me a 'Certified Fisher-girl.' I believed it was real. It was my most prized possession for a while. But one day my mom had enough of me talking about fishing. She told me to focus on school, that I couldn't make a living that way. The next day, my certificate disappeared. I thought I lost it, but after she passed, I found it in her things."

Tom pauses his rowing, then without a word, he pulls me into a hug, holding me close. I lean into him, feeling the steadiness of his heartbeat.

When I pull back, he's smiling. "When I was a kid, I wanted to be a pilot."

"Really? You never said."

"Yep. But there was one problem." His grin widens. "I was terrified of heights back then."

I burst out laughing, the sound echoing across the still water. We laugh together, the kind of easy, comfortable laughter that comes from being married for years. But just as the laughter fades, something catches my eye.

Something dark, floating just beneath the surface of the water.

A sharp, icy panic grips me. "Tom... What is that? Is that hair?"

He glances where I'm pointing and pauses for a moment. "Oh, that's just seaweed," he says casually, starting to row again.

But I can't look away. The shape—no, the texture—is all wrong. I lean forward, my stomach tightening with the same dread I felt on the drive here.

It's definitely hair.

Long, black strands of hair, tangled and drifting in the water. The hair moves slowly with the current, swaying close to the boat. Fear coils in my stomach and a cold sweat breaks out on my skin as the water laps against the side of the boat.

THIRTEEN

Tom was adamant that it was just seaweed, and it was swiftly dragged away by the current, but our date was ruined as I insisted we hurried back to shore.

All I wanted to do was hold my baby. Daisy was crying when we got home, but she stopped the moment I held her, settling into my chest. I pressed a kiss to her damp forehead, feeling the thrum of her tiny heartbeat against mine.

I'm just carrying her through to our bedroom where I'll take a nap alongside her when I overhear Isobel's concerned voice from the hallway. "What happened out there? Mom didn't seem herself. She looked scared."

Isobel is right. What we saw sent my mind into the darkest places it could possibly go. I am scared. No, terrified.

And if they knew what I've hidden from them for so long, they'd understand why.

A little after midnight, I sneak out of the bedroom, careful not to wake Daisy and Tom, who are fast asleep, and head to the study, dropping into the chair at my desk to get some work done. It's better than tossing and turning all night.

I grab my drawing tools and get started immediately. The scratch of my pencil against the paper almost soothes me as I lose myself in the rhythm of it, creating intricate patterns and designs while the night lamp casts a warm light across the room.

I dropped out of school at sixteen, just months before my final exams were due to start, my dreams of a bright future shattered by an unplanned pregnancy. But even in those darkest moments, there was a spark of creativity that refused to be extinguished.

When I became a mom, with my little baby Isobel by my side, I poured my heart and soul into illustrating the stories I made up for her, filling notebooks with colorful drawings and whimsical characters to bring my words to life.

As she grew older, she would beg me to read her the stories over and over again, and I knew that I had found my calling, my purpose in life.

Maybe one day, I'll dig out those old notebooks, dust off the pages and breathe new life into the stories that had once brought us so much joy. Perhaps I'll even gather the courage to self-publish them. Being an author has never been a dream of mine, but I'm sure that seeing my illustrations gracing the pages of my own books would bring me a huge sense of fulfillment. And the idea of sharing those memories with Isobel, of giving her something tangible to hold on to, fills me with a sense of purpose and pride. Maybe Daisy, too, will be able to share in the magic of those stories. Or new stories or poems I will write especially for her.

The night stretches on, the hours slipping away like grains of sand through an hourglass as I lose myself in my work. But as the clock ticks past 3 a.m., a sudden cold shiver snakes down my spine, causing me to pause. I stop drawing and the pencil hovers over the paper. I glance around the room, but everything appears as it should—the familiar furniture, the lamplight, the shadows dancing along the walls.

I try to shake off the unease, but it's as if the air in the room has turned dense, each breath I take feeling heavier than before. I listen intently, straining my ears for any sound, but all I hear is the steady thump of my own heartbeat.

With a sigh, I set down my pencil and lean back in my chair, massaging the back of my neck. Maybe I just need some fresh air, a change of scenery. I rise from my seat and make my way to the window, drawing back the curtains and peering out into the night.

The street below is deserted, bathed in the soft glow of the moonlight as it spills across the pavement. But something doesn't feel right.

It's not the first time I've felt this way. There have been nights like this before, after what I did that night. Moments of unease that come and go like shadows.

I draw in a deep breath as I look out into the night. And then, just as I turn away from the window, I catch a movement out of the corner of my eye, a figure standing in the doorway of the study, watching me.

It's Isobel, her expression unreadable. She's just watching me with a strange intensity that makes me squirm.

"Isobel? What are you doing up?"

She doesn't respond immediately.

"Is everything okay?" I chew on the end of my pencil the way I did as a child whenever I was nervous. "Is there something you need?"

Isobel shakes her head and shrugs. "I couldn't sleep. I thought I heard something and came to look."

I nod, my pulse thrashing in my ears as I struggle to maintain my composure. "Well, everything's fine. I was just doing some illustrations. You should go back to bed."

She hesitates for a moment, glancing around the room.

Then, with a nod, she turns and disappears into the darkness of the hallway.

My mouth dry, I return to my desk, drop into the chair, and pick up my phone, navigating to the Amazon app. I need something to distract me, to make me feel better. In the search bar, I type in the title of the children's book I illustrated for one of my clients last year, holding my breath as I wait for the results to load.

It's a story about a young girl who discovers a hidden world inside an old grandfather clock that she finds in the basement of their home. The illustrations I created for the book were some of my best work, each brushstroke infused with a sense of wonder and magic that seemed to leap off the page. I see the book listed among the top sellers in its category and scroll through the reviews, most of them five-star. For a brief moment, my fear and paranoia are replaced by a surge of pride and yet I can't relax, thinking about the way Isobel acted just now.

She's clever, Isobel. She is definitely getting more and more suspicious, wondering about what I'm hiding that could haunt me so much. With all my struggles lately I've been careless, and I've let slip too many clues. But even though everything I have done was for her own good, I don't think my family could understand. It's not the thought of prison that frightens me so much, it's the look on Tom and Isobel's faces when my secret tears their world apart.

FOURTEEN

Late the following night, I've just fed and changed Daisy and am standing by the nursery window with her in my arms, staring out as I often do these days.

Tom was still sleeping when I carried Daisy through to the nursery, and I'm sure he was having a bad dream because his brows were furrowed, his fists were clenched, and he was murmuring something unintelligible. I was tempted to wake him, but then he might not get back to sleep, and he needs his rest.

As Daisy nuzzles into my shoulder, I softly recite to her a poem I wrote for her earlier today.

"Little Daisy, soft and sweet,
With tiny hands and dimpled feet,
You came to me like morning light,
And turned my world from wrong to right.
Though you're small, you're oh so strong,
In my arms, you now belong.
A gift I never knew I'd see,
But now you're everything to me."

The soft light from the night lamp casts a gentle glow over her peaceful face as she yawns and her eyes drift shut, and I continue to stare at her, memorizing every detail of her features, from the soft curve of her long eyelashes to the dimples in her chubby cheeks.

I have fallen so deeply in love with this little girl and I know if I ever lost her, my heart would bleed just as much as it did when we lost Danielle.

Finally, I suck in a long breath and walk out of the nursery with her tucked in my arms, switching off the lamp on our way out.

Back in our bedroom, I settle Daisy in her bed and move to the window again, but just as I carefully push aside the drapes, Tom whispers from behind me.

"You'll drive yourself crazy, you know? I know what you're thinking, looking out of the window again."

I turn in time to see him sitting up in bed. There's not enough moonlight flooding into the room to reveal the concern etched on his face, but I can sense it.

"I can't help it." I blow out a long breath. "I can't shake this feeling that someone will come looking for her. The father, maybe?"

Tom reaches out a hand and I hesitate for a moment before joining him under the covers, seeking comfort in his familiar warmth.

"It's been over a week now, sweetheart," he murmurs and pulls me close to him. "I don't think anyone is coming."

I bury my face in the crook of his neck, and his hand rubs soothing circles on my back.

For a while, neither of us speaks as the night envelops us.

I finally start to sink into sleep, but then a rustling sound jolts me awake. Adrenaline surges through me as I sit up in bed, my breath coming quick and shallow.

"Did you hear that?" I wrap my arms around my body.

Tom sounds annoyed as I wake him up. "Nora, you're letting your imagination get the best of you. It's probably just the wind outside or Isobel going to the bathroom. We can't keep going on like this, jumping at every little noise." He groans. "I have a long day ahead of me tomorrow, and I need to get some sleep."

I nod, and lie there in the darkness, trying to will myself back to sleep. The rest of the night seems to stretch on forever, and eventually I drift off.

When I wake up in the early hours of the morning, Tom is not in bed next to me. I find him with Daisy in the nursery, fully dressed for work and feeding her a bottle.

"Nora, I've been thinking," he says as he rubs Daisy's back. "Maybe we should think about moving away from Ellery Creek."

"But what about your job? You just got the promotion."

"I'll find another one. We can start fresh somewhere new, where we're sure no one knows about... this, and we won't have to wake up in the middle of the night worrying." He looks up and his eyes search mine for a response. "We don't have to move immediately. My notice period is three months and that would give us time to tie up loose ends and plan everything carefully."

"Yes... yes. I think that's a brilliant idea. I'm in." I feel brighter at this glimmer of hope. A fresh start, a clean slate somewhere far from here.

Tom doesn't know that I've been looking over my shoulder for years, not just since Daisy came to live with us.

"We should also start thinking about getting some kind of documentation that would prove that Daisy is legally ours, like a birth certificate?" he suggests. "I'll do some research."

"Thank you." I wrap my arms around my husband and Daisy. "What about Isobel? I think she'll want to stay in Amber-field for college, probably move back into the apartment. I know she's fallen out with Lauren, so Lauren will just have to move out now, I guess. It *is* Isobel's apartment. But it's sad, isn't it?"

"What... what's sad?" Tom rises from the armchair, settling Daisy in my arms.

"That we might never see Lauren again. She was like part of the family." I press a kiss to the top of Daisy's head. "And it will be hard for Isobel. They have been friends since they were little girls."

Tom sighs and shoves his hands into the pockets of his gray suit pants. "It is sad, but sometimes people drift apart. Particularly at that age. Isobel will be okay, she's so resilient."

"True," I murmur. "Do you think Lauren will eventually move back to Ellery Creek?"

"I doubt it. I bumped into Jenny and David the other day at the grocery store and they said they haven't heard from her in a while."

"Well, that's not surprising given the kind of parents they are. They never supported her in any way."

Tom nods in agreement. "Yeah, I know. Poor Lauren." He walks over to where I'm standing and kisses me. "I have to get going."

As he walks away, I can't stop thinking about Lauren. She reminds me so much of myself at that age. Fierce and proud, battling alone in the world without parents that care for her. I miss that girl, and I know she was good for Isobel. I wish I knew what it was they fought about. What could have ended a friendship that we all thought would last a lifetime?

FIFTEEN

I wake up determined to take control of my home and my life, starting with doing something for Isobel. A mother should be the caregiver, not the other way around.

There's tension in her shoulders lately that speaks volumes of the stress she carries. She does her best to hide it, but a mother knows. And if I can do something, anything, to alleviate that burden, then that's what I'll do.

"Sweetie, Mommy's going to make things right again," I whisper to Daisy and as if sensing my resolve, she coos and kicks her legs.

Cradling Daisy close, I leave the kitchen and climb the stairs. I plan on giving the entire house a good scrub, but I'll start with Isobel's room. When she comes home this evening, she'll find it spick and span and a sanctuary for her to retreat to.

As soon as Daisy and I reach her door, I press down on the handle, and push it open.

Chaos greets me—scattered clothes draped over furniture, open textbooks everywhere with pages dog-eared and marked up with Isobel's meticulous notes. Her laptop sits open on her desk, the screen displaying a half-written essay.

It pains me to see my daughter's space turned into a reflection of her inner turmoil.

The room has lost its magic, suffocated by neglect. She's been so busy with school and taking care of me that cleaning a room was not top of her priorities.

"Let's fix this, shall we?" I murmur and head to our bedroom to get the baby sling.

With Daisy strapped to my body, my task begins with gathering the discarded clothes, smoothing out the wrinkles, then folding them with care.

Done with the clothes, I move to her white desk and clear away the clutter of books and loose papers, organizing her notes and textbooks neatly in a pile. Then I notice a crumpled photo peeking out from under a pile of essays. It's one of Isobel, Tom, and me from our family vacation at a mountain cabin in Warm Springs, Virginia, to celebrate our third wedding anniversary. The sun was setting in the background as we huddled together, our arms wrapped around each other.

"Isobel and I have come so far," I whisper and memories immediately flood in unbidden. A young me, cradling baby Isobel, my heart squeezing with both love and fear. Nights spent in shelters, our futures uncertain. I had never been more terrified in my life, and yet I knew I had to keep going because someone depended on me.

I brush away a tear that trickles down my right cheek. Then my hand pauses over a chaotic stack of flyers for a demonstration against animal cruelty. I remember the day Isobel had come home with those flyers, excited and determined to make a difference. She had always been an advocate for animals, or the voiceless as she called them.

I stand back to observe my handiwork, looking from the now orderly desk to the corner of the room, where cardboard boxes huddle in a messy pile, some still sealed by tape.

I smile to myself and shake my head. Isobel was never a fan

of unpacking. Even after a vacation, her luggage would remain untouched or half-emptied for days until I gently reminded her to put everything away. Before Tom came along, we moved many times from one place to the next, and often I didn't bother unpacking then, as I knew we would be leaving soon. It was easier to keep everything in boxes and suitcases, ready for the next move.

But now, things are different; we have a place to call home.

I stride over to the boxes, fingers tracing the flaps of the nearest box. This isn't just about unpacking; it's about restoring peace to Isobel's world, to our world. If these boxes are cluttering her space, perhaps they're cluttering her mind too.

With careful movements, I begin to slice through the packing tape, the ripping sound oddly satisfying. Each item I unwrap is a piece of the puzzle that is Isobel—a favorite book from her childhood, picture frames with smiling faces, trinkets from vacations.

I place each object with intention around her room and envision her surprise when she sees the effort, when she feels the love woven into every action I take.

As I unpack her belongings, I am also unpacking my own dreams for her—dreams of her reclaiming her confidence and defeating the inner battles. In the calmness of the space, with only the gentle sound of paper rustling, I dare to hope that even after everything we went through, things will eventually work out just fine.

Isobel deserves happiness and I'll do whatever it takes to help her find it.

With the soft burbles and gurgles of Daisy as my soundtrack, I sweep through the room, my fingers trailing along surfaces, getting rid of dust and dirt that have settled over time.

As I wipe, I come across an old photograph tucked into the frame of her mirror, of Isobel grinning widely beside Tom at a carnival on her twelfth birthday, cotton candy clutched in her hand. I tuck the memory back into place, anchoring it firmly so it doesn't slip away again. The room is gradually shedding its layers of neglect and becoming a cocoon of warmth and calm.

As I reach under her bed for an errant shoe, my fingers brush against something unexpected. It's a book, wedged tightly between the wall and the bed frame. It must be a diary, I think. Why else would Isobel hide it so carefully? I tug at the book, freeing it from its hiding spot. It's a diary, and the cover is worn, the edges frayed, indicating that it has been well-used.

I'm tempted to read it, but something stops me. It's an invasion of her privacy, a breach of trust. But then, Isobel doesn't say much to me lately about what's going on in her life and I don't know how to help her if I don't understand what she's going through.

Her recent emotional distance and the circles under her eyes, which she thinks I haven't noticed, push me closer to crossing a boundary that I can never come back from.

"Forgive me, Izzy." With a conflicted heart, I decide to open a random page and read.

I threw up again today. I tried to keep the food down, but I couldn't, not even water. I hate it. I hate that food has so much power over me again. But I need to be careful. Mom cannot know that my eating disorder is back. She already has enough on her plate. I overcame it before and I'll do it again. I know what triggered it.

My hands tremble as I turn the pages to a few weeks before the entry, reading about more struggles with food, sleepless nights, and her breakup with Joe.

Then I find it, the entry that shifts the ground beneath my feet.

I feel like I'm stuck in some kind of nightmare. I don't know how to handle this, if I bring it up it will destroy her and us. If only I could turn back time and unknow the truth. The secret I have to keep, because of her.

SIXTEEN

The tomato slices easily under the sharp edge of the knife, surprising me with how effortless it is.

It's been a long time since I've cooked dinner, but tonight feels like a turning point. I'm determined to be the strong and reliable woman my family needs right now.

When I move on to the onions, my mind drifts back to yesterday and the discovery of Isobel's diary. I have decided not to bring it up, because maybe I jumped to a conclusion. She might not have found out my deepest secret. After all, how could she? She could have been referring to something else. There is no reason for me to think the worst.

Now, I need to regain a sense of control over my life. Tonight, I'm determined to be present, to be the mother and wife my family deserve. Enjoying the sizzle of onions hitting the pan, I watch them caramelize, the sweet aroma wafting through the air. I hope my meatballs and sauce will turn out right, but I remind myself that tonight is not about being perfect; it's about trying my best. As I stir the sauce and see it thickening, I feel the tension in my shoulders dissipate.

Cooking has never been a strong suit of mine, but maybe I

should consider taking it up as a hobby. It seems to have a soothing effect on me. My sauce is a little too salty, so I add a dash of sugar to balance it out, remembering that my mother used to do that.

I drop ready-made meatballs from the freezer into the simmering red sauce, but as I do so, I can't shake the memory of Isobel's words scrawled on the pages of her diary, the ink bleeding like a wound.

"Do you need help?" Isobel says, walking into the kitchen with Daisy in her arms.

"No, sweetheart," I reply, stirring the pot more vigorously than necessary. "Helping out with Daisy is more than enough."

She leans against the doorframe. "Are you sure?"

"Positive." My voice is steadier than my hands. "I want to do this. Dinner will be ready soon!"

"All right then." She retreats with Daisy, and I'm left alone with the bubbling sauce and my lack of culinary skills. My mother was an excellent cook, but unfortunately, her cooking skills didn't transfer to me. Maybe I avoid cooking to keep from thinking about her so much. There are so many painful memories that come with losing her and being left alone to navigate life on my own, and then becoming a mother before I was ready.

When Tom joins me in the kitchen, he's fresh from the shower, the hint of his cologne mingling with soap.

I prepare a simple salad and remove the spaghetti from the stove while he lights candles and sets the table. We all gather around it, with Daisy now in her sling attached to Isobel, and there is a sense of formality in our arrangement that feels strange after weeks of scattered meals.

"Thank you for this, Nora." Tom reaches out to squeeze my hand. "This is so good. Who are you and what has happened to my wife? Have you been lying to us about your cooking skills all this time?" He grins, the corners of his eyes crinkling.

"No." I chuckle, feeling flattered. "Maybe the culinary gods are showing me mercy today."

But Isobel picks at her food, her fork pushing around the greens. I don't miss the glances she sends my way as if she wants to say something to me but can't find the right words, and instead goes back to tightening one arm around Daisy.

Desperate to break the tension, I glance over at Daisy, her tiny head resting peacefully against Isobel's chest. That's when I notice it—a small, faint scratch near her ear. "Oh, sweetheart, look at that scratch on your face." I lean in to get a closer look. "She must've done it with her nails. I'll have to trim them after her bath tonight."

Tom frowns a little and stretches out an arm to pat Daisy's back. "Poor thing. I swear, those tiny fingernails are sharper than they look."

Daisy stirs, making a soft sound.

"You know," I say, "when Isobel was a baby, her nails were like tiny daggers. Her face constantly had little scratches, and I had to put those baby mittens on her just to save her from herself."

Tom laughs, the sound warm and rich, breaking the tension. "I can totally see that. Isobel, the tiny warrior, even back then."

Isobel says nothing, and I take a sip of water, trying to stay calm. When she came home yesterday and found her room tidy, she seemed pleased, but after she had changed and showered, her mood had completely changed.

Does she know I read her diary?

Close to eleven that night, Daisy wakes up desperate for a diaper change. As I reach for her, I notice that Tom is not in bed, and there's no light spilling out from under the bathroom door. Maybe he's downstairs getting something to drink. He's been doing that a lot lately.

I head into the hallway and glance briefly out the window where I spot two figures in the moonlit garden. It's Isobel and Tom, their postures rigid. I may not be able to hear their words, but from their animated gestures, it's clear they're having some kind of disagreement.

Wrapping Daisy in a blanket, I go downstairs and slip out of the house through the back door in the kitchen. The cool damp of the grass seeps into my slippers.

They turn as I approach them, their expressions shrouded in shadows.

"Isobel? Tom?" I look from one to the other. "Are you two arguing? What's going on, why are you out here at night?"

A wordless exchange passes between them.

"It's nothing. I went down for a drink," says Tom slowly, "and Isobel couldn't sleep so we decided to get some fresh air."

Isobel opens her arms for Daisy. "I'll take over and sleep in the nursery."

I watch as she disappears into our home, the door slamming shut behind her.

Tom sighs. "I wanted to find out what's bothering her. But that girl is as stubborn as a mule. She simply refuses to share what's on her mind."

Tom says he wants to stay out a little longer to think, and I make us both a cup of coffee and a bowl of chocolate chip ice-cream, carrying it all out on a tray. But instead of staying in the garden, we move to the porch swing.

"You seem to have a lot on your mind," I say gently as I hand him his cup. "Is it about Isobel? Daisy?"

He shakes his head slightly. "Not only that, there's some school stuff going on too. We're dealing with some issues... vandalism in the boys' locker room, and the superintendent is on my case about test scores."

"I'm sorry to hear that." I reach for the folded quilt on the arm of the swing and drape it around his shoulders before nestling beside him. "Here." I hand him a spoon. "Whatever is on your mind, ice-cream always helps," I say, trying to muster a smile.

He accepts the spoon with a grateful nod. Nothing else is said between us and the only sound is that of the soft chink of our spoons against the glass bowls and the distant chirp of crickets in the night.

Finally, I can't take it anymore. His silence is killing me. Sometimes it's better to walk through the fire than to continue circling around it. I put my spoon down, the remaining ice cream now a sweet soup.

"Tom. What was the argument with Isobel about, earlier?"

He hesitates, then scoops up a spoonful of melted ice cream and stares at it for a while. Under the porch light, the chocolate chip specks look like tiny islands in a sea of cream. He puts the spoon back down untouched.

"She... she just didn't want to talk to me, and I was upset about that." He clasps his hands together. "You know how much I love her. It's tearing me up seeing her struggle and not knowing how to reach her. I just want to help her, Nora."

Before I can respond, a piercing cry shatters the fragile peace. My body responds before my mind does, launching me from the swing as Daisy's screams burst from the house.

Daisy has screamed before, but this sounds different.

Something is really not right.

Tom is right on my heels as we bolt into the house and collide with Isobel in the hallway, her eyes wild with alarm. All three of us run to the nursery.

Inside the crib, Daisy's tiny face is contorted in anguish, her skin flushed an angry red, her fingers clenched tight as she wails.

"I was just coming to get you. Mom, something's wrong with her." Isobel gasps for air, her words cracking.

I hurry over and gather Daisy up into my arms. Her body

feels terrifyingly hot against mine, her cries frantic, and in this moment I have never been more afraid.

I wrench the thermometer from Daisy's armpit, the digital numbers screaming back at us: 104.8.

My breath hitches, a cold rush of dread settling in. This isn't just a little fever; it's a wildfire raging through her tiny body.

"Daisy, baby, it's going to be okay," I try to soothe her as best I can.

While Isobel holds Daisy, I hurry out of the nursery and drench a washcloth in cool water. I did this a lot of times with Isobel when she was a baby. But when I return and press the cloth to Daisy's forehead for a while, her skin continues to burn beneath my fingers and her wails grow louder, more panicked. Her little body is fighting something fierce, and she's losing.

I wish I could give her paracetamol, but Daisy is less than a month old and it's not recommended.

"Tom..." I start, my eyes meeting his. We're thinking the same thing, the unspoken terror that has haunted us since we took Daisy in. We can't take her to the hospital. Not without exposing our secret. They'll take her away.

"Maybe... maybe the fever will break soon," Tom whispers, but he doesn't believe his own words. And neither do I.

"What do we do?" Panic claws its way up my throat, threatening to choke me. "We can't take her to the hospital, right? Everyone will know—"

"No, we have to find another way," he says, his jaw set.

"But, Tom, we need to do something now, there isn't time to think," I say through gritted teeth. "Call Larry, your doctor friend. Hurry. We'll just have to deal with the consequences."

SEVENTEEN

Tom puts his phone on speaker and paces anxiously as it rings.

Larry is the school doctor at Ellery Creek High, and he works part time at the local hospital. He's been Tom's friend for a long time. But he's on annual leave right now and Tom can't remember when he's leaving for his planned vacation.

"Come on, Larry," Tom mutters, the palm of his free hand pressed against his forehead. The call drops to voicemail, and Tom hangs up.

Isobel watches us from the day bed, tears streaming down her cheeks as Daisy continues to scream in my arms.

"Again," I urge. "Try again."

"Damn it," he curses under his breath then dials again. And again. And again.

Finally, when the mechanical message of the voicemail plays out once more he hangs up and runs a hand through his hair.

"Tom, we have to do something, right now."

"What do you want us to do? March into the hospital and admit we've got a baby that isn't ours? They know you lost our baby. It only just happened."

"We can't just watch her suffer!" I insist, feeling the sting of tears. "We have to get help."

"Dammit, Nora! You think I don't know that?" His words are sharp, laced with fear and frustration.

Then Daisy lets out another heart-wrenching scream and without thinking, I head for the door. Tom follows wordlessly, knowing the decision's been made.

Maybe we just have to drive her to the hospital and leave her there, disappearing from her life as easily as we entered it.

The thought shreds my heart, it's unbearable, but the sight of Daisy's labored breathing, her tiny chest heaving with each struggle for air, pushes me onward.

Less than ten minutes later, I buckle Daisy carefully into the car seat, her screams slicing through the stillness of the night. As Tom starts the engine, I glance back at my baby, consumed by the fear of losing her.

The drive to the hospital is a blur, the streets devoid of life this late at night.

Finally, the hospital building emerges from the darkness, its windows glinting in the harsh glow of streetlights. I clench my teeth as Tom swings the car into the emergency lane, his hands shaking on the wheel.

I take a deep breath and grip the car door handle before swinging it open. Daisy's screams fill the night as I unfasten her from the car seat, drowning out everything, even my fears. In this moment, nothing else matters but getting her the help she needs.

"Stay here. I'll handle this. I have an idea."

Tom says something, but I'm already gone, heading to the entrance, clutching Daisy to my chest.

The automatic doors whoosh open, and I step into the sterile, buzzing atmosphere of the emergency room. Without hesitation, I approach the front desk, swaying gently to soothe Daisy.

"Help," I gasp out. "I was babysitting for a friend and the baby—she won't stop crying. She's burning up."

A nurse behind the counter with thick glasses and a pointy chin looks up, her expression shifting instantly from routine indifference to concern. "Name?"

"Daisy," I say without skipping a beat. But then she asks for a last name, insurance information, questions that corner me into a harsh reality and send my pulse racing.

"Uh, I don't have all the details. I'm just the babysitter." The lie thickens on my tongue and my mouth feels parched. "I can't reach her parents. They're out of town."

"Ma'am, we need the parents' contact information immediately."

"Right, yes, let me just—" I'm fumbling with my phone, pretending to search for details I don't have, when movement at the corner of my eye snags my attention.

A policeman strolls through the sliding doors and my chest tightens. I shrink back slightly, pressing Daisy closer to my body. But he doesn't even glance in our direction. He strides past, focused on some other emergency, someone else's story.

Relief leaves my legs weak. I'm invisible, unnoticed, and for now, that's exactly what I need. But the relief is short-lived; the nurse is waiting.

"Ma'am?" she prompts again, eyebrows knitting together.

"Sorry," I stammer. "The baby needs help first, right? I'll get the details. Please."

The nurse's patience is wearing thin, and my heart is hammering in my chest as I wait for her to read through my lies and call the policeman over. But before she can press further, Tom bursts through the entrance.

"Larry called back," he breathes out, words rushing past his lips like water through a burst dam. "He'll see her at his house."

Thank God.

With the nurse calling after us, we slip away, leaving her questions unanswered, and the automatic doors slide shut behind us.

Tom starts the car with a frenzy, then the streets are unfurling before us again.

"Does he know that we lost Danielle?"

Tom shakes his head. "I didn't tell him. I told him what we agreed on, that Daisy is our baby. I said the birth was traumatic and we don't want to go back to the hospital if we can help it."

"Do you think he can help Daisy? Or will we have to go back to hospital anyway?" I ask.

"I don't know, Nora," Tom replies, his shoulders hunched and rigid. "But we have to try. We don't have a choice."

EIGHTEEN

Larry Donell's home is a sleek display of modern architecture, a glass and steel structure with minimal walls and a design that could easily be featured in an architectural magazine.

We find him waiting for us on the porch, wearing casual, black pajama pants over his athletic frame, his blond hair messy from sleeping.

"Let me see her," he says as soon as we step out. Tom lifts Daisy from her seat, blankets and all, and presents her to Larry like an offering.

I can barely breathe as Larry walks into the house ahead of us and examines our baby girl right there in his living room. Daisy's cries have quieted to whimpers, but each one is still filled with pain. The seconds drag on until Larry straightens up, his face unreadable for a moment before it breaks into a weary smile.

"It's just an ear infection," he announces, and relief crashes through me, so potent it leaves me dizzy. "Painful, but not serious. And the fever has gone down, which is a good thing. I'll write you a prescription for some antibiotics."

"Thank you," Tom exhales, the relief in his voice mirroring my own. "Thank you so much, Larry."

We'd been teetering on the brink of disaster, and now, suddenly, there's solid ground beneath us. It's not over—not by a long shot—but for now, Daisy is going to be okay. That's all that matters.

"Let me get that prescription." Larry disappears into his home office.

Tom and I exchange a glance, the unspoken question hanging between us: Are we truly in the clear? But there's no time to dwell on it because Larry returns, scribbling on a pad, then tearing off the top sheet and handing it to Tom.

"Get this filled first thing in the morning," he instructs. "She needs to start on it right away."

"Of course," Tom replies, pocketing the paper as we step outside. "Again, thank you."

"Wait," Larry says just as we're about to take Daisy back into the car. "Can I have a quick word, Tom?" He gestures for Tom to follow him, and they move away from me, their voices hushed but intense. I try to eavesdrop, but their words are snatched away by the night breeze.

Larry's arms are folded across his chest, his posture rigid in contrast to Tom's pleading gestures. There's a tension there, an undercurrent of disagreement that has my heart racing.

I watch, helpless, as they continue their debate. My mind goes wild as it tries to come up with possibilities—what could they be arguing about?

Finally, they seem to reach an uneasy agreement. Tom nods stiffly, and Larry waves a dismissive hand, his body language suggesting resignation. They head back toward us.

"Everything okay?" I ask Tom.

"Everything's fine," he assures me as he slides into the driver's seat, but even in the dim light of the car's interior, I notice his jaw is clenched tight.

"Tom," I say over the hum of the engine, "what did Larry want to talk to you about?"

He exhales slowly. "I had to tell him everything—about Daisy, about us. He was pissed, Nora. Really pissed." Tom shakes his head, as if trying to dispel the memory of the confrontation. "But I talked him down. He promised he wouldn't tell anyone."

"Why? Why did you have to tell him?"

"Because he knows. He knows we lost Danielle. Doctors talk, I guess. This is a small town."

"But what if he tells someone?"

Tom doesn't respond.

"Tom?" I prod again, needing him to say something, anything, to chase away the dread that threatens to strangle me.

Still, he says nothing, and the weight of his silence is a tangible thing, pressing down on me until I can hardly breathe.

Finally, he speaks. "I guess we need to prepare ourselves for what to do next if he does. Leave it to me, Nora."

What does that mean? What can we do? I really wish we could move right away, but Tom has given in his notice at the school and can't just up and leave. He's also only just started the process of getting our house up for sale. But if Larry speaks, we might just have to run.

"Please don't let them take her away from us, Tom. I can't bear it," I say, as I watch Daisy in the mirror. She's finally sleeping, and I watch her chest rise and fall.

"I won't, sweetheart. I promise. I'll think of something."

NINETEEN

Tom has just left for work this bright April morning and I'm making my way to Isobel's room with Daisy in my arms. Thankfully, within a few days of being on antibiotics, my baby is herself again, happy and content.

I find Isobel in the midst of unloading a basket of laundry, her shoulders slumped and her mind elsewhere.

From a young age, she has always helped me with household chores, but I don't want her to be burdened with additional responsibilities on top of helping with Daisy, especially now that her studies are becoming increasingly demanding as summer break approaches.

It was no shock to me when my daughter announced her plans to study to become a veterinarian. She has always had a natural connection with animals, tending to wounded birds and rescuing lost pets that found their way onto our property. With soft words and bits of food, she's able to gain the trust of even the most skittish creatures.

When Tom and I sell our house and leave Ellery Creek with Daisy, and Isobel moves back into her apartment, I plan to surprise her with a kitten or a puppy. With Lauren gone, she'll need some company.

I lower myself next to her on the bed, watching as she meticulously folds each piece of clothing.

"Izzy, are you okay?" I place a hand on her back.

"Yeah, I'm fine, Mom." She gives me a strained smile.

"Look, Isobel, I want you to go out and enjoy your day. Why don't you go help out at the animal shelter?" Placing Daisy down on the bed and taking a black and white T-shirt from Isobel, I continue, "I can handle the rest. You deserve a break, sweetheart."

Isobel's face lights up at the suggestion, and she sets down the clothes. "Thanks, Mom. That's a good idea. I'll go right now."

She quickly gets dressed and grabs her backpack. Picking up Daisy, I follow her downstairs, but when she opens the front door, we find Martha on our doorstep. And next to her is Mrs. Lewis, who has bright-pink curlers in her salt and pepper hair, and several other women from the neighborhood, all carrying casseroles and baked goods.

Martha steps forward. "Nora, sorry to show up unannounced, but we figured that after over two weeks, you would finally be open to us visiting and meeting the new baby." She peers down at Daisy in my arms and her expression softens even more. "My goodness, is that her? She's absolutely precious!" The rest of the women follow suit, gathering around to get a better look at Daisy and gushing over her small features.

Mrs. Lewis places a beautifully wrapped gift in my free hand and smiles. "We wanted to welcome the newest member of our community properly."

Gritting my teeth, I smile warmly at the group of women and invite them inside, thanking them for their generosity. I usher Martha and the others into the living room, then Isobel and I take some of the food to the kitchen.

"Is that a good idea, Mom?" Isobel drops her backpack on the kitchen table and takes Daisy from me. "What if—?"

"Look, they won't go away until they get what they want. The last thing we need is for them to go around spreading rumors and making assumptions." I pause as I take out some plates and glasses from the cupboard. "It's better if we just play along for now."

Isobel nods, but I can see the worry etched on her face.

"Izzy, you don't have to stay, you know, honey? Go on to the shelter. I'll handle this."

"And leave you with the vultures? No way, Mom. I'm staying right here. We'll get through this together."

I give her a grateful smile and say nothing more as I arrange the plates of food on the kitchen table.

I place Daisy in a bassinet and join Isobel in serving our guests, and they eagerly dig into the food, their chatter filling the room as they take turns to coo over the baby.

When Martha stands over her, I feel so uncomfortable, I can't help feeling like she's staring at her with an unusual intensity. But finally, she looks away and clears her throat. "What a beauty she is, you must be so proud. Would you mind terribly if we took turns holding her?"

I give her a polite nod, "Of course, please feel free to take turns, just make sure you've put some antibac on your hands first."

Martha volunteers to be the first one to hold Daisy, cooing and whispering sweet nothings.

"Oh, Martha, why don't you let someone else have a turn with the baby?" I suggest after a few minutes, trying to keep my tone light and casual. But Martha's grip on Daisy tightens, her smile turning into a grimace as she shakes her head.

"No, I think I'll hold on to her a little longer."

The other women exchange hesitant glances, a tension hanging in the air.

Then Daisy starts wailing and squirming in Martha's arms. Martha's smile falters as Daisy's cries grow louder by the second.

I seize the opportunity and step forward, reaching for Daisy. "Let me take her, Martha. She hasn't been feeling too well lately."

Martha gives up and releases Daisy and I quickly gather her into my arms, soothing her with whispered words and gentle swaying. But she refuses to calm down, her cries escalating into full-blown wails.

"She's not used to having many people around," Isobel offers as an explanation, then turns to me. "Mom, maybe you should take her upstairs."

Grateful for her intervention, I nod. "I think that would be best. Please excuse us."

As I carry Daisy out of the room, her cries gradually subside, replaced by soft hiccups and sniffles.

As soon as we enter the nursery upstairs, I let out a long breath of relief. Then I lower myself into the armchair to catch my breath and figure out what to do next. As Daisy starts making soft cooing sounds, I look at her innocent face and feel the anxiety inside me loosen a bit. I stroke her soft cheek, a wave of protectiveness washing over me.

Finally, just as she drifts off, Isobel comes into the room and offers to stay with her.

"Thanks." I say to her. "But after the neighbors leave, you should still go to the shelter. I think it will be good for you."

"I will, I promise. I just didn't want to leave you alone with *them*."

Closing the door behind me, I head back downstairs to our uninvited guests.

"I'm so sorry, ladies. Daisy just needed some time to settle down. She's calm now and will probably fall asleep soon. I hope you all understand."

Jolene Martinez, a brunette with hazel eyes and long, fake lashes, who owns a teahouse at the corner of Maple and Elm Street, speaks up. "Don't worry about it, Nora. Babies can be unpredictable sometimes. We completely understand." Her words are mostly met with nods of reassurance and understanding.

Martha, on the other hand, says nothing as she reaches for a plate of hors d'oeuvres.

As the food disappears, they start discussing current headlines and local gossip. Then Doris, Martha's sister-in-law who moved in with her after Martha's husband died, asks if everyone has heard the news about "that poor girl" and the entire room goes quiet.

Relishing the drama, Martha's voice drops to a conspiratorial whisper. "A young woman has been found dead at the beach near the border with Amberfield. They say she fell from a cliff."

My heart thuds, and in the heavily silent room, I'm sure everyone can hear it.

"Oh, yes, I read about that. Such a tragedy." Mrs. Lewis takes a gulp of red wine. "They say foul play may be involved, but the police are keeping hush about the details. Let's see if they can solve this one quickly."

Rose Bridges, a kindergarten teacher, nods in agreement, her pigtails bobbing. "It's unsettling to think about things like that happening so close to home."

Their conversation takes a somber tone as they hypothesize about the events leading up to the woman's death. Each theory they suggest grows increasingly morbid and dramatic.

"If I had to guess, I'd say it has something to do with a love gone sour," Doris adds and pops a grape into her mouth. "Or perhaps she took her own life."

"Enough, Doris!" Mrs. Lewis snaps. "This is not a gossip column. A young woman lost her life."

Saying nothing, Doris simply shrugs before picking up another grape.

"That's right," Martha adds. "There's no use in speculating. She was only found yesterday, so I'm sure we will be hearing more about it soon. It's just so sad to think about what she must have gone through in her final hours."

To my relief, the conversation eventually shifts to lighter topics as the ladies finish their food and share stories about their families and recent vacations. I try my best to engage, nodding and smiling at appropriate intervals, but my mind keeps drifting to the woman whose body was found on that nearby beach.

Finally, the ladies grab their empty dishes and head out the door. As everyone walks down the path, Martha lingers behind.

"Thank you, Nora, for inviting us into your home. Your baby is truly a little angel." She hesitates, her eyes flickering over me. "But I must say, she looks nothing like you."

I do my best to appear unruffled. "Oh well, you know how these things go, Martha. Babies can take after anyone in the family, right?"

Martha is silent for a moment longer than is comfortable for me, then she smiles. "Yes. She does remind me of someone, that's for sure."

TWENTY

At midday, Tom surprises me by coming home for lunch, and the moment he enters through the door, I can see on his face that something is terribly wrong.

"We need to talk," he says, taking Daisy from me and cuddling her to his chest.

As I follow him to the living room, my mind races with all the worst-case scenarios.

Did Larry go to the cops?

Once we're seated on the couch, he takes a deep breath before speaking. "I'm not sure if you've heard, but this morning everyone around here was talking about the woman found dead on some rocky beach."

"Yeah, Martha and her crew mentioned it when they—"

"They were here again?" Tom's face darkens.

"I couldn't turn them away this time. They brought food and gifts for Daisy."

"Right." He takes my hand in his, with Daisy snuggled against his chest, her little legs pointed toward his torso. Her face scrunches up briefly, a little furrow forming between her brows, and she lets out a soft, restless whimper. I notice her small fists clench and release, her body wiggling slightly as if she's struggling to get comfortable. Tom rocks her gently, his hand instinctively patting her back in a steady rhythm. "Nora, there's something else you should know about that girl," he says.

Our eyes lock. "What is it?"

"The authorities have identified her." He pauses. "It's Lauren."

"Oh, my God!" My hand flies to my mouth as tears spring to my eyes. "Not our Lauren?"

"I'm afraid it's her," Tom says, his own eyes filling with tears. "She's dead."

My stomach drops. Before Lauren and Isobel parted ways, Lauren was such a big part of our family, sometimes even joining our family celebrations. She was almost like a second daughter to Tom and me.

I can't imagine her lying dead, on a mortuary slab somewhere. Sweet, smart, beautiful Lauren.

"Are they sure?"

"Yes. I'm sure it's all over the news now. Nora, there's something else. They suspect she recently gave birth."

The room starts to spin and my fingernails curl into my hands. "She was pregnant? How... Why didn't she tell us? Oh God, Tom, do you think... Could Daisy be hers? Oh, poor Lauren."

Tom wipes his brow with the back of his hand. "Maybe. I seriously don't know what to think. It was all such a shock."

We sit there, the weight of the news heavy between us, until gradually we shift and make our way to the kitchen, barely able to talk to each other. Our movements dazed, Tom and I have lunch together, reheating leftovers from yesterday's chicken and vegetable stir-fry. The entire time, I find it difficult to breathe.

Tom finally puts his fork down. "Jenny and David must be so—"

"Devastated?" I finish for him. "You'd think so. But to be

honest, they never cared much about their daughter while she was alive," I say bitterly and wipe away the tears trickling down my cheeks.

The reason Lauren visited us so often and attended many of our family functions was because her parents seemed utterly disinterested in her. Instead of helping out their daughter financially, Jenny was more focused on spending the money she earned at the local post office on beauty procedures and fancy clothes, in an effort to stay young. And David, a used car salesman, was always more interested in his antique car collection than spending time with his own daughter. It was no wonder Lauren found comfort in our family, where she was treated like one of our own.

"How are we going to tell Isobel it's Lauren?"

"I'm sure she already knows. The way news in this town travels, she probably heard it before we did. I should call her."

"That's a good idea," Tom says, getting to his feet. "I'm sorry, sweetheart, but I need to get back to work."

"Okay. I'll see you later." I kiss him and escort him to the door.

After Tom leaves, I call Isobel, but her phone is switched off. I just hope her friends at the animal shelter are looking after her.

Two hours later, I'm sitting in front of the TV while Daisy, happily fed and changed, is babbling to herself in my arms.

A breaking news alert flashes on the screen, and the reporter's voice fills the room, confirming the identity of the deceased woman found on the beach: Lauren Montgomery, a 20-year-old woman, who was born and raised in Ellery Creek but was studying in Amberfield.

As I watch the reporter, a woman with sleek black hair and bright-red lipstick, my hand clutches the arm of the couch tightly.

Lauren's face stares back at me from a corner of the screen, back when she still had her long black curly hair, her dark-brown eyes sparkling with life. Memories flood my mind of her and Isobel when they were younger, playing in the woods behind our house.

"Lauren Montgomery was found dead on the beach shared by Ellery Creek and Amberfield by a dog walker in the early hours of yesterday morning. The police are treating her death as suspicious and are urging anyone with information to come forward. Lauren was born and raised in Ellery Creek, but after high school, she moved to Amberfield to study psychology at Sagebourne College. She was described as kind, generous, and full of life by her friends and family."

The reporter glances behind her at flowers on the edge of the cliff Lauren may have fallen from because one of her shoes was discovered there. Then the camera zooms in on a bouquet with a note that reads, "You're forever in our hearts, Lauren."

I find myself aching all over for that poor girl, for the life she had led and the life she could have continued to live. A sob rises in my chest, followed by a single tear that slides down my cheek.

When the reporter turns back to the camera, she delivers the final piece of information. "Even more tragic is that according to the preliminary autopsy results, Lauren Montgomery seems to have given birth not too long before her untimely death. The identity and whereabouts of the baby remain unknown at this time, adding another layer of mystery to this already heartbreaking story."

Unable to handle it, I find myself quickly flicking off the TV screen, and in that moment, I hear the sound of a key turning in the lock of the front door. I put Daisy down in her chair for a minute and rush to the entrance. There Isobel stands, her eyes red and swollen from crying.

I pull her into a tight hug. "Oh, Izzy, I'm so sorry. I can't even imagine what you must be going through right now."

Isobel clings to me, her body shaking with sobs. I guide her to the living room and sit her down on the couch, where she takes a deep, shuddering breath before finally speaking.

"I can't believe she's gone, Mom. She was my friend, and now... now she's just... gone. I feel so terrible for the way we ended..." Hiccups escape her lips as tears stream down her face, leaving wet trails on her cheeks.

"We'll get through this together, Izzy." I put my arms around her again, unable to hold back my own tears. Despite their falling out, I know that Isobel still cared deeply for Lauren, and her grief is palpable. "It's going to be okay," I whisper, rubbing circles on her back in a futile attempt to offer comfort.

After she calms down a bit, I gently ask, "Did you know that Lauren was pregnant?"

Isobel pulls back and quickly gets to her feet. "Yeah, I did." She sniffs, saying nothing more.

"But why didn't you say anything? You know what this means, don't you?"

She simply shrugs. "Look, I'm sorry, Mom. I just... I need some time to process everything. This is all too much."

I rise to my feet as well and give her shoulder a reassuring squeeze. "Take all the time you need, sweetheart."

Before leaving the room, she stops briefly by Daisy's chair, just staring down at her. Then she draws in a deep breath, as if trying to gather strength from within before walking out and heading upstairs.

My daughter knew. All this time, she knew who Daisy's mother was.

What else has she kept from me?

TWENTY-ONE

"We need to talk," I say as soon as Tom walks through the door at 5 p.m.

"I know." His expression is grim as he takes Daisy from my arms, and we head to our bedroom, where he puts her in the co-sleeper.

We sit in silence for a few minutes, until he continues, "What do you think we should do? The police will be looking for Lauren's baby."

"We can't go to the police. There's no way Jenny and David would want Daisy; she will end up taken to a foster home, or worse."

"I agree." Tom scratches his beard. "Daisy was left on our doorstep. I think we shouldn't say anything. Lauren clearly wanted us to care for her."

"Yes. It's the right thing to do in Lauren's memory." Fresh tears spring to my eyes as I think of Lauren again and how she reminded me so much of myself at that age.

She had no one watching out for her and had to make it through life struggling to make ends meet on her own. Like me, she had to deal with pregnancy when she was far too young.

And now her baby is in our care, a tiny, innocent being who will depend on us for everything.

Tom's hand finds mine, holding it tight.

"Nora," he asks, "do you think it was suicide? The police believe there could have been foul play, but if Lauren left Daisy on our doorstep, she must have known that she was not going to be there to take care of her."

I stare at the wall, lost in thought. Lauren was a fighter, a survivor. She wouldn't leave her baby behind willingly, would she?

"I don't know," I reply. "I can't wrap my head around it."

"Me neither, but whatever happened, Daisy is our responsibility now, our baby girl."

I sigh as I watch her kicking her little legs in the air, then get to my feet. "I need to check on Isobel."

I lean over to brush a gentle kiss on Daisy's forehead before leaving her with Tom. As I go, I silently vow to do everything in my power to give Daisy the love and care she deserves, that Lauren would have given her. I will not allow anyone to take her away, to become part of a system that would toss her around like a ragdoll, from one foster home to another, like Tom was after being left in his pram at a local church. I will fight tooth and nail to ensure that she has a stable, loving environment to grow up in.

Suddenly images of Lauren lying dead on the beach flash through my mind, her lifeless body surrounded by murky water, rocks, and tangled weeds. The thought sends a wave of nausea crashing through me. Lauren had been in and out of my home for years, she and Isobel had been so inseparable since they were around the age of twelve. The idea of her being gone, leaving behind a baby who would never know her mother, is almost unbearable. But I have to be strong for Daisy now.

When I reach Isobel's door, I hear the sobs, deep, raw, and heart-wrenching. My hand hesitates on the doorknob. My daughter is not someone who cries often and even when she's overwhelmed, she usually keeps her emotions all buried inside. Even when we lost Roxy, our dog, a year ago, her tears were few and far between. Sometimes I feel that she holds back her pain to be strong for me. God knows I've shed enough tears for both of us over the years as I raised her and navigated the challenges life threw our way.

I push open the door to see her curled up on her bed, her face buried in her hands as she cries uncontrollably. I lower myself down, wrapping my arms around her.

"Isobel, sweetheart, I'm so terribly sorry." Her sobs are muffled against my chest, but slowly she lifts her tear-streaked face to look up at me.

"Mom," she chokes out, "I can't believe she's gone. Lauren was... she was like a sister to me. And it's all my fault. She wouldn't be dead if it weren't for me."

TWENTY-TWO

I pull Isobel closer, holding her tight. How could she possibly think she's responsible for Lauren's death?

"Baby, listen to me," I say firmly, tilting her chin up gently. "What happened to Lauren was not your fault. It was a terrible tragedy, a twist of fate that none of us could have seen coming. You were a true friend to her. You allowed her to stay with you when she couldn't find a place she could afford. You brought her home with you so she would have a family to celebrate the holidays with."

"But I was supposed to be there for her, Mom. I promised we would always have each other's backs. If I had just been there for her when she needed me, if I had listened to her, she would still be here." She buries her face into my shoulder.

"Isobel, you were a true friend to Lauren. I know you two had a fall-out, but deep down, I'm sure she knew how much you cared for her." I take a deep breath. "Baby, we can't predict or control everything that happens in life, no matter how much we wish we could. Sometimes, despite our best efforts, things happen that are beyond our control."

Isobel lifts her head slowly, her tear-stained face searching mine. "But she was pregnant, Mom. She was pregnant and afraid and I walked away when she needed me the most." She stands and goes to the window as her shoulders continue to shake, then she turns around. "I'm sorry I didn't tell you about Lauren's pregnancy. It's just that she didn't want anyone to know."

I walk over to her and place a gentle hand on her shoulder. "It's okay, sweetheart. You were respecting Lauren's wishes, protecting her privacy. You were being a good friend, even when it was hard."

"But now she's dead. And I never got to tell her how much she meant to me, how sorry I am for everything..." She presses her lips together. "I think Daisy is Lauren's baby, and she wanted us to have her."

I nod and swallow hard. "I think so too. Tom and I have decided that we're not going to the police with the information. We'll continue to raise her as our own. No one needs to know."

"Okay. I'll always be here to help you take care of Daisy. It's the least I can do for Lauren."

"Thank you. Lauren would have been happy that you're here for her daughter."

"Lauren's mom called me," she continues through her tears. "Tonight at ten, the hour Lauren was born, there's going to be a vigil for anyone who wants to pay their respects. She wanted to make sure we knew and could be there if we wanted."

I sigh. I wish they had been there for their daughter in life, and I wonder if now they regret how they treated her. Now that it's too late. "Yes, okay, thank you for letting me know. I think it would be good for us to go together as a family. We'll make sure to honor Lauren's memory and keep her spirit alive in our hearts. And Daisy will grow up surrounded by love from all of us."

. . .

Around seven that evening, when the sun is just starting to set and Tom is out running errands, the doorbell downstairs rings. Isobel appears in the bedroom doorway moments later, looking pale and uneasy.

"Mom, it's the police," she whispers and blood drains from my face.

TWENTY-THREE

Beads of sweat are forming at the back of my neck as I stand stock-still in my bedroom. Am I about to be arrested?

I glance toward the window and for a few seconds I watch the sunset painting the sky in hues of fiery orange and soft pink.

The doorbell rings again.

"Mom, what do we do?" Isobel's eyes are wild with panic.

I take a deep breath, trying to steady my racing heart. "You need to open the door for them. Answer their questions. But before you do that, I'm going to leave the house by the back gate, with Daisy. They can't know she's here."

I scoop up Daisy from her crib, her tiny hand grasping on to my finger.

Our garden has a small gate that leads into the dense woods and it's our best chance to slip away unnoticed. Hurrying to the nursery, I quickly grab Daisy's diaper bag, stuffing it with a few essentials before racing to the stairs just as the bell rings again.

Isobel follows close behind me down the stairs and as soon as I slip into the kitchen, I give her a small nod, tell her not to look nervous, and close the door.

Outside, shadows from the setting sun cover everything, and

the trees whisper softly in the late April breeze that ruffles my hair.

Holding my breath, I make my way to the small gate at the edge of our property.

The rusted latch gives way with a soft click, and I push it open just wide enough to slip through, careful not to make a sound as I imagine Isobel back inside the house with the cops, dreading the questions they will be asking her.

Soon, we step into the woods, the earthy scent of pine and moss filling my nostrils. Daisy stirs in my arms, her chubby fingers grasping at my shirt.

I make my way to a small nearby lake and while normally soothing, the rippling surface of the water fails to calm my jangled nerves. I hope Isobel is holding up okay, that they don't see guilt in her expression.

A bench beckons to me from the water's edge; I sit down and press a gentle kiss to Daisy's forehead, murmuring soothing words in an attempt to calm her crying. The pacifier is gone; she must have spat it out somewhere along the way. But at least we're far enough for the police not to hear her.

Just as I start to relax a little, she starts crying louder and I shush her, rocking her gently in my arms as I scan the area for anyone. But it's just us for now.

When Daisy refuses to calm down, I realize she must be hungry. It was a good call for me to bring along her diaper bag and a bottle. It's only half full, but it will have to do. I shift her in my arms and cradle her head as I offer her the milk.

Her cries soften to contented suckling sounds, her small hands reaching up to grip my thumb. I watch the fading light glinting over the water, the beauty of the ripples reflecting the changing colors of the sunset.

Everything is going to be all right, Nora. There's nothing to worry about.

As Daisy relaxes more in my arms, I lean back against the

worn wood of the bench and enjoy the sight of the shifting colors of the sky above us. The hues blend together like an artist's palette, streaks of pink and orange melting into a deep indigo that takes my breath away.

After a while Isobel calls to let me know that the police have finally left.

"They heard that Lauren and I were best friends and lived together. They're just talking to anyone who might have known her."

"Did they say what they think happened to her?" I'm still shaking so much it's getting hard to hold Daisy.

"A suicide note was found, Mom. It was tucked under some rock on the clifftop." The last words are swallowed by her sobs. "I can't believe she chose to go like that..."

"I'm so very sorry. I'm coming home now, I'll be there soon. Hold on, darling."

When I get home, I hold Isobel to me as heart-shattering sobs rack her body. "I'm so sorry, sweetheart. I know how much she meant to you." Isobel says nothing and instead just holds on tighter. As I let her grieve, I can't hold back my own tears.

"Did they say anything about the missing baby?" I ask when we finally pull apart.

"No, just that they're searching." Isobel glances at her watch. "I think we should get ready for the vigil."

"Yes, you're right. Tom will be here soon. He'll stay home with Daisy."

Something tells me that it's only a matter of time before the police come knocking on our door again.

TWENTY-FOUR

Soon we arrive at the site of the vigil on the clifftop where Lauren is suspected to have jumped. It's the same beautiful place I came to with Isobel not too long ago, but now the air is thick with grief and shock.

The flickering candles cast shadows on the faces of the mourners and the air smells of burning wax.

Apart from Isobel and me, there are at least thirty people here and they're gathered in clusters as they light candles and place them along with bouquets of roses and lilies on the ground next to a black and white blown-up photo of a grinning Lauren with braces. She's wearing a cap and gown at her high school graduation, her long hair hanging in waves down her shoulders.

Tears burn the backs of my eyes because I remember that day like it was yesterday. I remember congratulating her and Isobel with a hug before taking the two girls out for lunch at their favorite pizza restaurant. For Lauren's parents, it had been enough to show up for ten minutes, take this photo that now marks her death, and get back to their lives like it was just another ordinary day.

The soft murmur of the crowd merges with the distant cries of seagulls and I watch the faces around me, searching for any sign of cops. But from what I can see, most of the people seem to be students from Isobel and Lauren's college. Their faces are streaked with tears as they console each other in hushed tones. Many of them know that Isobel used to be close to Lauren and so they approach her with sympathetic smiles and words of condolence.

It annoys me that there are also several local reporters present and I don't think that's okay. It doesn't feel right for them to record intimate moments of grief that should be private.

A young man with sunglasses even at this late hour catches my attention. He stands apart from the crowd, his hands shoved deep into the pockets of his jeans as he watches the flickering candles.

"Who's that?" I whisper to Isobel.

"Mark, Lauren's ex-boyfriend. They broke up before she died. I'll be right back." Without waiting for my reply, she makes her way over to Mark, and a jolt shudders through me. Mark must be Daisy's biological father, but does he know that? What does he know about what happened to his child, and to Lauren?

As my mind wanders, a cool breeze sweeps across the clifftop, rustling the leaves of nearby trees and teasing the candle flames. Feeling a sudden chill despite the warm evening, I wrap my arms around myself and move closer to where Isobel is standing with Mark.

His shoulders tense up at first, but then he relaxes slightly, his expression shifting from anger to resignation. Isobel reaches out to touch his arm in a gesture of comfort, and for a moment, they stand together, united in their grief. The sound of waves crashing mixes with the sounds of voices, as more and more stars pierce through the blanket of darkness above us, around a pale moon.

As the vigil begins, a solemn hush falls over the crowd. Lauren's father, David, a stocky man with a receding hairline, which he combats with an ill-fitting toupee that fails to hide his fifty-something years, steps forward to say a few words about Lauren and is soon joined by Jenny, her mother, who's dressed in a sparkly black dress that hangs loosely on her frail frame. Even though her dress is dark, as the candlelight reflects off the thin material, she almost takes on a ghostly appearance.

Their voices tremble with emotion as they speak of their daughter, their words a tribute to a life cut short. The crowd listens intently and some, including me, wipe away tears as memories of Lauren flood their minds.

Jenny sniffs and reads from a piece of paper, "Our darling Lauren was a bright light in our lives, a beacon of hope and joy. She brought laughter and love wherever she went, and her absence leaves a void that can never be filled. We will never forget her infectious smile, her kind heart, and the way she lit up a room just by walking into it."

David takes Jenny's hand and adds, "We may never understand why this tragedy occurred, why our precious daughter was taken from us so soon, but she will live on in our memories and our hearts forever."

As he finishes speaking, the crowd erupts into soft sobs and whispers of agreement. Tears of sadness trickle down my cheeks, but mostly I feel anger toward David and Jenny.

Tom and I were better parents to her than they ever were. She celebrated more holidays at our house than with them. For them to stand there and speak of her like they cared for and loved her dearly makes my blood boil. But I swallow down my anger. Now is not the time or place.

As the vigil continues, different people step forward to share their memories of Lauren. Friends recount funny stories from college parties, professors praise her intelligence and dedication, and others speak of her kindness and generosity. Each story paints a picture of a vibrant young woman with a bright future ahead of her, a future that died with her.

When it's Isobel's turn to speak, she takes a deep breath and steps up to the makeshift podium. "Lauren was more than just a friend to me. She was like a sister, my ride or die. She was always there for me, through the good times and the bad. She had a way of making everyone feel special and loved, even on their darkest days." She pauses to catch her breath and stop herself from breaking down. "Lauren was the kind of person who would go out of her way to help others, without ever expecting anything in return. And that's why it's so hard to believe that she's gone." She suddenly stops talking and presses the tips of her fingers to her eyes. "I... I... sorry. I can't do this."

I can feel the tension rising in the air as the reporters start to approach the podium, their cameras flashing in our faces. And before I know it, one of them shouts out a question.

"Were you aware that she was pregnant?"

Caught off guard, Isobel's mouth opens and closes as she struggles to find the right words. I step forward, placing a protective hand on her shoulder.

"That's enough," I say firmly. "This is a time for remembrance, not speculation."

The reporter takes a step back at my tone, but others start chiming in with more questions.

"Where is the baby?" one of them shouts.

Isobel grips my arm tightly, her nails digging into my skin as she looks at me. I can sense her anxiety radiating off her in waves. But instead of responding, she steps away from the podium.

Refusing to quit, a female reporter with a tight bun turns to the parents. "Mr. and Mrs. Montgomery, do you have any comments on the allegations that Lauren was struggling with mental health issues prior to her death?"

David's face reddens with anger as Jenny reaches out to

grasp his hand. But he detangles himself from her grip and steps up to the microphone.

"My daughter was a strong and resilient young lady and while she had her troubles, she did not kill herself."

His voice cracks, and Jenny comes to stand next to him and dabs at her cheeks with a napkin. "We are her parents, and we refuse to believe she chose to end her own life. She had so many dreams for her future. She wanted to travel the world, to carve out her own pathway. And she was always scared of swimming, of open water. Even if she wanted to die, she'd never have done it this way. Someone did this to her. To our baby girl." Her words are punctuated by a hiccup, and David wraps a protective arm around her, guiding her away.

The reporters hesitate for a moment, perhaps sensing the raw emotion radiating from the grieving parents. Then some begin to pack up their cameras and microphones. They know that they have pushed too far and are giving up, allowing us to return to our memories of Lauren.

As they start to disperse, I hear audible sighs from the crowd. I suck in the scent of the ocean and the aroma of candle wax, and I know it's a scent I'll take with me. From today onward, whenever I smell that combination of salt and flame, I'll remember this moment, tonight. I'll remember what happened to Lauren.

Isobel moves on to speak to some other students and I'm close enough to overhear their conversations.

"I don't believe she killed herself either," a girl with dreadlocks and a long cardigan says with conviction. "A few days before she died, she told me how excited she was to be a mother. And now..."

"Did she tell you who the baby's father was?" someone asks. "Was it Mark?"

The first girl responds. "Yeah, exactly, and she said they weren't together anymore. I got the sense it wasn't a good breakup, but she seemed so determined, so confident that she could parent her baby alone."

As I strain my ears to listen, Jenny and David approach me, their faces grief-stricken.

Then Jenny blurts out a question that slams into me like a freight truck. "Where is our grandchild, Nora?"

TWENTY-FIVE

It takes a few seconds for me to process Jenny's question, my mind spinning.

"I... I don't know," I stammer out.

Jenny sniffs, her eyes red and swollen, and reaches out to touch my arm. "Sorry, it's just we know how close Lauren was to your family and we thought maybe she said something before... before—"

David steps in to finish his wife's sentence. "When Lauren told us she was pregnant, we didn't react in the best way. We were shocked and disappointed, but we loved her. We would have supported her and that baby no matter what."

Lies. All lies. They did not even support Lauren on her own without a child. But I have to keep such opinions to myself. It's not my place to judge them, especially now that they're grieving.

"I didn't know that Lauren was pregnant. I'm really sorry, but I don't have any information about your grandchild."

I can't tell them about Daisy. They could go to the police and they will certainly take her from us. And if they don't end up raising her, the father might decide to step up. Mark. A young man, barely out of his teens. How could that be better for Daisy, than staying in our care?

When all is said and done, Lauren wanted us to have the baby. She obviously didn't trust her own parents enough to raise her daughter.

Sobbing now, Jenny wrings her hands in desperation. "We have to find out. We have to know what happened to our grandchild. I know we failed Lauren when she was alive, but we want to do right by her now. Please, help us, Nora."

"I'm so sorry Jenny, David. I wish I knew something."

Jenny's shoulders slump in defeat, and David wraps his arms around her, offering what little comfort he can.

"We understand." Jenny attempts a small smile. "Thank you for being there for our daughter and for coming tonight. It means the world to us."

I watch them walk away, their figures fading into the darkness of the night. Guilt cuts deep, twisting and churning. But I have to do everything in my power to keep this secret. Soon, Tom, Daisy and I will leave town and they will never suspect a thing.

As the vigil comes to an end, the crowd begins to disperse, friends and family offering their condolences to David and Jenny before drifting away in small groups.

As I stand there alone, Isobel returns, holding two envelopes. "I want to get out of here. I can't... anymore."

I wrap an arm around her shoulders and pull her to me. "Yes, let's go."

Inside the car, she hands me one of the envelopes.

"What is this?" I ask as I settle behind the wheel.

"Some memories of Lauren, I think. One of the students put them together. Let's look inside at home."

I'm not surprised that it wasn't Jenny and David who created the keepsakes. After all, they don't have enough memories of their daughter to fill a small box.

When we arrive home, Daisy is asleep in her baby basket next to Tom, who is watching the local news.

"There were reporters at the vigil?" he asks, standing up to give me a kiss. "What the hell?"

I nod and drop onto the couch while Isobel excuses herself to go to bed. "They were desperate for a story. You should have seen how disrespectful they were, lurking around like vultures preying on the grief of others. And there's something else you should know." I pinch the bridge of my nose. "Jenny and David asked if I knew anything about Lauren's baby. I told them I didn't know anything, of course."

"You think they suspect something?"

"I don't know. But we need to leave town, Tom, and soon."

The night wears on, and Tom and I remain in the living room for a while, taking turns holding Daisy and watching the news on repeat.

The only break I take is to go make Daisy a bottle, but before I head to the kitchen, I pull the memorial envelope from my purse—which I left on the console table by the front door—intending to open it with Tom. A few minutes later, I'm back in the living room and realize I've left it in the kitchen. Too exhausted to get up again, I decide I'll look inside later.

An hour later, Tom heads up to bed, taking Daisy with him. But I stay up, heading into the kitchen to make some tea. It feels like the walls are closing in on me and I let out a heavy sigh. Then I notice the envelope on the kitchen table, the one Isobel gave me in the car.

I slowly tear it open. Inside are various photographs, a printed poem, and small trinkets—each one a piece of Lauren's life.

Then something falls to the table, a folded piece of paper.

A jolt runs through me when I open it to see Tom's handwriting.

Lauren, I want to ask you to reconsider keeping the baby. Nora recently lost another baby, and it has broken her heart. We both know you're not prepared to be a mother at such a young age. As your child's father, I have a say in this too. Nora and I can offer a loving and supportive home for our baby. It would be the best thing for all of us. Please take some time to think about it.

TWENTY-SIX

ISOBEL

Seven Months Ago

The desire to become a veterinarian has been ingrained in me since childhood. From the earliest memories of clutching toy animals in my hands to the countless hours spent poring over books about animal care, the passion for veterinary medicine has never left me.

Now, as I step into the corridors of the Sagebourne School of Veterinary Medicine in Amberfield, I feel a surge of excitement.

It's a typical Monday morning, the campus buzzing with the energy of students rushing to their classes after summer break.

The lecture hall is spacious and well-lit, with rows of neatly arranged seats facing a large projector screen. The walls are covered with colorful posters depicting various animal species.

As I settle into my seat, Dr. Wilson, an adjunct professor, strides to the front of the room. He's wearing a suit that looks like a patchwork quilt and his hair brushes the tips of his shoulders.

"Today," he begins, his voice commanding the attention of the room, "we'll be diving into the fascinating world of canine communication."

Throughout the lecture, he navigates through the complexities of dog body language, using funny anecdotes and real-life examples to get his points across.

Halfway through the lecture, my phone buzzes in my pocket. I try to ignore it at first, but the buzzing persists, and curiosity gets the better of me.

Glancing down at my device, I see a text message from Lauren, my best friend and roomie, who studies psychology at the same college. She knows I'm in a lecture right now, so seeing her message tells me it has to be something important.

I tap on the notification to see a picture filling the small screen—a long, glossy black braid tied up with a pink ribbon. It's an odd choice for a text, even coming from Lauren, whose love for all things hair is no secret.

My mind races with questions, but before I can dwell on it further, Dr. Wilson's voice pulls me back to the present. For now, I push aside my confusion, pocket my phone, and redirect my focus to the lecture.

By the time the lecture ends, I have forgotten about the text. I grab my stuff and make a beeline for the library, for an hour of undisturbed study time before the next lecture comes around. Nestled in a cozy corner with my textbooks spread out before me, I dive into my studies, relishing the solitude and focus that the library offers.

I flip open the book Dr. Wilson suggested we read, *Animal Behavior: An Evolutionary Approach* by John Alcock, and before I know it, an hour flies by in a rush of highlighted passages and quickly scribbled notes.

The rest of the day passes in a blur of lectures, practical classes, and study sessions. It isn't until evening descends that I drive to our apartment. Finally home, I insert the key into the lock, turn it with a click, and then push open the door.

The familiar scent of vanilla greets me, from the plug-in air freshener that sits in the hallway. I also catch a whiff of something more earthy, most likely the remnants of last night's meal. The entryway is cluttered, with shoes piled haphazardly beside the coat rack and a few jackets hanging off of it. On the small console table next to the door, there's a scattered stack of unopened mail. We should really get to those.

As I walk farther into the main living area, I'm met with a cozy yet slightly chaotic scene. The living room is inviting but shows signs of a busy student life. The deep-blue sectional sofa is covered with colorful throw pillows that have started to slip onto the floor. A gray fleece blanket is bunched up on one armrest. The coffee table in front of it is cluttered with magazines, several half-empty coffee mugs, and a couple of stray snack wrappers.

I'm not in the mood for tidying up now or ever, so I go straight to the bathroom, which is a tiny but comforting space. The floral shower curtain is drawn back, revealing a tub that's been well-used, the porcelain slightly chipped here and there.

There's a pile of laundry in the corner and a few bottles of shampoo, conditioner, and body wash lining the rim of the tub. But I jump into the small shower instead since I don't have much time. I need to hurry and get to work at the Sunny Side Restaurant, where Lauren and I work as part-time waitresses.

The warm water slides down my body, washing away the stress of the day and soothing my tired muscles. But as I let out a sigh of relief, I remember the cryptic message Lauren sent me earlier.

Once I'm done and dressed in my blue and gray waitress uniform, I leave the apartment again and drive to the restaurant.

The place is bustling with activity as usual, with the smells of sizzling food filling the air and lively chatter among customers. It is a beautiful mix of the past and present, old and new, reminding me of Ellery Creek, my hometown. The brick walls and aged wooden tables give off a rustic charm, while the modern touches of chrome counters and advanced kitchen equipment add an element of sophistication.

Our menu perfectly reflects this fusion as well, featuring traditional dishes with a modern twist. One standout dish is our pan-seared salmon topped with a zesty mango salsa, which has quickly become a popular choice for repeat diners.

It's time to jump right in, to serve tables and interact with customers. As I weave my way through the packed tables, I quickly scan the room for Lauren, who started her shift earlier. I spot her behind the counter, talking to a regular customer.

"Hey, you," I say when they're done. "How's it going?"

For a moment, the cheerfulness she's been showing to customers falters and I catch a glimpse of exhaustion in her eyes before she regains her composure. "Pretty good," she replies, but she won't meet my eyes. "It's been non-stop since I started. So sorry, I can't talk now, I have an order to fill."

I nod in response, but she has already hurried away. She seems distracted by something more than work, but for the time being, I push it to the back of my mind and continue with my shift, losing myself in the repetitive tasks of refilling glasses, clearing plates, and taking orders. The hours seem to blur together as a steady stream of orders flows in and out of the kitchen.

As Lauren and I finally leave the restaurant and stroll side by side onto the bustling street, I bring up the text she had sent me earlier today.

"By the way, what did that text mean that you sent? Whose hair was that? It's kind of creepy."

Lauren stops walking and reaches up to remove her Sunny

Side Restaurant cap. And that's when I see it—the absence of her long, flowing, jet-black hair replaced by a short, choppy cut.

I'm immediately deeply concerned for my friend, who has always taken pride in her beautiful hair.

"Lauren, what did you do?" I blurt out before I can stop myself.

"I sold it. It'll grow back. I needed the money," she says with a brave smile.

I know Lauren has financial problems from time to time, but I had no idea just how bad it had got.

"Why didn't you tell me? I could have helped out. I don't have much but I'd have been happy to loan you some."

"You know I hate charity, and I didn't want to burden you. You worry enough as it is."

But I'm already worrying about her, and my heart breaks for the weight she has been carrying all on her own. While my parents only charge her nominal rent and her living expenses are low, her college fees must be crippling.

"I'm pissed at you." I pull her into a hug. "You should have told me, Lauren. We're in this together, remember? You didn't have to sell your hair."

We stand there for what feels like hours, holding on to each other and as I comfort my friend, I can't help but wonder how far she would go to keep her head above water.

The low growl of a shiny black motorbike cuts through our silence, and I turn to see Mark—Lauren's on and off boyfriend—pulling up at the curb. He kills the engine and slides off the seat with the kind of ease that only comes with confidence or cockiness, depending on how you look at it. Mark isn't the type you forget easily, with his rugged good looks, shaved head, and leather jacket that's a little too worn, a little too perfectly distressed. And, of course, the ever-present sunglasses, which he wears no matter the time of day.

Lauren glances at me with a small, apologetic smile. "That's my ride. I'm spending the night at Mark's."

Mark saunters over, giving me a nod of acknowledgment but clearly focused on Lauren. "Ready to go, babe?" He pulls her into his arms and kisses her before running a hand through her hair. "I love the short hair. Feels like you're letting go of all the extra weight, huh? Freedom looks good on you."

"Hi there, Mark. I didn't know you were back in town," I say before I can stop myself. "You've been gone for a while."

"Yeah, had to clear my head. You know how it is." He says it like it's the most natural thing in the world, like vanishing for a week without notifying Lauren is perfectly fine.

I have no idea how she puts up with his disappearing acts. He just keeps coming and going, drifting in and out of her life. Mark dropped out of college in the first semester, but somehow he's always managed to land on his feet. He's one of those guys who makes money wherever he goes—detailing cars, fixing up bikes, working construction gigs. He lives by his own rules, refusing to be tied down by anything or anyone, not even Lauren. He goes off for days sometimes, just vanishing off to wherever the wind takes him—whether it's a road trip, a spontaneous camping adventure, or working odd jobs out of town. He always comes back with no apologies and somehow, Lauren always forgives him.

Now, she hesitates for a second, glancing back at me before she takes his outstretched hand. "I'll see you tomorrow?" she asks.

"Yeah, of course," I say, but the words feel hollow as I watch her climb onto the back of his bike. She wraps her arms around his waist, and before I know it, they're speeding off, leaving me standing there on the sidewalk, watching the taillights disappear down the street.

My heart aches as I think about what Lauren said before

Mark showed up. She has done so many things in the past to earn extra money, including missing many classes in order to work, and even selling her plasma.

I'm honestly terrified to think what she would do next to make ends meet.

TWENTY-SEVEN

At 8 a.m. on Friday morning, I wake up to see a bunch of missed calls from Mom.

I roll over in bed and punch in my passcode.

There's also a message from my boyfriend, Joe, an engineering student from another college, telling me how excited he is that we're finally seeing each other today for lunch and even a movie. Even when I'm in Amberfield, it's a struggle to see each other sometimes due to my hectic study schedule and frequent visits home to see my family, especially when my mother is going through a rough time.

The rest of the messages are from Mom, but they are all requests for me to call her back. She sounds quite cheerful, actually. I dial her number and she picks up immediately.

"Hi, sweetheart, so sorry I called you early. I woke up at the crack of dawn and didn't know what to do with myself, I thought you might be awake too and we could have a little chat." Her voice bubbles with an excitement I haven't heard in quite some time.

"Mom, is everything all right? Are you okay?"

"Of course, Izzy, everything is really great."

I prop myself up on one elbow. "So, nothing happened?" I'm still not convinced.

"No, it's just another ordinary day." She sighs. "Oh, Isobel, you worry too much. It's just that I remember you saying yesterday that today you only have one morning lecture and the rest of the day free. I was thinking that it's been a while since you and I had a mother–daughter day out. Remember when we used to paint ceramics at that little shop downtown? Or when we had a picnic by the cherry blossom trees in the park, just you and me?"

The memories she brings up feel so distant and so much has happened since then. The day we painted those ceramics was actually two days before she lost the last baby. But I smile anyway.

"Of course, I do, Mom. We had so much fun."

"Then let's do it again, create some new memories."

I slide out of bed and open the curtains to reveal the small garden at the back of our apartment building that never comes alive. No matter the season, those plants are always dead. The grass is always a parched pale yellow and brown, the trees rarely have leaves on them, and the flowers wither before they can bloom.

"What did you have in mind?" I have to admit that her excitement is starting to rub off on me a little.

"Well, what do you think about a trip to the bookstore followed by coffee and pastries at a nice café?" Her voice is full of bubbly anticipation. "And then, if we're still up for it, we can visit that art museum I used to take you to when you were little. Maybe we'll even have time to go shopping. As you know, Tom and I will be celebrating our anniversary soon, and I'd love it if you could help me with finding something special to wear at the party. What do you think?" She's breathless now, but I can imagine the excitement in her eyes as she waits for me to give her an answer.

"That sounds perfect, Mom." I can't help but be drawn in by her infectious enthusiasm. "I'll drive out as soon as my lecture ends."

"Wonderful. We'll have so much fun, baby. See you soon."

It's only after she hangs up that I remember that I promised Joe we'd spend the day together. A sinking feeling takes over as I anticipate his reaction. He's always been so particular about our plans, and the thought of disappointing him stirs that familiar knot of anxiety in my chest.

I get that we haven't seen each other in a while, but Mom hasn't been as cheerful as this in months.

Dreading the conversation, I pick up my phone again and dial Joe's number.

"Baby, please don't hate me," I say as soon as he picks up.

A brief silence, followed by a heavy sigh. "Let me guess, you're calling to cancel, aren't you?" His tone is flat, and it stings.

"I'm sorry, Joe. But I am. Something came up with my mom. She's having—"

"Another crisis?"

"No, it's not that." I rub my forehead. "Look, she just needs me for something important and I need to drive home after my lecture."

I wonder if I should tell him it's more of a fun day than anything else, but the thought of his reaction keeps my lips sealed. He just won't understand why I have to do this, so I don't bother trying to explain it to him. Every time I bring up my mom or even sometimes Lauren, he makes it seem like I'm choosing my family and friends over him, and I'm so tired of defending myself.

"You do realize that you just got back this week, right, and we haven't even seen each other yet?" His tone hardens. "It feels like I'm always the last priority for you. It's not normal, Izzy. You can't just keep canceling like this. What about our relationship?"

"I know, Joe, and believe me, I do feel terrible." I try to come across reasonable and understanding, though part of me wants to push back, to tell him it's not fair for him to keep guilting me like this. "How about tomorrow? I'm working in the morning, but we could go to the cinema in the evening, if you like."

"Fine," he says, but it's clipped. "Just remember that relationships take effort from both sides. You can't keep bailing."

"I know, baby. And I really appreciate your understanding." When I hang up, the uneasy feeling in my stomach deepens. I hate letting him down.

Trying to ignore the feeling, I turn from the window to see Lauren standing in the doorway to my room, eating from a tub of Ben & Jerry's cookie dough ice-cream. Leaning against the frame, she looks like she heard my entire conversations, like she's been standing there for a while. I didn't even hear her open the door.

"Izzy," she says slowly, like she's picking her words carefully, "I know you're trying to juggle a lot right now, and... I don't know. Joe doesn't sound like he's being fair to you." She punctuates her sentence with a pointed spoonful of ice-cream.

I frown, caught off guard. "What do you mean?" I know exactly what she means. I also know for a fact that she has never been a fan of Joe.

The day I introduced them to each other, she told me there was something about him that made her uncomfortable, but she could not tell me what.

"Izzy," Lauren continues, "Joe is always making you feel guilty about stuff you shouldn't feel guilty for. I don't like it. Just... be careful, okay? Guys like that—sometimes they start out a little controlling, and it gets worse. I've seen how you're always trying to explain yourself to him. You deserve someone who doesn't make you feel bad every time you take a bit of attention from him." She licks a small blob of ice-cream from a corner of her lips. "I'm not saying dump him or anything, but... just, don't ignore the red flags."

TWENTY-EIGHT

The evening air buzzes with excitement as I navigate the chaotic parking lot of the Starlight cinema. Cars jostle for spaces in the packed lot, but I manage to find a spot.

I still feel terrible for canceling on Joe yesterday, but the day with my mother was everything I had wished it would be. We did all the things she wanted to do and ended the day shopping for a pretty chocolate and emerald blouse and a knee-length skirt for her anniversary. When we parted ways, she hugged me for a long time and told me to stop worrying about her, that she was fine now.

But how can I not worry? No matter how many times she reassures me, there's always this undercurrent of fear tugging at me. The thought of anything happening to her makes my chest tighten.

I smile to myself, thinking back to a memory from when I was little. We didn't have much back then. Money was tight, and I knew it, even if she tried to hide it. But on my birthday, she'd always find a way to make the day special. One year, we couldn't afford a cake, so she baked cookies instead and arranged them into the shape of a butterfly. I was so excited, I didn't care that it wasn't a real cake. It was the most beautiful thing I'd ever seen. She even made wings out of construction paper and hung them on the walls, turning our tiny apartment into a fairytale just for me.

Dressed in my favorite blue scuffed jeans and a cream sparkly blouse, and still smiling at the memory, I push through the throng of people.

As I approach the entrance, which is flanked by towering posters advertising the latest blockbuster releases, I spot a couple nearby. They're lost in their own world, wrapped up in each other's arms with smiles lighting up their faces. I can't help but smile at their happiness.

In the carpeted lobby, I inhale the nostalgic scent of freshly popped, buttered popcorn as I search for Joe among the sea of faces. Finally, I spot him near a concession stand, a grin spreading across his face as he holds out a tub of what I know will be caramel popcorn, my favorite.

Smiling back, I make my way over to him until his tall, athletic frame towers over me as he gives me a soft kiss on the lips. Joe's sandy-blond hair is slightly disheveled, and his eyes sparkle with warmth and excitement. His casual clothes, a simple green T-shirt and a pair of well-worn jeans, add to his easygoing charm. But what I find totally sexy about him—that others might find weird—are his ears. They jut out a bit, giving his face an elfish touch. Some people may think it's peculiar, but I think it's that feature that drew me to him when he and his friends walked through the doors of Sunny Side.

After a year of dating, I still can't say I'm deeply in love with him, but I do love being around him and it feels right being his girlfriend.

"Hey, sorry I'm late," I say, offering him a sheepish smile as I reach for the tub of popcorn.

"No worries," he replies with a grin. "At least you didn't cancel this time."

The words are laced with something I can't quite place, but I push it aside even though Lauren's warning nags at the back of my mind. *Be careful, Izzy. Don't ignore the red flags.*

"Yeah, sorry about that," I murmur. "But I'm here now, and I'm ready to enjoy our night together."

"That's all that matters." His smile widens, and he gives my hand a reassuring squeeze in return, but it's just a little too tight.

With snacks in hand, we make our way into the theater and find our seats near the back. The lights go down and the opening credits roll, and I allow myself to relax in front of the romantic comedy we chose. Joe just wants more of my time. That's all. Lauren was overreacting.

Leaning back, he drapes an arm heavily over my shoulder and I shift slightly under the weight, but his arm stays put.

As the story starts unfolding on screen, my thoughts drift back to Lauren. Ever since she cut her hair, I'm really concerned about her. She's so proud, I know she won't accept my help, but she's my best friend and I wish she'd let me in.

Soon enough the movie comes to an end and to be honest, I can't recall much of it.

As the credits roll and the lights flicker back on, Joe turns to me with a smile. "What did you think?"

I decide to be honest, sharing my worries about Lauren and the struggles she's facing.

"I'm sorry to hear that," he says when I'm done. "It sounds like Lauren is going through a lot right now. But you've done everything you can for her. She barely pays anything to stay in your parents' apartment and I know you're always cooking for her, buying the groceries."

"I'm just trying to help," I mutter.

"And what about your own needs?" The intensity in his eyes makes my skin prickle. "Every time something comes up with Lauren, you act like nothing else matters. What about us? What about our plans, our relationship? This is our time, Izzy."

"Don't be so dramatic, Joe." I try to pull my hand away, but he grips it hard. "This is just about me worrying about someone who needs me, someone who's been there for me a lot of times."

"And what about your mother?" Joe interjects. "Every time she has one of her *episodes*, you drop everything and run home to her. You can't keep running to everyone else's rescue."

His mention of my mother strikes a nerve, and I feel my anger boiling over. "Don't you dare bring my mother into this. You have no idea what it's like to watch someone you love struggle with severe depression, let alone your own mother. I have to be there for her, Joe. I have to make sure she's okay. She's been through a lot. It's only been five months since she had a miscarriage. Some people need longer to recover, if they ever do. I need to go home." I stand up abruptly, my hands clutched at my sides.

"Izzy, wait." Joe reaches out to grab my hand again. "I didn't mean to upset you."

I shake my hand free, turn away from him and quickly make my way out of the theater.

I know that I've hurt Joe, but I find his lack of empathy for my mom, and his inability to accept that Lauren will always be a priority for me, hard to accept.

Twenty minutes later, I enter the apartment to find Lauren sitting in the now extremely tidy living room with her fists clenched and a panicked expression on her face.

"Lauren, what's going on?" I ask, hurrying to her.

Like me, Lauren is not the tidiest person, but when something is going on with her, she goes on a cleaning rampage. And right now, the blue sofa is clear of pieces of clothing, books, or any other items that are usually tossed onto it without thought, and the colorful cushions are lined up perfectly, everything in its place. Even the coffee table, which is usually littered with magazines and takeaway containers, is spotless except for a pile of neatly gathered mail that we still need to open.

"Oh, it's nothing. I'm just exhausted. Long day, you know?"

But I know Lauren well enough to recognize when something is wrong, and this clearly goes beyond just being tired.

"Lauren, please," I press. "You can talk to me. I'm here for you."

For a moment, it seems as though she might open up, but just as quickly, she shakes her head and looks away. "I'm fine, Isobel," she insists. "Really. You don't have to worry about me."

I let the matter drop for now, but later, before I drift off to sleep, I reach for my phone and dial my mom's number to confide in her about my concerns for Lauren. She suggests that as it's Lauren's twentieth birthday next week, we should give her some money. Since it's a birthday gift, she'll have to accept it.

I drift off to sleep around midnight, but not long after, there's a gentle rap on my door. Assuming it must be Lauren, I invite her in as I sit up and yawn, but she doesn't come in. Puzzled, I slowly get out of bed and open the door.

No one is standing outside, and the light in Lauren's room is switched off. Still, I know I didn't imagine it. Lauren was at my door, wanting to confide in me about something. But for some reason, she changed her mind and disappeared without saying a word.

TWENTY-NINE

My mother and Tom's eighth wedding anniversary is tomorrow, and Lauren and I are back in Ellery Creek to celebrate with them. Of course, Joe had something to say about that, but I don't really care.

He has been calling a lot since I left Amberfield, his name lighting up my phone screen every few minutes. I ignore it. Each time the phone buzzes in my bag, I remind myself I need this time with my family.

Lauren is pretty much considered part of the family too. On many weekends and some holidays, instead of going back to her parents, she comes home with me to have some home-cooked food and do laundry.

As I drive down the familiar streets toward my childhood home, I glance at her quickly. She's gazing out the window, taking in the sights of the small town we both grew up in.

It's great to see her looking more relaxed than she did a few days ago. Mom, Tom, and I gave her a bit of money on her birthday and at first, she refused to take it, but we insisted, and she eventually accepted. It won't cover all her college fees, of course, since we don't have enough for that, but hopefully it's eased her stress a little.

"I really appreciate you inviting me to celebrate your parents' anniversary." She sounds genuinely grateful, even though I had to talk her into it.

"Well, if I remember correctly, you didn't really want to come."

She rubs a hand down her face and sighs. "I know. I'm just starting to feel like I've been intruding too much. Your family has done so much for me already. I can't keep taking."

I shake my head. "That's ridiculous. Lauren, you're never an intrusion. You're family. Mom and Tom love having you around, you know that."

She reaches out to squeeze my arm and says nothing.

Soon we pull into the driveway, and when we get out of the car, Lauren takes a few steps, then pauses, glancing at the familiar stone path before finally following me to the front door.

Just as we reach it, the door swings open and my mom is standing there, her face breaking into a wide smile. It's so great to see that the antidepressants she's been on for months after her second miscarriage are working. But in my experience these moments don't last. In a day or two, she'll refuse to get out of bed again.

"Oh, you two made it." She pulls us both into a warm hug.

Inside, the aroma of Tom's lasagna wafts through the air. Mom is not much of a cook, but luckily for her, Tom loves nothing better than standing in front of a stove. Over the years, he taught me how to cook and it became one of the things that bonded us.

He greets us with the same warmth Mom did and returns to the kitchen.

"Why don't you two go and freshen up while I finish setting the table?" Mom suggests, giving us a knowing look.

Lauren nods gratefully, and we head upstairs to the guest

bedroom that she stays in every time she comes over. It's decorated in shades of blue and white, a peaceful retreat from the noise of the world outside. The bed is covered in a soft quilt and the air is fresh with the scent of lavender from a small bouquet on the bedside table.

This room has started to feel more like Lauren's own rather than just a guest room. The en suite bathroom even has a few of her personal items like her toothbrush, her favorite coconut and lemon shampoo, and body wash on the counter.

Lauren sits on the edge of the bed, her hands twisting nervously in her lap. In the car she had seemed lighter, but now she's retreating into herself again.

Closing the door behind us, I go and sit down next to her. "Hey, what's really going on? I know something is on your mind. Please talk to me."

Although a part of me wonders if this has something to do with Mark, I highly doubt it because they've been getting along better lately and he's been spending more time at our apartment than usual, until he went off on his road trips again yesterday. No, this must have something to do with Lauren's finances.

She takes a deep breath before speaking. "I... I don't know. I've just been thinking a lot about my parents lately and their lack of support. It's hard to see the obvious difference between my family and yours, and sometimes it makes me feel out of place, like I don't belong here." She shrugs and her lips curl into a bittersweet smile.

I pull her into a hug. "Come on, Lauren. You need to stop feeling like that. You're loved here, by me, by my parents. You've become a part of our family because we see the incredible person you are and we're so grateful to have you."

I do get why all this is coming up now. Her parents didn't even bother calling to wish her a happy birthday. In the past, even though they never really showed much interest in her and her life, they at least called. This year, however, passed by like any other day. Lauren had put on a brave face, but I could see the hurt hidden underneath her silent strength.

I assure her again that she belongs in our home and when she gets a call from Mark, I leave her room to go to mine.

When I get to my room to freshen up, I pull my phone from my bag to see it lighting up again. Joe's name is flashing across the screen for the fifth time in the last hour. I sigh, ignoring the call, and toss it aside. I already know what he'll say, how he'll try to guilt-trip me about not answering, about leaving town instead of spending time with him.

Later, as we make our way downstairs to join my parents for dinner, Lauren is still not herself. Throughout dinner, she looks increasingly uncomfortable, picking at her food and barely saying a word. I catch her stealing glances at Tom and my mom, her brows furrowed in what seems like deep thought.

After dinner, my mom and I clear the table and wash up the dishes while Lauren and Tom are in the living room choosing a film for us to watch.

"Is everything all right with Lauren?" Mom asks softly, her brow creased. "I can't believe she cut her beautiful hair. I wish we could help her more financially, but we plan on giving IVF another shot and—"

"Really, Mom? You still want to go through that again?"

She reaches for a dishcloth and busies herself with wiping the dishes. "Tom and I really want a baby and it's been five months since the miscarriage. I'm ready."

As much as I want to support them in their desire for a baby, after two miscarriages, followed by periods of my mother struggling with chronic depression, I'm worried about the toll it might take on her mental health if they go through another round of IVF. But I know better than to voice my concerns now.

"I understand, Mom. I just want you to be happy. If that's what you want..."

She nods, her expression softening. "It really is, sweetheart. A baby would make me very happy."

With the dishes done, we join Lauren and Tom in the living room, where they've settled on an end-of-the-world thriller. As the movie plays in the background, I steal glances at Lauren. Her eyes are fixed on the screen, but her mind is clearly elsewhere. I wish there was something I could do or say to ease her worries, to make her feel at home and loved in our family.

I wish she could see how deeply I care for her. When I love someone, I love them more than my own life. I'd do anything for her, if only she'd let me in.

My phone buzzes again, vibrating on the armrest of the couch. This time, it's a text from Joe, not a phone call.

Having fun without me, huh? Guess I'm not as important as your family.

I roll my eyes and switch the phone off.

The next day the house is decked out in silver and white decorations, and the scent of Tom's cooking fills the air. The guests, mostly neighbors and a few close friends, mingle in the living room, their laughter bouncing off the walls.

I find myself getting caught up in the excitement of the celebration, chatting with our neighbors, and enjoying the delicious spread that Tom and I have prepared, several varieties of pastas, homemade breads, salads, and a lovely roast chicken that is the star of the feast. But then my mind drifts to Joe.

He was also invited to the party, but he didn't want to come. He's never made any effort to meet my family or get to know my friends, almost as if he doesn't want to share me with anyone else. I finally called him back before the party because he had been calling all day and leaving messages.

As expected, he was furious that I ignored his calls. He didn't say it outright, but I could hear it in his voice. His words, though—they were all about how much he loves me, how he can't stand being apart. I get it, but it's like I'm caught in this cycle of feeling guilty, confused, and then relieved because, in the end, he loves me.

As the celebration kicks into full swing, Tom stands up to make a speech. "Thank you all for joining us today to celebrate this special occasion." He glances at Mom with a smile. "It's been an incredible journey, and I feel blessed to have Nora and Isobel in my life. They've brought so much joy and love into this home, and I couldn't be more grateful."

There's a round of applause as he raises his glass in a toast, and I stand up to say a few words of my own. "I just want to thank Mom for choosing Tom to be the father I never had. He's been there for me through thick and thin, always offering love, support, and the occasional bad dad joke."

Laughter ripples through the room and there's a chorus of "hear, hear" as I raise my glass of sparkling water. When I'm done, Tom comes over to give me a big hug.

As the evening wears on, I notice him and Lauren slipping out onto the porch. I watch them from afar, and I hope that he can somehow get through to her.

After the guests are gone and we all head to our rooms, I decide to check one last time on Lauren, but she's in the shower. Her phone is on the bed and its screen lights up with a message notification, probably Mark wishing her a good night. The message flashes briefly on the screen, catching my eye.

But it's from Tom.

You're not alone. Call anytime you need to talk. Anytime.

THIRTY

It's around 9 a.m. on the last Sunday in September, two weeks after Mom and Tom's anniversary party, and I'm just waking up even though I planned on being up earlier to do an online Pilates class.

Stretching and yawning, I hear Lauren humming in the kitchen and it makes me smile.

Since our visit to Ellery Creek, she's been in a much better mood. It's like a weight has been lifted off her shoulders. Hopefully now, she knows that whatever struggles she's facing, there are people who love and care for her.

After I pull myself out of bed, Lauren and I bustle around our small kitchen, preparing for another day at Sunny Side.

"I hate that we have to work on a Sunday," Lauren groans, pouring coffee into a plain, white mug. "I wish I could spend the day at the beach with Mark before the travel bug catches him again."

"Look on the bright side, at least we get to work the same shift. I may not be as exciting as Mark, but I'll do my best to keep you entertained."

"You could never bore me, silly." She chuckles as she makes

me a cup of steaming black tea and hands it to me. She always drops in a spoonful of sugar and way too much milk, just the way she knows I like it, while she loves her coffee and makes it with a dash of cinnamon and a hint of nutmeg. "You're nowhere near as handsome as Mark, but you'll do until he comes over tonight."

As we sip our hot drinks, my phone buzzes with an incoming call. Glancing at the screen, I see it's from my mom. With a quick apology to Lauren, I answer.

"Hello, Mom, are you okay?" I ask, balancing the phone between my shoulder and ear as I head to the stove and crack eggs into a pan.

"Yes, sweetie. I just wanted to let you know that I found those earphones Lauren was looking for. I know you're not coming over for a while, so how about I send them over in the mail?"

I glance over at Lauren, who's busy checking her phone, a furrow of concentration between her brows.

She and her earphones, a new pair that Mark gifted her on her birthday, were virtually inseparable before they disappeared.

"Mom, that would be great, thanks," I reply, flipping the eggs in the pan. "She'll be so relieved not to have to go another day without them."

Lauren looks up at me as I hang up the phone. "Everything all right with your mom?"

"She found your earphones under your mattress," I explain. "She's going to mail them to us."

"Really?" Lauren claps her hands in excitement. "Oh, thank goodness! I thought I'd lost them for good. Your mom is a sweetheart. I'm glad I didn't tell Mark they got lost." She suddenly goes quiet, then jumps to her feet. "I... I'll be right back." She bolts out of the kitchen while I plate the eggs and pour more tea for myself.

When I follow to ask what's going on, I find her in the bathroom, but the door is locked and behind it she insists she's fine.

She's obviously not fine because I end up eating breakfast alone. After washing the dishes and cleaning up the kitchen, I check on her again, and as I approach her room, I can hear muffled sniffles coming from inside.

I knock gently on the door. "Lauren, can I come in?"

There's a moment of silence before she responds, "Yeah, come in."

Pushing the door open, I find her sitting on the edge of her bed in tears.

Without a word, I sit down beside her and wrap my arms around her shoulders.

"Lauren, are you okay? What happened?"

"I just had a fight with Mark. Don't worry about me." She shrugs. "It's nothing. But he won't be coming over tonight. He's decided to go to Vegas with his brother."

Lauren and Mark have had an on-and-off relationship for almost two years, constantly bickering and making up. But this time, something feels different. In all the fights they had in the past, she never cried.

"Hey, you don't have to pretend everything's fine if it's not. What exactly happened?"

She shrugs and sighs. "We were arguing about something silly, as usual. But then it just escalated, and I don't know... I just got so frustrated and upset. I really don't feel like talking about it. I just need some time to figure things out. We should probably get ready for work."

As I walk out of her room, it hits me that before Mark supposedly called Lauren, she had already run from the kitchen. If she was on the phone, I would have heard.

THIRTY-ONE

Despite being one of the best waitresses at Sunny Side, today Lauren is dropping utensils, mixing up orders, and rushing off to the restroom every chance she gets. Each time she returns, her complexion seems paler, her movements more labored.

At one point she approaches me and says, "Hey, Izzy, could you handle table four for me?" She hands me an order slip.

"Sure, no problem." I want to ask if she's okay, but she runs off again in the direction of the restroom.

This time, I decide to follow her, and pushing open the restroom door, I find her hunched over the toilet, her shoulders shaking.

"Lauren, you're sick. Why didn't you just stay home? You know we can't be serving food when we're ill." I rub her back in circular motions.

She straightens up slowly and stands, her face a mask of shock at my sudden appearance. "Izzy, I'm fine, really, it's nothing contagious. Just something I ate." She flushes the toilet and steps out of the cubicle, heading to the sinks. Turning on the tap, she rinses out her mouth and splashes water on her face.

Then Donna, our no-nonsense boss, strides into the

restroom, her expression stern and her arms crossed over her chest. She's a formidable woman with sharp features and a voice that could cut through steel. Her short, brown hair is pulled back, a few unruly strands escaping to frame her face, and she's wearing her usual attire—a gray apron over a white chef's coat and black trousers.

"Come on, we've got a rush on!" she snaps. "I'm not paying you to stand around gossiping in the bathroom!"

Lauren quickly grabs a tissue from the dispenser by the sink to wipe her mouth, her face flushing with embarrassment. "Yes, Donna, sorry, we're coming."

As we return to the dining area, the morning rush hits us at full force. Donna barks out orders, and I do my best to keep up and cover for Lauren who, needless to say, is not in best form. After the breakfast service, my shift is over and I'm about to head out, but Lauren decides to take on another shift for some extra cash.

I try to talk some sense into her, offering to give her money instead, but of course she refuses and in the end, I give up and leave. They're expecting me at the animal shelter and I've been looking forward to going there all day.

The familiar scent of hay, pet food, and fur greets me as I step inside, and a chorus of barks and meows fills the air. I make my way to the dog kennels, where a playful Labrador catches my eye. His tail wags eagerly as I approach, and I smile as he nuzzles my hand through the wire mesh.

I soon lose myself in the work, forgetting all my cares as I feed and groom the animals, cleaning their cages, and showering them with love and affection which is always unconditionally returned.

When my shift is over, I walk out to my car in the parking lot, feeling tired but fulfilled. I'm about to open the door when I notice something tucked under the windshield wiper. At first, I assume it's just a flyer, but when I pull it free, my breath catches. It's a handwritten note, folded carefully, with my name on it.

I unfold it, my pulse quickening as I recognize Joe's handwriting. It's a love note, short but heartfelt.

Thinking of you. I can't wait to meet up again. One minute away from you feels like a lifetime. Love J

Butterflies wrestle for space with a creeping anxiety. I appreciate the gesture, who wouldn't? But I never told him I was coming to the shelter today. Did he follow me?

I shake my head and laugh it off. I must've mentioned it on a call and just forgot. My mind has been so cluttered lately. And things between us are good. We've seen each other a few times since I got back from Ellery Creek, and it's been great. I should see this for what it is, a romantic gesture from my loving boyfriend.

I fold the note carefully and slip it into my bag, brushing off the unease still lingering in the back of my mind. After sliding behind the wheel, I send Joe a quick thank you text.

As evening approaches, I return home to our apartment and even though I'm a vegetarian, I prepare Lauren's favorite meal, a beef stir fry, hoping to lift her spirits.

The delicious aroma fills the air as I chop vegetables and fry the ingredients. When Lauren finally returns from her shift, she looks exhausted, but when she catches sight of the steaming pot on the stove, a small smile tugs at the corners of her lips.

"You made beef and broccoli stir fry?"

"Your favorite." I spoon her food into a square plate and set it on the table and plate up my own meat-free version. "I thought it might cheer you up." I offer her a fork.

But she shakes her head. "That's so sweet of you, Izzy, but

I'm not hungry. I had something to eat at the restaurant and I really want to jump into the shower and go to bed. I'll enjoy that tomorrow, though."

My heart sinks as I watch her go and the words spill out before I can stop them.

"Are you pregnant, Lauren?" I blurt out.

Lauren's eyes are wide as she turns to face me. "No, no, it's not that," she stammers. "I must have eaten something that my body doesn't agree with, that's all."

But I can see it all over her face. She's lying.

It's close to midnight when the shouting starts between Lauren and Mark, who came over around nine to stay the night. Apparently, his trip to Vegas was postponed.

At first, it's just muffled voices, too quiet to make out any words, but then the volume rises. Mark's voice. Harsh, sharp. It cuts through the thin walls like a knife. I strain to hear, but the words are drowned in his anger. Then, suddenly, a loud crash—something shatters against the floor, followed by the unmistakable sound of Lauren sobbing.

"Please, Mark," I hear her voice break through the noise, trembling, desperate. "I'm sorry... I'm so sorry... I wish I could fix this."

"You can, but you don't want to," he shouts back.

The sobs get louder, and I can hear the shuffling of footsteps. My heart pounds as I press my ear against the wall, listening for just another minute before I go in all guns blazing.

Another crash. Louder this time, like a chair being knocked over, and then more muffled yelling. Mark's voice has risen to a dangerous level, but still, I can't make out what he's saying. Lauren's voice cuts in again, shakier, more frantic. "I'm sorry... please..."

That's it.

I hurry into the hallway. The apartment is dark except for the sliver of light coming from under Lauren's door. I hear her crying, but the words between them are still impossible to catch. Then, suddenly, just as I'm about to open it, her bedroom door flies open with a force that makes me jump.

Mark storms out, his face twisted in fury. He's like a storm cloud ready to explode—his jaw tight, fists clenched, every part of him bristling with rage. For the first time in a long time, he's not wearing his sunglasses.

Behind him, Lauren stumbles out, barefoot, her bathrobe hanging loosely off her shoulders, her hair glued to her scalp by sweat. She's still crying, her eyes red and swollen.

"Mark, please!" she begs, grabbing his arm as he charges down the hall. "Please, don't go! I'm sorry, I shouldn't have—"

He rips his arm out of her grasp and spins around to face her, his face a mask of pure rage. "You destroyed us!" he shouts, his voice booming through the hallway. "You messed everything up, Lauren! I'll never forgive you for this!"

Destroyed them? What did she do? I watch as Lauren collapses to her knees, her sobs echoing through the apartment, clutching her bathrobe tightly around her like it's the only thing holding her together.

Mark doesn't even look back. He marches out, slamming the door behind him so hard the walls shake.

The silence that follows is deafening.

For a moment, I just stand there, frozen. My heart is racing, my mind spinning, trying to make sense of what just happened. What did Lauren do? What could possibly make Mark so furious that he'd say those things? I have no idea, but whatever it is, it's bad.

Lauren's crying pulls me out of my thoughts. I rush over to her, kneeling beside her on the floor. "Lauren, what happened? Are you okay?"

She shakes her head violently, her tears falling harder. "It's over," she gasps, her voice barely above a whisper. "We broke up. For good this time."

I blink in disbelief. "But... why? What did he mean—destroyed you? What's going on?"

Lauren doesn't answer. She pushes herself up and stumbles toward her room, her sobs choking her words. "I can't... I don't want to talk about it," she stammers, slamming her door shut behind her before I can ask anything else.

I stand in the hallway, staring at her closed door, my chest tightening with worry. I've never seen her like this before. Never seen Mark like that either.

That look of ice-cold hatred in his eyes was enough to drive terror into anyone's soul.

THIRTY-TWO

When I enter the apartment, the weight of my backpack, full of textbooks from a long day at college, falls from my shoulders with a thud. Collapsing onto my bed feels very tempting right now. It's lucky I don't have to work today. The thought of carrying trays and serving drinks all evening is exhausting.

As I kick off my shoes, my hopes for a peaceful moment alone are interrupted by the sound of someone crying. I thought Lauren took on a shift today, but I guess she called in sick.

A week ago, Mark broke up with her and she's still hurting terribly.

"Lauren?" I call as I head to her room, but no answer comes, just sniffles and sobs.

I make another attempt at calling out to her but there's still no response.

My hand hovers over the knob, before I steel myself and turn it.

Lauren is sprawled across her bed, a tangle of limbs, and her short hair is sticking in all directions. I flick on the light and gasp. Her room is in total chaos. Clothes are strewn on the floor, and textbooks lie abandoned and haphazardly tossed aside.

"Isobel..." Her voice trembles, barely audible. The shadows beneath her eyes give the appearance of bruises, and her skin is pale and blotchy, her nose visibly red and raw.

"God, Lauren, what happened?" I step closer, my breath quickening and my palms growing clammy. This isn't just a bad day; this is a breakdown. "What's wrong, sweetie?"

"Everything's wrong," she gasps. Her words are punctuated by hiccups, her body curling defensively. "It's all wrong."

"Talk to me." I reach out a hand and place it on her back. "Tell me what's going on."

"Can't... I just can't..."

"Of course you can." I stroke her back. "We'll fix it together."

"Isobel, you don't understand," she chokes out, pressing a balled-up tissue onto her face to soak up fresh tears.

"Then make me understand."

"Isobel, I—" Lauren starts, then she stops.

"Whatever it is," I say again, fixing her with a determined stare, "we're in this together. Always."

Instead of answering in words, she reaches under her pillow and pulls out what looks at first like one of those old-fashioned black and white photos. I inhale sharply.

A sonogram flutters in her hand, the stark black and white image of an unborn child, a confirmation that my suspicions were right. I was hoping, praying I was wrong, but there's the proof.

"Oh, my God, Lauren," I breathe out, my throat tight.

She doesn't look up at me, just continues to cry, a sound so raw and jagged it's painful to even listen to. I reach for her, but she recoils as if my touch burns, clutching the sonogram closer to her chest.

"Does Mark know? Is that why you broke up, why he was so angry?" I need her to say something, anything, but she just shakes her head, then her mouth opens only to let out a strangled sob that tells me everything and nothing all at once.

To be honest, I wouldn't be surprised if she told Mark about the baby and that's why he broke things off. My mind reels at the thought of him becoming a father. I try to picture him with a newborn in his arms, waking up for late-night feedings, changing diapers. It feels almost laughable. He barely stays still long enough for Lauren to catch her breath before he's off again.

A baby wouldn't just slow him down, it would anchor him to something permanent, something real and harder to walk away from. And knowing Mark, he'd hate being tied down like that. No wonder he was so furious. What if he demanded that Lauren has an abortion and she refused? During their fight, he did insist that Lauren could *fix this*.

The thought that he might believe walking away from Lauren would somehow absolve him of his responsibility makes me sick. Did he actually think that breaking up with her was some kind of escape from being a father?

"Lauren, please." I pick up the sonogram that has fallen to the floor. "You're not on your own, I'm here. Just talk to me."

Her emotions are spiraling out of control, and it's clear that she's on the brink of an even worse meltdown. She covers her face with her hands and tries to hold back the tears but fails. As I watch her crumble before me, I feel powerless.

Finally, she looks up. "Tom," she says simply.

"What about Tom?" My mouth is dry.

"He's... He's the father. I... I slept with Tom."

Time freezes, and all at once, I'm drowning.

"No. It can't be true." Still holding on to the sonogram, I get to my feet, my knees buckling. I stumble backward, putting as much distance between us as possible. "This isn't real," I whisper to myself. "You're lying."

"I'm so sorry, Izzy," she stammers through her tears. "I'm really—"

"How could you—" I breathe out as my words get stuck in my throat, suffocating me.

My entire being recoils, every instinct telling me to turn and run away.

"Isobel," Lauren pleads, reaching out with a trembling hand. "Please, you have to understand—"

Understand? How could I possibly wrap my mind around this? The man who has been a father figure—the man who helped raise me—has betrayed Mom and me in the most unforgivable way. He was meant to be a constant, a steady force in our lives, the complete opposite of the turmoil my mother and I had experienced before him. And now he and Lauren, my best friend, who I viewed like a sister, have shattered our bond and my trust in one fell swoop.

I suddenly remember them talking at the anniversary, the text that followed. It was all so much deeper than I ever realized.

"Isobel!" Lauren pulls herself up to a seat.

"Stop," I gasp. This isn't happening. It can't be real.

But it is real. Despair tightens its grip on my heart. Betrayal. Deception. A wound so deep it may never heal.

"Isobel, please," she whispers.

"Lauren." I struggle to say her name. "I don't even know who you are anymore."

Her devastation mirrors mine, reflected in the tears streaming down her cheeks. But there's nothing left for me in this room.

"You are dead to me," I whisper, a final farewell to the girl I thought I knew. "You've destroyed everything."

And with that, I walk out, each step a mile, each breath a struggle as tears stream down my face.

In my bedroom, my clothes are wrenched from drawers and

flung into the gaping mouth of a large suitcase. My fingers tremble as they fumble with the zipper.

Then I'm carrying it, heading to the front door, desperate to get out. But before I can leave the apartment, Lauren appears, her arms wrapped around her body.

"Isobel, wait! You don't understand. Please let me explain. It's complicated."

"Complicated?" I spit out the word. How can this enormous betrayal be anything but black and white?

"It is." Her hands reach for me, shaking. "There's so much you don't know."

"Lauren, we're done. I'm moving out. I'll be back soon for more of my things." I sob, putting on my headphones and cranking up the volume. The music blasts into my ears, drowning out her pleas.

"Never talk to me again," I growl at her.

"Isobel, I'm so sorry!" Her words are mouthed, silent behind the barrier of music. "You can't leave me like this!"

But I can, and I will.

As the door slams shut behind me, I know it's over between us. There's no coming back from this.

THIRTY-THREE

I turn the key, and the car lurches forward as if it's also desperate to escape this place. As I pull away from the apartment parking spot, I bite back tears. My heart is aching, not just from Tom and Lauren's deception but mostly for my mother, who's already been through so much.

I can't bear to picture how she'll react to this new blow. The man she loves, who she has been trying so hard to have a baby with for so long now, got someone else pregnant. Someone she loves like a daughter. The thought is so sickening that I have to force down the bile rising up my throat. I switch on the radio in the hopes that the mindless pop tunes can drown out the whirlpool of thoughts inside my head.

As dusk begins to paint the sky in shades of bruised purple, I'm crying so hard that I can barely see through the blur of my tears. I keep wiping them away, but they come back faster than I can control. I don't want to stop because stopping means thinking. But driving blindly isn't a good option either. I keep driving until I decide to stop at a roadside café on the edge of town. Tears blur the neon sign of Luke's Pit Stop Café as I pull into the gravel lot.

I kill the engine and then the only sound that can be heard is that of the sobs that rack my body. Suddenly, I hear the beep of a message coming from my handbag in the passenger seat. I dig my phone out and swipe away the notification without reading, along with all the other messages Lauren has left. Then I stumble out of the car and into the café. A chime rings out as I enter, and the door swings open.

The atmosphere is warm and welcoming, with the soothing smells of freshly brewed coffee and baked goods filling the air. The cozy interior features wooden tables and chairs that don't quite match, and above the counter hangs a chalkboard menu, filled with tempting choices such as hot cocoa and homemade pie. The woman behind the counter is an older lady with a kind smile and soft eyes framed by laugh lines. The name on her tag is Janine.

I'm the only customer in the café, so my order is brought to me quickly.

"Sweetheart, you look like you could use this more than most." Janine slides a steaming mug of coffee across the table. "On the house."

"Thank you," I murmur, cradling the warm cup between my numb fingers. It's an unexpected kindness from a stranger and it means a lot to me.

"There's not much going on around here tonight," she continues, glancing at the clock on the wall. "I'll be closing up soon, but take your time."

I offer her a grateful smile and take a sip of the scalding liquid. I wince at the slight sting on my tongue and think of my weekend morning rituals with Lauren, sitting at our tiny kitchen table with me sipping my tea and she her coffee. I do my best to push away the memories.

I need to talk to someone who is not Tom, Mom, or Lauren. So, I pick up my phone and dial Joe's number.

"Izzy? Hey, what's wrong? You sound like you've been crying."

"I have." A sob pushes its way up my throat, but I swallow hard and press on. "Lauren... she's pregnant. With my stepfather's child." The words spill out, bitter and sharp like the steaming coffee in front of me.

"Jesus, Isobel..." He exhales sharply. "Are you okay? Where are you?"

"Not okay, no. And I'm at a roadside café. I'm going home, Joe. To Ellery Creek. I can't live under the same roof as her."

I can't stand to be around Tom either, even more so in fact, but I have no choice. My mother needs me. The truth is, I'm not sure what to do, how I'll handle this situation. I'll have to confront Tom, that's for sure, but then what? Do I tell my mother, who deserves the truth but may be too fragile to handle it?

There's a pause on the line, a hesitation that feels like an eternity. I imagine Joe running a hand through his tousled hair, the way he does when he's searching for words. "Home? But, babe, that apartment is yours. Lauren was just staying with you. Why should you leave because of what she did? Your life is here. What about—"

"What about us?" I finish for him. "Nothing changes. Ellery Creek is less than an hour away. I'll still be coming to campus. But I can't stay at the apartment, not now, and I'm not going to kick Lauren out, I'm not that cruel. We'll find a way to make it work. You can even drive up on weekends."

"Come on, you know it won't be the same. Things will change. We already don't see each other much, even in the same town."

I let out a breath. "Joe, don't make this complicated. Please, let's talk about this some other time."

"All right," he says through clenched teeth. "Be safe, Izzy. Call me when you get there."

"Okay," I say, but the line is already dead.

Groaning with frustration, I shove the device into my bag and spot the sonogram I took from Lauren's room. I had not planned on bringing it with me, but in my hurry to leave, anything and everything had been stuffed into my bag. The desire to go home to my mother overcomes me again, so I drink up, thank Janine for her kindness and hurry back outside.

This time, despite the tears, I keep driving until I reach Ellery Creek. The rush I normally get when entering my hometown is not present tonight. I don't see the beauty of the place, the charm that once captivated me and made me so proud to belong here. It's there, somewhere beneath the surface, but I'm blind to it.

The landmarks blur into one—the library where I first fell in love with words, a diner where secrets were shared over milkshakes with friends from school, a park where I would often spend my afternoons reading under the old oak tree.

I pull into the driveway a few minutes after half past eight, and it's hard to keep my hand steady as I turn off the car and reach for the door handle.

The porch light flicks on, spilling warm yellow light onto the front steps as the door creaks open. My mother's figure fills the doorway, then she's hurrying to the car just as I'm getting out, her blonde hair glowing in the porch light.

She already looks too thin from the depression, and I hate to think what will be left of her if she finds out what I learned today.

"Isobel? Honey, I didn't know you were coming... and so late? Are you okay? Have you been crying?"

"Mom." I throw myself into her arms, clinging to her like she's the only solid thing left in my world. When I pull away, I look her straight in the eye. "I moved out. Lauren and I... we're no longer friends."

"Oh, no, what happened? Did you have an argument?" She

wipes away a tear from my cheek with a thumb. "Do you want to talk about it?"

For a second I consider telling her everything, but I stop myself.

"Yes, Mom, but can we talk in the morning? I just need to rest."

"Of course, love. Let's get you to bed." She helps me take out my luggage and we head for the front door.

The house smells of lavender and lemon, well-known scents from my childhood. But right now they make me feel nauseous.

"Where... Where's Tom?" I glance at the stairs.

"He's already asleep, I'm afraid. He had a long day at the school today."

I give a small nod and climb the stairs, glad I won't have to confront him tonight.

In front of my bedroom door, I turn to my mother and hug her again. "Goodnight, Mom."

"Goodnight, love." She squeezes me back. "I'm sorry about you and Lauren. We'll talk in the morning."

In the sanctuary of my room, I drop onto the bed and don't even bother to undress before pulling the quilt up to my chin. The darkness of the room closes in around me, and all I can hear is my own breathing. I try hard to fall asleep, but my thoughts are a carousel, spinning too fast. Each passing image, every memory of Lauren is like a heavy weight pressing down on me. I bury my face into the pillow, inhaling the scent of vanilla and cotton, wishing it was enough to drown out the hurt.

Not knowing what else to do, I do something I haven't done in a while. I pray. Maybe, just maybe, Lauren is confused. Or maybe she's lying. I don't know why she'd do that, but this is so unbearable I need to feel like there's just a fraction of a possibility that it isn't true.

"Please, God, let it not be true," I plead into the stillness. "Please don't let Tom have slept with Lauren."

I know that if this happened, and Mom found out, it would break her. It would completely shatter our family, and I'd never forgive either of them; my best friend, or the man who has been the closest thing I've ever had to a father.

The last thing I think as I drift off to sleep is that I must protect my mother, whatever it takes.

THIRTY-FOUR

At one in the morning, I'm awake again. I can't stop thinking about it all and hoping desperately that it isn't true. That for some unfathomable reason, Lauren is lying. Tom loves my mom and me; in my wildest dreams I'd never have imagined he would do this to either of us.

But how could Lauren do this to my family, accuse Tom of such a horrific thing? And why?

My mind flashes back to the time Tom taught me how to cook my first dish, lasagna, the smell of garlic and tomatoes permeating the air in our kitchen as he patiently explained the order of the layers. I remember his laughter in the living room as he watched one of his favorite comedy shows on TV.

Then I think back to the speech he gave at their anniversary not too long ago. He has been more than just a stepfather; he was the dad I'd always longed for, the one who made Mom smile again after years of raising me alone.

I can't stay still any longer. I get up from my bed and drift over to the window where I part the curtains. The moonlight streams into the room and I catch my breath. It's Tom. He's out there sitting on one of the iron benches in the garden, his head bowed, something glowing between his fingers as he raises it to his face, followed by smoke curling upward. He's smoking.

Tom doesn't smoke. He's never touched a cigarette in all the years I've known him. He said he used to in his early twenties, and he warned me constantly to stay away from it. Yet there he is, late at night, betraying another promise. It's almost laughable, the irony of it all.

Why now? A sinking feeling seeps in my chest.

Could this be his way of dealing with the guilt that's eating away at his conscience? Sitting out there alone underneath the crisp moonlight, he certainly looks like a man haunted by something.

I watch him exhale another cloud of smoke that's almost ghostly as it swirls and dances into the night.

A nauseating wave pushes up my throat and my legs propel me forward as I scramble to the bathroom, push open the door and rush inside. The room spins around me as I reach for the porcelain rim of the toilet and my body violently ejects my stomach contents.

It brings back horrible memories of my bulimia days when I was in high school. I will never forget the endless episodes of binging and purging, the way it left me feeling exhausted, disgusted, ashamed.

Sweat trickling down my forehead, I rise from the floor, using the sink to support my weight. The coolness of the water I rinse my mouth with brings me back to reality, like a lifeline that prevents me from falling into despair. I can't break down now. My mother needs me.

The trust I held in Tom, the certainty that he was a good person, crumbles within me like a sandcastle. He's the best father ever, I used to say to everyone who would ask, and I once gave him a mug that read "World's Best Dad."

Now I have an impossible decision to make. Speaking the truth would destroy my mother, whose mental state is already hanging by a thread. But if I say nothing, I will be aiding and abetting a lie. I'd be an accomplice to this unspeakable betrayal. And she deserves to know, no matter how much it hurts. I owe her that much. The woman who has sacrificed so much for me, who has loved me unconditionally, deserves to know the reality of the man she trusted. The man we trusted.

I take a deep breath, feeling the cool air fill my lungs, and exhale slowly. I can feel the fear and uncertainty creeping in, but I push it aside as I throw a bathrobe over my clothes.

I switch off the light and tiptoe to their bedroom, pressing my ear to the door, wondering if my mother is also awake, battling her own demons.

The recent miscarriage left her empty and broken, but lately we've all noticed a glimmer in her eyes, a spark of hope returning to her life. How could I possibly be the one to take that away?

I lean my forehead against the door, and then I take a shaky breath and think for a while, before I slowly step away. No, I'm not the person who should tell her. But someone must. Tom needs to take responsibility for his actions. It's his confession to make.

THIRTY-FIVE

The kitchen door clicks shut behind me. Outside, the night is eerily quiet, the only sound the faint rustle of leaves in the gentle breeze.

I tighten my bathrobe around myself and follow the cobblestone path that cuts through the large garden, leading me to the bench.

He's still sitting there, still smoking his cigarette. Husband, father, pillar of the community. Cheater? Liar?

As I approach, he gasps out my name and drops the cigarette onto the dew-soaked lawn, his face as pale as the soft glow of the moon. Even without saying a single word, his fearful eyes betray him. He clearly knows why I'm here, why I came home. Lauren must have called to tell him that I know.

I sit down on the bench as far away from him as possible, but his cologne of sandalwood and bergamot, a scent I once found comforting, hovers between us. Instead of speaking first, I allow him to stew in his guilt, hoping that it will force him to be the one to break the ice.

"Izzy, sorry I was asleep when you arrived and couldn't welcome you home."

"Did you know I was coming?" I sit on my hands to keep them from shaking and stare straight ahead because I can't bear to look at him just yet.

He shifts uncomfortably and clears his throat. "I... no. I woke up when your mother came to bed, she told me."

"Right." I turn to him then, my temples throbbing with rage. "Do you know why I'm here?"

His eyes widen and suddenly I want to punch him right in the face. He better not be about to lie to me.

"Lauren..." Tom's voice trails off, then he clears his throat. "Your mom told me you had a fight with Lauren."

"A fight." I let out a soft chuckle as anger surges within me. "Lauren is pregnant. But you know that, don't you?" I throw the words at him, picturing them like shards of glass.

I watch Tom closely, noticing his jaw tense up. His hands, hands that have built and fixed countless things in our home and guided my own as he taught me to cook, now fidget pathetically with the hem of his pajama top.

After a while, he shifts in his seat and clears his throat. "She's pregnant?" His tone attempts to convey surprise, but it falls flat.

"I know you're the father of her baby. She told me." There's no room for denial or excuses, not now. "Please tell me it's not true."

When he peels his gaze away from mine, my stomach drops.

THIRTY-SIX

Time seems to slow down until, at last, he turns back to face me.

"It's not true, Izzy, or not the way she's saying it, anyway," he says, but his hands twitch as he fumbles for the words. "I've been dreading her doing this to you. Lauren is a fantasist," he begins bluntly. "She has an intense infatuation with me; it's been going on for a while now. She always wants more and I've tried to be kind to her, but to keep clear boundaries between us. It's been hard, because I know how much she means to you, she's your best friend. I hoped it was just a phase. But when I reject her, she creates a delusion. It's absurd, I know."

I study him, trying to discern truth from fiction in the lines of his face. "Are you really saying she's lying about being pregnant with your baby?"

"Yes." He rakes a hand through his hair. "The weekend you brought her to stay with us in July... That Saturday night I couldn't sleep, so I went downstairs to watch a movie and had a few drinks."

"What do you mean by a few?" I know Tom has a habit of having one or two drinks in the evening after dinner, especially when he's stressed.

"I came across a bottle of aged bourbon in the pantry and I couldn't resist. I'll admit I had a few more than usual. As the movie played, I must have drifted off on the couch."

"And what does that have to do with Lauren?" Her name tastes like a bitter pill on my tongue.

"I woke up in the early hours of the morning and she was there, on the couch... with me."

I feel sick, my nails digging into my palms as he continues.

"I had a massive headache from the alcohol and there she was, lying next to me." He pauses to push a hand over his face, exhaling deeply. "I asked her what she was doing, and she started crying, saying the most awful things... that we had slept together. But I don't remember any of that, I really don't, Izzy. I only remember waking up. I would never, never have slept with her, not even when I was drunk. You have to believe me."

"Were you dressed?" I ask slowly.

Tom frowns, but he answers my question, "She... she was in her underwear, and I..." He shifts uncomfortably. "I was just in my boxers, my T-shirt was off."

"So, it's possible that you two..." The words, like lead, sink heavy and cold to the pit of my stomach.

"Like I said, I don't remember, and I really don't think so. I honestly think she set me up." His voice is desperate. "You have to believe me," he says again. "I would never betray your mother like that. I'm in love with her, I always have been."

"So, let me get this straight: you think Lauren is pregnant with someone else's child but she decided to pretend you're the father by making you believe you'd slept with her?"

"Yes," he whispers. "To trap me and make me leave Nora for her. She confessed to me that night that she was in love with me. It's so twisted."

"Does Mom know about any of this?"

He shakes his head, then turns me to face him. "Isobel, please listen to me." Urgency creeps into his tone. "Your mother can't know. She's been through hell and she's so much better. She only just came off the antidepressants. If she hears what Lauren has been claiming..." He trails off.

The thought of my mother going back to that depressing place is unbearable. I can't allow that to happen. What if I lost her, forever?

"Promise me, Isobel. Promise me you won't say a word to her."

I suck in a deep breath and think for a moment. If he's telling the truth, telling my mom could cause irreparable harm, and it would all be over a lie.

"Only if you really didn't do anything with Lauren." I look him straight in the eyes, which are brimming with relief and gratitude. "You have to swear on your life, Tom."

I call him Tom most of the time, and Dad only sometimes. My friends have never understood this, but I still remember a life before him, and he's never pushed me to call him Dad. He's always been so understanding, so sensitive.

"I swear, Isobel. I'd never lie to you, you know that." He gives my hand a squeeze. This time, his eyes are clear and honest.

And I believe him.

I'm disgusted by Lauren. I thought I knew her. I thought I could trust her.

With a soft exhale, I make my vow. "But is there anything else I should know about? Any other secrets? Please, Tom, you have to tell me everything. Now is the time."

He runs a hand through his hair and clears his throat. "Yes, there is something else. After Lauren told me about the pregnancy, I made a deal with her."

A deal? The word reverberates in my mind and I draw my bathrobe around me tighter.

"I... I said I couldn't be who she wants me to be, that I don't feel about her that way. But she is terrified of being a single mom, she doesn't really want to be pregnant so young. So I offered to adopt the child."

"Adopt?" The question comes out as a strangled whisper.

How could he possibly think that's a good idea?

"But why would you want to do that? It's not your baby. She lied about you, set you up."

"I know it's crazy, but Isobel, you know how much your mother wants a child. And after everything—"

"You can't be serious." I shoot to my feet and start pacing. "This is crazy."

Tom gets to his feet as well and grabs hold of my shoulders, making me stand still. "Isobel, listen to me. Your mom desperately wants a baby and it hasn't worked for us. It hurts me deeply to see her in so much pain, over and over again. She has always been open to adoption. It was me who resisted the idea. I thought that we had to have our own child, I really wanted to make that work somehow. But her grief... I can't bear it. And now—"

"But what if Lauren doesn't want to give away her baby in the end, Tom? You can't just take someone's child."

"Lauren already agreed to it, as soon as she reconciled herself to the fact that I would never be with her. She does not want the baby and planned to put it up for adoption anyway, but this way she knows the baby will be in a good family, and I'll give her some money too." His voice holds a gravity that roots me to the spot. "In this way, we can help her, and she can help us fulfill a dream we've held on to for so long. Can't you see that, Isobel?"

"But she betrayed you... us. How can you trust her? What if she decides in the end not to give you the baby? Or that she wants the baby back?"

"I don't think that will happen, but I understand it's a possibility. That's why I've decided not to tell your mother just yet, not until Lauren has had the baby. Then if she's still sure, we will go ahead. I don't want Nora to be told until then, because if Lauren backs out, it'll crush her."

"I just don't know about this, Tom. We're keeping too many secrets from Mom." I shake my head. "It feels... wrong."

"Please, Isobel," he implores. "Just wait until the baby is born. Your mom doesn't need any more pain."

A wave of exhaustion hits me then. I need to sleep. "I need to think it through. Let's talk again tomorrow. Goodnight."

Tom releases his hold on my shoulders, stepping back with a sigh. "I understand," he says as he watches me go.

The moment I reach my room and climb back into bed, I replay our conversation. It's so hard to accept that Lauren would do something like this to me and my parents, after everything we've done for her and all our years of friendship. But I choose to believe Tom. He's my dad, or at least the closest I have to one.

Having made my decision, I reach under the pillow and fumble for my phone. I find Lauren's number, and with a finality that surprises even me, I block it.

I may not know what to do about Tom wanting to adopt Lauren's child, but I do know one thing. Lauren is dead to me. And I'm not going to let her hurt my family any longer.

THIRTY-SEVEN

It's the first Friday of October and I haven't been in Amberfield or on campus for a whole week. The town is painted with the cozy colors of autumn with leaves dancing at my feet and the air carries a slight chill that hints at the winter to come.

Tom had already come back to pack up the rest of my stuff while Lauren was out, and I pretended to be sick so I didn't have to go to lectures in person. To be honest, the emotions I went through the last few days did mimic the symptoms of an illness.

As I navigate the campus grounds, red, brown, and orange leaves crunching under my feet, I search for Lauren's face, and let out a sigh when I don't see her.

Once I'm inside the veterinary medicine building, it's unlikely that I will cross paths with her, so far away from the psychology students, who hang out on the far end of the campus.

Finally, I walk the maze-like hallways, but I don't feel the usual excitement that comes with being in this place, where I'm pursuing my dreams.

"I can do this," I reassure myself under my breath, but I

don't sound convincing. A part of me still wishes for the warmth of my bed, to be wrapped in a cozy blanket, with the soft glow of the TV screen flickering as I watch *Gilmore Girls* on repeat and try to forget the world outside.

But I have responsibilities here, commitments I can't ignore. No matter how much my personal life is in turmoil, I can't let it interfere with my studies. I have worked too hard, given too much of myself to get to this point, and my future depends on it. Flunking out is not an option. So, I shove the worries into a corner of my mind, lock them tightly and forget about them for a while.

Passing by the notice boards plastered with reminders and upcoming exam schedules, I make my way toward room 214, where Dr. Daniels's Introduction to Veterinary Nutrition class is about to start. I approach the old oak door, painted a sterile white like the rest of the building, and push it open. The squeak of the hinges reminds me of how early I am.

The room is still empty except for Dr. Daniels, who's hunched over his desk shuffling through a stack of papers. He's an imposing man, with salt and pepper hair and bushy eyebrows that bunch together when he concentrates on something. A pair of glasses is perched on the bridge of his nose, threatening to fall at any moment. But they never do.

"Ah, you're early," he says, pushing his glasses back up his nose.

"Yes, sir. I thought I'd get a head start." Since I've barely spoken the past few days, my voice sounds unfamiliar.

"Good for you." He flashes me a quick smile before going back to his papers, leaving me to settle into the routine of preparing for the class. I select a seat near the front, close enough to see the blackboard clearly but far enough to avoid being singled out. I pull out my notebook, its pages crammed with notes and annotations, and my favorite mechanical pencil that has seen more than its fair share of all-nighters.

Not long after, other students begin to filter in, bringing with them a wave of chatter and the smell of fresh notebooks and coffee. The room quickly comes alive as they greet each other and swap stories about their weekends.

I remain at my desk, mostly unnoticed as I flip open my notebook and begin to review my notes. Even though I wasn't here in person last week, the online lecture recordings have allowed me to keep pace.

The lecture starts with a review, then Dr. Daniels walks us through the digestive systems of cats and dogs, emphasizing the importance of nutritional timing and composition.

"Today, we will focus on the dietary needs of canines in recovery," he announces, flipping open a large textbook.

The time goes by quickly and ends with Dr. Daniels assigning us a detailed study on a canine species of our choice, to be discussed in the next class.

At lunchtime, I meet up with Joe at a fast-food joint down the street from campus. It's a beautiful afternoon. The air carries the scent of autumn leaves and pumpkin spice from nearby cafés, and the sun spills golden light across the pavement.

Though we didn't see each other the last few days, he doesn't seem angry as he kisses me and draws me into a long, warm hug, something I desperately need right now.

"Tell me everything," he says, when we take a seat at one of the greasy tables by the window. "I'm ready to be a more supportive boyfriend. I know you filled me in a bit, but are you really sure what your stepfather said is true, that he never slept with Lauren?"

I swallow hard. "I... Tom wouldn't lie to me."

Joe leans back in his chair, a skeptical look on his face. "Really? You honestly believe that? But he did lie. He didn't tell you or your mother about what happened in the living room that night. If nothing really happened between him and Lauren, why hide it? And do you really think Lauren would make up something so... extreme? Come on, Isobel."

"Lauren is obsessed with Tom." I lower my tone, leaning in. "She's lying about him, Joe. You have to believe me. Tom is just not capable of what Lauren is accusing him of."

He studies me for a moment, those intense chocolate eyes trying to read the truth in mine. "If you say so."

"I do. Now let's just eat," I suggest, anxious to move past the interrogation. But as Joe nods and turns his attention to the menu, I can't deny that this conversation has left another crack in the foundation of our relationship.

We order our usual burgers—mine vegetarian and his beef—and fries and I am grateful for the comforting smell of the sizzling grease and onions. Joe talks about his engineering classes and his latest garage band endeavors. But his words are barely penetrating the fog that has settled over my thoughts. Each bite of the burger, each sip of soda, is an automated act. I feel so disconnected from everything.

"Isobel?" Joe is looking at me with a strange expression, his mouth set in a tight line. "You've barely touched your food."

I glance down at my burger, its juices seeping into the wax paper, and realize I'm not actually hungry. I push the plate away with a weak smile. "Sorry, just... I'm not hungry. Do you want it?"

"No, I'm fine." Joe lowers his fork. "You're not really here, Izzy."

"I know," I murmur, pushing a fry around my plate with my finger. "I'm sorry. Just... this whole thing with Tom and Lauren is messing with my head."

"Have you decided if you'll ask Lauren to move out of your apartment so you can move back in?"

"No, I'm staying home for now."

Tom told me that he is letting Lauren stay in the apartment rent-free until the baby is born.

"So you won't be coming back at all?" Joe's eyebrows knit together.

"It's not just about Lauren, Joe. My mom needs me."

Joe leans back, his expression unreadable. "Fine," he finally says, though his tone suggests otherwise.

As I shift my gaze away, focusing on a worn sticker stuck to the side of the ketchup bottle, doubts creep in. Is he right? Was Tom lying?

"Isobel, you can't keep doing this. Your life..." He pauses to take a sip of soda. "It can't just revolve around your mother."

I feel his words like a sharp blow to the chest. He's doing it again, trying to make me feel guilty for giving my mother more time than I give him.

Swallowing my annoyance, I reach out to touch his hand. "Joe, nothing has to change between us. We'll still be seeing each other. I'm here, aren't I?"

"Barely," he scoffs and dabs his lips with a napkin. "You really believe that things will stay the same?" His eyes darken. "Every time there's a crisis with your family, you vanish. Our plans get put on hold."

"I..." I rake a hand through my hair. "Look, I'm tired of having to justify my choices to you. All you do is criticize."

"Right," he mutters and stands abruptly. Then he throws down his napkin, the white paper crumpling like the promise of our afternoon together. "Sorry, I have to go. I forgot I have another lecture. And Isobel, I'm starting to think this thing between us just isn't working anymore." He throws his parting words over his shoulder and starts to walk away.

"Joe, wait!" I call, but he doesn't turn back.

Did he just dump me?

Dread squeezing my chest, I gather my things and leave the restaurant. The warm afternoon sun does little to ease the chill settling in my body. As I make my way back to campus, my thoughts circle back to Joe's words.

Your life can't just revolve around your mother.

What am I supposed to do? Turn my back on my own mother when she needs me most? Isn't family supposed to come first?

Reaching the campus, I find a bench under an old elm tree and sit down. The fallen leaves rustle softly around me, and the cool breeze carries a faint scent of earth and decay.

It's true; my mother's illness has consumed my life, and it's hard for me to see anything beyond it. She has begged me so many times to focus on my life, to go after my dreams, to enjoy my time at college. But how can I leave her side when she's so vulnerable?

"Isobel?" a familiar voice rings out.

I look up to see Lauren, standing only a few feet away. She's wearing a yellow dress with a black cardigan over it and her short hair is glinting in the sunlight, but there are bags under her eyes.

I jump to my feet, ready to get away from her. "I have nothing to say to you, Lauren."

"Please, Izzy, we need to talk about... about—"

"Save it," I spit before she can say anything more. "I don't believe a word you said last week."

Her face falls. "You have to listen to me."

"No, I don't have to do anything. You're a liar. That baby isn't Tom's."

Lauren's eyes glisten as tears fill them. "Isobel, please—I want to—"

"You want to do what?" I snap back. "Continue to spin your lies? To try to destroy my family despite everything we've done for you? Tom told me everything." I grit my teeth and force out each word. "You only got pregnant to manipulate Tom because you have some weird crush on him. I'm glad you're giving the baby to my parents. You'd be a terrible mother, just like you're a terrible friend."

"Please, just listen to me," she pleads, reaching out. But I step back.

"Goodbye, Lauren." I turn on my heel and walk away.

I hear her cry out my name, but I continue to walk and don't look back because I don't want her to see my tears.

THIRTY-EIGHT

A few hours later I push open the living room door, my textbooks weighing heavily under my arm. The smell of oil paint and turpentine hits me, a scent that has slowly faded over the past few months.

The room has been transformed into an artist's studio, with canvases and sketches scattered around in an organized chaos. And there, in the center of it all, is Mom. She sits on the edge of the couch, hunched over in deep concentration as her hand glides across a sheet of paper, creating a trail of vibrant colors.

"Hey, Mom." As I step deeper into the room, through the windows, I catch sight of the willow tree in the drive, its golden branches swaying gently in the autumn breeze. There's something about autumn that enables us to pause, to breathe deeply, to appreciate the beauty of change.

Mom looks up at me with a smile just like the day when we had our mother–daughter date. "Isobel, you're home early." It feels so good to see that genuine spark of joy radiating from her again.

"Class let out sooner than usual." My backpack slips from my shoulder, landing softly on the floor as I move closer.

Her whole body seems less tense, her shoulders no longer weighed down by depression. Even her usually limp hair is shiny and pulled back into a ponytail, with a few strands framing her face like brush strokes.

"You haven't drawn in a long time," I say to her.

She sets down her pencil and leans back to admire her work with a critical eye. "I just felt inspired today. It feels good to be creating again."

I feel relieved, but I know her return is delicate and I'm not going to get my hopes up so soon.

"Your work is beautiful, as always."

"Thank you, sweetie." She pats the space beside her, and I sit, the cushion dipping under our weight. "It's nice to have this again. To feel like myself." She reaches for my hand and squeezes. "How are you, Isobel? Really?"

I fidget under her penetrating stare, ready to deflect with a pre-prepared response. "Just the usual, you know. School is intense."

She nods with a smile. "You're working hard. I'm proud of you. I hope you know that."

"Thanks, Mom."

"Is everything else all right, apart from college? Even though you've moved back home, I feel like I don't see you much. We rarely talk."

"Of course, everything is great," I say, too quickly. I hate lying to my mother.

Her gaze softens as she studies my face, a mother's intuition no doubt picking up on my unease. "Isobel, darling. I may not have been the best mother recently, but I'm still your mother. I can tell when something's wrong. How are things going with Lauren? You haven't really told me what happened between you two."

The name stiffens my spine. "I'd rather not talk about it." I glance at the vibrant drawings scattered around her. "Is that a new children's book you're working on? Those illustrations really are amazing, Mom."

I focus on one image in particular, of what looks like an African princess in a multi-colored gown, her rich skin shimmering under a radiant sun. On her head is a crown of vibrant hibiscus flowers, each petal exquisitely detailed.

My mother turns to look at the drawing. "Ah yes, this one," she says affectionately. "Her name is Adanna. This is a story about her journey, from being a common girl in her village to becoming a brave and loved queen of her people." She picks up the drawing and her fingers trace over the princess's face. "It feels good to do something different from the usual fairy tales and mythical beasts. Both the publisher and author are quite pleased with this batch."

As I listen to my mother speaking so passionately about her project, I feel so proud and inspired by her. Despite everything she has suffered, she finds strength enough to create beautiful stories that captivate the imagination of children around the world.

Then suddenly, the living room door clicks open and Tom strides in, his presence filling the room. He flashes his usual charming smile as he leans down to kiss Mom. "Hello, darling wife."

Right now they are the picture of domestic bliss, but my mind is filled with disturbing images of Tom and Lauren, together.

"Isobel?" Tom comes to give me a peck on the cheek. "You okay?"

"Fine." I manage a smile. "Just tired from college."

"Of course." He nods, but his gaze lingers a second too long on my face, probing, searching for something.

I force myself to look away, to pretend to study another illustration.

"Tom, did you remember to call the plumber about the

sink?" Mom asks casually. She's utterly oblivious to the tension between her husband and daughter.

"Uh, yeah, they're coming tomorrow," he replies, but his eyes flicker to mine again and I feel a shudder of doubt run through me.

Who do I trust? My best friend, or the man I love like a father?

One of them is lying.

THIRTY-NINE

On Saturday morning, I crack an egg into the sizzling skillet and watch as the yolk bubbles and pops. The scents of melting butter, toast, and coffee fill the kitchen.

The house is quiet, except for the ticking of the clock on the wall and the gentle scrape of my spatula against the cast-iron pan.

"Morning, Izzy," Tom says, and my fingers tighten on the spatula.

"Morning," I reply without turning. I had hoped he'd be out playing tennis like he does on most Saturdays, and it would be just me and Mom this morning.

I've been avoiding him as much as I can, but he keeps showing up whenever Mom and I are alone.

"Need help?" He steps closer, reaching for the coffee pot. "I can make some bacon to go with those eggs."

I shrug. "Yeah, okay."

A few minutes later, as the bacon sizzles, I glance at him. He's still in his pajama bottoms, a rare Saturday indulgence for a man who is usually up and about before the sun has even had a chance to lift its head. His hair is tousled and he looks younger than his forty years.

"Isobel," he says finally, and I brace myself.

"Let's just focus on breakfast," I say, more to myself than to him.

"Something smells good," Mom says, entering the kitchen wearing her purple satin robe.

"Morning, Mom." I feel instant relief at her presence. "Have a seat. Breakfast is almost ready."

"Perfect. I'm so lucky to live with two cooks in the house." She ties her robe tighter around her waist, padding over to join us, her slippers shuffling against the cold tiles.

She seems so innocently peaceful right now, and I can't bear the thought of anything hurting her.

"Anything interesting planned for today?" she asks when we're all sitting at the kitchen table.

"I thought I'd spend the day with you." I reach for my orange juice and take a sip. "We could catch a movie or stroll down to the park."

Her face lights up immediately. "That sounds lovely, Isobel," she says, her fork clinking against her plate.

"Perhaps I can join you," Tom cuts in. "Thought I'd stay home today as well. I canceled tennis with the guys to spend the day with my family."

"Oh, how nice!" Mom exclaims. "It's rare for us to spend a Saturday together."

"All the more reason to make it a family day then," I say through gritted teeth, forcing a smile at Tom.

"This is such a lovely breakfast, Isobel," Mom praises.

"Thanks," I mumble, my appetite gone. If I continue to eat now, I'll throw it all up as soon as I leave this table. I've been doing a lot of that lately.

"Isobel, darling, I'm really sad about what happened to you

and Lauren. You used to be so close. Are you sure you don't want to be the bigger person and reach out to her? Whatever happened, I'm sure your friendship is strong enough to make it through."

I stiffen, the fork pausing midway to my mouth, and before she can press further, there's a crash. Tom's hand has knocked over his glass of water. It spills across the table and wets the white tablecloth.

"Oh!" my mother gasps, as the cold water trickles down and onto her lap. She quickly rises from her chair while Tom fumbles with his napkin, stretching across the table to blot the spreading pool of water.

"Damn, sorry," he stammers. His cheeks are flushed.

We resume eating while speaking about other mundane topics. Then Mom and Tom get up to clear the table.

The clatter of the dishes and silverware in the sink reverberates through the room and I close my eyes only for them to fly open again at the sound of a soft beep.

Tom's phone is on the table in front of where he sat and it looks like a text has just come in.

Tom and my mother have their backs to me as they wash the dishes, and my gaze flickers between them and the phone.

"Isobel." My mother's voice makes me jump. "Could you bring me those glasses?"

"Sure, Mom," I say and take them to her before I'm tempted to read the notification.

When I return to the table, I see that Tom's phone has lit up again. This time it's vibrating with a call from someone with the initials L.M.

"Excuse me." Tom is suddenly at my side, snatching up the phone.

"Important call?" my mother asks, drying her hands on a dishtowel.

"Work," Tom replies quickly, the word sharp, final.

He walks out of the kitchen and into the garden.

"Everything okay, Isobel?" Mom questions, sensing the shift in the air.

"Fine," I answer. But nothing is fine. Nothing at all.

I watch her open the fridge to put back the milk and juice cartons.

"Mom," I start, the words thick on my tongue. "What if—what would you do if a man cheated on you?"

She stills and turns to face me.

"Honey, why would you ask that? Did Joe cheat? Did you two break up? Is that why you don't mention him anymore?"

Joe and I haven't spoken since yesterday when he walked out on me during lunch. I tried calling last night, but he never returned my calls or replied to my texts. I guess maybe we have broken up.

"No, it's not about Joe. It's... I'm just curious."

She nods and comes to sit with me at the table.

"Well, cheating..." She pauses, her gaze distant. "It's the ultimate betrayal, isn't it? Trust is shattered and love is questioned." She pauses to look out at Tom, who is pacing and talking on the phone. "But I'm lucky. I have a husband who would never do that to me. I don't think it's something I'd handle well."

FORTY

The lecturer's voice fades away as I quickly gather my books and pack them neatly into my backpack. It's 2 p.m. on Monday, three weeks since Joe walked out on me, but he called yesterday asking to meet up.

I thought we had broken up this whole time, so I wanted to say no and tell him he had lost his chance. But for some reason, the words wouldn't come out. I do understand where he's coming from. I just need to calmly explain everything to him instead of getting upset.

Not wanting to be late, I hurry to my car, but as soon as I slide behind the wheel, I get a call from my mother.

"Hello?" I answer, pressing the phone too hard against my ear.

"Isobel, you need to come home—now... please."

"Mom?" Panic claws up my throat, sharp and insistent. "Are you okay? Is everything all right?"

"Just come, please," is all she manages before the line goes dead, leaving me with a dial tone that might as well be an alarm bell.

I shove the key into the ignition and the engine roars to life beneath me.

As I pull out of the parking lot, it hits me that I must cancel on Joe.

He won't understand—how can he? Yet again, I'm putting my mother first.

At a red light, I dial his number, put the call on speaker, and hold my breath.

"Joe," I begin when he picks up. "I'm so sorry but something's come up with Mom. I have to go home."

There's a pause, and then his long sigh.

"Joe, are you there?"

"Look, I'm tired. Tired of always coming second to your family drama. I can't do this anymore. Go home to your mother. I'm done."

"Wait, Joe—"

Click.

I stare at my phone, willing it to ring again. But when I hit redial, it goes straight to voicemail.

As I stare at my phone, I feel only one thing. Relief. I'm not able to give him what he wants, not now at least. It's not fair of me to keep dragging him along. Perhaps it's for the best. His jealousy has become suffocating and I'm starting to think that if we stay together, he could end up turning into the guy Lauren warned me about.

Stop thinking about her, I scold myself, and I hit the gas as soon as the light turns to green.

The roads are slick with the day's earlier rain as I drive through, the streetlights reflecting off them in a mosaic of colored puddles.

When I arrive home and park the car, the front door swings open and Mom comes rushing out.

"Isobel!" She pulls me into the house with an unexpected strength.

"Mom, what's going on?"

"Sweetheart," she starts as soon as the front door is closed behind us, "I'm pregnant. We didn't even have to restart IVF. It worked naturally."

"What?" The world tilts on its axis, and for a moment, all I can feel is the blood roaring in my ears. Pregnant? After another loss that nearly broke her, that left our family reeling?

"Mom..." I stammer, grappling for words that won't come. "Are you sure? After—"

"Isobel." Her hand cups my cheek, cool and steady. "I know it's a risk. But I feel it, here." She places my hand over her heart. "In my heart. This time... this time it will be different."

I want to wrap her in my arms, to shield her from the heartache I fear is looming on the horizon. She looks so happy and I know she's waiting for me to join her in her excitement.

"Mom, if you're happy, then I'm happy for you. I just hope—"

"Isobel," Mom cuts me off, "honey, we have to believe, not hope. For this little one, we have to believe."

"Okay, Mom," I whisper, the words a vow. "We'll believe. Together."

But as soon as Tom comes home, I get to him first because my mom is having a late nap.

I find him in the kitchen, setting down his keys. Mom said she already told him the news this afternoon when he came home for lunch, but he doesn't look all that thrilled. He just looks tired.

"Tom, we need to talk." I close the kitchen door, so we can be alone.

"Everything okay?" Concern flickers across his features.

"Mom told me about the baby."

"Right." He drapes his coat over a chair before turning to face me again, a small smile on his face, but it looks forced.

"Yeah." I take a deep breath, forcing the next words out.

"So, how is this going to work? Are you still planning on adopting Lauren's baby?"

The sigh he releases is heavy with unspoken thoughts. "No, Isobel. We won't be doing that anymore. I forgot to tell you that Lauren has changed her mind. She wants to keep the baby."

"Okay, well, good. I think that's for the best. It would be so complicated."

He scratches at his beard and leans against the countertop, looking down at his shiny, black shoes. "I agree. Now let's just focus on the good news and hope for the best."

After talking to Tom, I step outside for some fresh air, trying to clear my head. As I stand on the porch, a car speeds past. It's a beat-up, old blue sedan, one that looks just like Joe's.

I watch it disappear down the road. But it can't have been him. If it really was, it would mean he was close by when we were talking on the phone. Watching me? Stalking me? And would it be the first time? I immediately think about that love note he left on my car, when I wasn't sure he knew where I was.

No way. He wouldn't follow me home, and certainly not after making it sound like we were done.

And yet a shiver runs down my spine as I head back into the house.

FORTY-ONE

On a cold Monday in January, I'm sitting on the edge of my seat in Dr. Monroe's waiting room. A breeze slips through the slightly cracked window, bringing with it the biting chill of winter outside.

I glance between the hands on the clock and my mother's beaming expression. Tom is sitting next to her, holding her hand tightly, the lines of his face softer than I've ever seen them.

In spite of myself, and despite everything that happened last year, I'm happy for them.

"Isn't it wonderful?" Mom whispers, more to herself than to us.

"It is, Mom. I'm so happy for you both." I reach for a dog-eared magazine with a cover story about parenting tips.

Just then, the door to the inner office creaks open, and Dr. Monroe emerges from the room, dressed in a crisp white coat, his silver hair ruffled just slightly as if he's been running his hands through it. "Nora Swanson, you can come in."

"Here we go." Mom stands, but I immediately notice the slight tremble in her hand.

We shuffle into the ultrasound room, a cramped space filled

with the hum of machines. Mom lies down on the examination table and Tom hovers close. I take a seat by the window, the subtle hum of the town seeping through the glass. Through the speckled window, I watch as an aging maple tree dances with the wind, its leafless branches swaying.

I could sit down beside Mom, close enough to catch a glimpse of the screen, but like her, I'm also filled with anxiety. Mom's past miscarriages have shown us how fragile this moment could be, how hopes raised too quickly can come crashing down in the cold sterility of a doctor's office.

I remind myself that Mom has made it to the end of the first trimester, a milestone she hadn't reached with her previous pregnancies. We are all hoping the doctor will confirm that she's no longer in the riskiest stage, and I came because I wanted to be there for her, whatever happens now.

The gel squirts onto Mom's belly and she grasps Tom's hand just as the monitor flickers to life, and the doctor begins his search. Suddenly, a rhythmic sound fills the room—a quick, steady thrumming. The baby's heartbeat.

For a moment, everything else fades away. The cold outside, the worries from the past year, everything.

"Nice and strong," the doctor assures us, and a weight slides off my shoulders.

"Thank you." Mom lets out a sigh that is almost a mix between a laugh and a sob, a sound of release from her pent-up emotions.

After receiving a kiss from Tom, she turns her gaze to the screen, fixated on the tiny life moving inside her.

I stand up to get a closer look for myself. My little brother or sister is inside there, and soon enough, we'll be welcoming them into our world.

The doctor prints out the images and hands them to Mom, who holds them close to her chest as Tom hugs her.

"Can you believe it, Izzy?" Mom says when we're walking

out of the clinic into the snow-covered streets. "Everything's going to be okay."

"Of course. I'm so excited." For her sake, for their sake. "Time to celebrate."

Our plan after leaving the clinic was to celebrate with the other locals of Ellery Creek at the yearly Warm Up Fest, a cozy yearly event designed to beat the winter chill. Despite the cold, the festival is in full swing, with stalls set up along Main Street, and the scents of freshly brewed tea, warm cinnamon, hot chocolate, and roasted chestnuts wafting through the crisp winter air.

We walk past stalls that sell everything from home-baked cakes and pastries to hand-knitted scarves. The icy wind bites at my cheeks and nose, making me shiver. I pull my woolen coat tighter around me, a Christmas gift from Tom and Mom. It's a deep, rich burgundy, with large, sturdy buttons that fasten securely down the front, a faux fur lining and a high collar that I now flip up to shield my neck from the cold.

I smile at the children darting between legs, their laughter drifting upward into the clear, cold sky, as a local band sets up on a makeshift stage in the gazebo close to the town's library.

Since we haven't eaten yet, we grab a couple of sandwiches and pretzels from a nearby bakery stall, set up under the naked Ellery Oak. The stallholder, Mrs. Donahue, giving Tom the royalty treatment he usually gets as the town's school principal, stuffs our bags with extra pastries and insists we take home a jar of her famous apple jam.

As we continue our walk, Mom grins up at Tom. "I think we're ready to tell people now. What do you think?"

Even though I see no risk in sharing their good news at this point, I'm still a little nervous. I want to ask her to wait a little longer, but she looks so happy that I don't want to dampen her joy.

"We definitely should." Tom draws her nearer and kisses

her cheek. "Isn't this the time people usually share their happy news, anyway?"

"Yes," Mom says, chewing on her warm pretzel, "And I think it's the perfect time."

As soon as we reach Whispering Pines Park, which is still decorated in fairy lights from Christmas, we hear someone call my parents.

"Hey, Nora! Tom! Over here!" Mrs. Henderson from the Knitting Booth is sitting on a chair at her stall, busy creating one of her famous quilts while trying to keep it from touching the snowy ground. She's in her eighties, but given the speed at which her fingers are moving, old age has not robbed her of her skills.

Next to her is a large basket filled with some of her products —a couple of multicolored blankets, a few pairs of wool socks, and an array of knitted hats. We cross over to her small corner of the festival.

"Guess what? I'm pregnant!" Mom blurts out before she can say another word.

"Oh, my dear Nora and Tom, that's wonderful news." Beaming, the older woman rises with difficulty to her feet and hugs both of them.

"Thank you," Mom replies, her cheeks flushed from the cold. After that, word spreads like wildfire, and before we know it, everyone is congratulating them.

"How far along are you?" Martha from next door—and the chief gossip in town—asks, patting Mom's stomach intrusively.

"Still early," Mom replies with a smile. "But it looks like a summer baby."

"A summer baby," Mr. Malloy, the local barber, chimes in, his hand stroking his gray, braided beard. "That's wonderful indeed. Congratulations, you two."

Standing nearby, I watch my parents surrounded by our

community's joy, but with every person who hears the news, my anxiety grows stronger.

"Are you okay, Izzy?" Mom asks when we're finally alone again. "You've gone very quiet."

"Yes, I'm good. Just happy for you both. It's finally happening."

"Good." She pulls me to her side. "Because you're going to be an amazing big sister."

"Wouldn't miss it for the world," I respond, and I mean it.

The air buzzes with the excitement of the festival as I detach from Mom and Tom, weaving through the crowd to join a group of people my age who I grew up with.

There's Katie, wearing a green hat with a white pom-pom, who used to be the prom queen of our year and is now studying nursing in Portland, Maine. Next to her is Ethan, a guy I used to have a crush on in my first year of high school before finding out he was a bully. Instead of pursuing further education, he took over the management of his family's farm.

And then there's Sophie, who waitresses at a local diner. In school, she was known as the girl with the pink umbrella because she hated getting her bone-straight hair wet and always carried one no matter what the weather forecast predicted.

For a while, everyone exchanges small talk, catching up on what's been happening in our lives. Katie talks about her latest exams and the chaos of dorm life. Ethan shares a story about a recent cow birth on the farm, which has Sophie scrunching up her nose in disgust. Meanwhile, I keep my family's news to myself.

"Izzy!" Sophie beckons me closer, her grin wide. "Did you hear about Lauren? I heard she's pregnant. I didn't see that coming. Do you think she will drop out of college?"

My pulse quickens, and I can feel the weight of their stares. If they're expecting to get the juicy details from me, they will be very disappointed.

"No idea," I say quickly and take a step back. "Anyway, Mom's probably wondering where I am. Catch up later?"

"Of course, Izzy," Sophie calls after me, but I don't look back.

"Mom, Tom," I call out, spotting them by the cotton candy stand. "I think I should go home. I have a bit of a headache."

"Already?" Mom lays a hand on my forehead. "Do you want me to come with you?"

"No, I'll be fine. I just need some rest."

"You know what, I think I'm also tired from all the excitement and I have some sketches to finish." She turns to Tom. "Honey, I'll go back home with Izzy. Will you stay and enjoy the fair?"

"No. I'm ready to get out of here as well." Tom gives me a pat on the shoulder. "We can all head home together."

Back at the house, I retreat to my room and remain there for most of the evening, coming out only to eat dinner and say goodnight.

Just as I'm about to start another episode of *Gilmore Girls*, Tom comes up to my room.

"Are you sure you don't want to take something for the headache, Izzy? I can bring you an aspirin."

"No, I'm okay," I insist. I hate medication unless I'm literally on the verge of dying. "Go on and enjoy your evening with Mom."

Tom nods, pausing in the doorway for a moment too long before finally retreating.

Surprisingly, I fall asleep pretty quickly, but jolt awake again around ten. Unable to sleep again, I decide to go downstairs for a warm glass of milk. As I pass by the hallway windows, I catch sight of something that freezes me in place.

There, on the path leading up to our house, is a figure wearing a dark coat, their gaze fixed on the house. The coat's bulky cut makes it difficult to determine whether the person is a man or a woman.

Is it Joe? What is he doing here, and how long has he been out there in the cold, watching our house?

Or could it be Lauren?

My veins surge with panic as I quickly rush down the stairs. If it's her, what makes her think she can just show up here after everything that's happened? Did she come to tell my mother the truth?

At the front door, I take a deep breath and yank it open, rushing outside to confront whoever it is. But there's no one there. Not Joe, and not Lauren.

FORTY-TWO

Three Months Later

An ear-splitting shriek cuts through the night.

I jolt upright and fumble for the lamp switch on my nightstand. For a few frantic heartbeats, I sit there, wondering if I was dreaming.

Then the scream cuts through the silence once more, even louder this time.

Mom.

I throw off the covers, jump out of bed and race toward my parents' room. Another anguished cry fills the air and without even bothering to knock, I push open their door.

"Mom!" The word is a gasp, torn from my throat. "What... What...?"

She can't be losing the baby. Not when she's come so far.

Her body is curled in a ball on the bed, her hands clutching her swollen belly. Tom is by her side, his face drained of color. He looks like he's about to pass out.

"I already called 911," he says, not looking at me, his entire being focused on Mom.

The wait for the ambulance feels like an endless stretch of time, the minutes ticking by slowly as we watch her suffer. We attempt to offer words of comfort, but nothing seems to ease the weight of her immense pain.

And then, finally, with the wail of sirens and the rush of paramedics, she's whisked away into the night, Tom with her in the back of the ambulance and me driving behind in my car. I barely register the countless turns, traffic signals, and angry honks.

Not long after, we arrive at the hospital. I pull my car to a halt in the parking lot, leap out, and sprint through the sliding doors just in time to see Tom following the stretcher with Mom on it.

Tom and I are asked to stay in the family waiting room while the doctors attend to her.

The room is filled with the steady ticking of clocks and faint murmurs in the distance. Every now and then, a loudspeaker crackles to life to announce a series of codes and names that mean nothing to us.

We wait, each trapped in our own thoughts. Tom is hunched over, his hands knitted together, his gaze fixed on the floor. He looks years older.

After what feels like hours, a very tall doctor strides into the room. He doesn't need to say it; the truth is written in the lines of his face and the downward shift of his gaze.

Tom jumps to his feet as the doctor approaches him. "How's my wife... and the baby?" He swipes the back of his hand across his brow.

"Mr. Swanson, your wife is okay, but I'm so sorry, the baby did not make it." The doctor's voice is neutral, but his expression is soft and sympathetic. "There was no heartbeat."

The words hang in the air like a putrid smell.

Another part of our family gone before we ever got the

chance to welcome her into the world. It was going to be a girl and Tom and Mom already named her Danielle. Now she's gone before I could see who she would become, who we all would become with her in our lives.

Tom approaches a wall and presses both hands against it, his body shaking visibly as he lets out a raw cry. "Not again," he mumbles through his tears.

I remain frozen in my seat and blink numbly at the floor tiles.

From the corner of my eye, I see the doctor place a hand on Tom's shoulder, offering apologies and condolences that mean nothing to him right now.

"Can we see her? Can we see my mom?" My voice is distant and I feel a strange detachment, as if I'm watching us from a distance.

"Of course." The doctor leads us down the corridor.

When we reach the room, I let Tom go in first. He pauses in the doorway, then he takes a deep breath before stepping inside, the door closing behind him with a soft click.

But not long after, the door swings open again, and he walks out. "Your mother doesn't want to speak to me."

"Tom..." I reach for him and, for the first time in months, we hug. I've been angry with him for so long, but right now all that anger seems so meaningless.

"I'm sorry," I murmur against his chest. "I'm so sorry we lost her."

Tom just holds me tighter, and I know that we're both grappling with the same unanswerable question: How do we move forward from here? How does Mom? Will she?

"I'll be in the waiting room," Tom says, releasing me and walking away.

I push open the door and see Mom curled up on the bed. She's there, but she isn't. Her eyes are dull and distant.

"Mom, it's me." I inch closer to the bed. "I'm here. I'm so, so sorry."

Her gaze flits to mine, then away, as if the effort takes up too much energy. I reach for her hand, but her fingers don't curl around mine. Her hand just lies limp in my palm.

"Please, talk to me, Mom." I brush a damp strand of hair from her forehead. She seems to be looking right through me, trapped somewhere deep inside herself.

"Go home, Izzy," she whispers, with a finality that chills me to the bone.

"Mom—"

"Please... I need to be alone."

Her dismissal stings like a sharp slap, and as I leave the room, I wonder if this is it, the final straw that breaks her.

"I don't want people to know," Mom says the day she's released from hospital and we're driving home. "Not yet. Let me be ready first." They're the first words she's said in almost a week.

Tom and I nod.

The car pulls into the driveway and Mom unbuckles her seat belt before the engine even has a chance to fully shut off. She quickly exits the car and makes a beeline for the house.

"Mom, wait, let me help you," I call out, but she doesn't pause.

Tom reaches out, his touch light on my shoulder. "Let her be. She needs time."

The rest of the day drags by and the house seems frozen in time with Mom staying upstairs in their room, refusing to talk or eat.

When the day finally bleeds into night, I'm sitting by the window when I see her out in the garden with Tom and they're in each other's arms. Mom is crying.

As I watch them grieve from a distance, for a fleeting moment, I wonder if it's too late for us to have Lauren's baby.

I'm certain nobody could love that baby as fiercely as my mom.

FORTY-THREE

Doing my best to balance the silver tray with steady hands, I make my way down the hallway toward Mom and Tom's room and knock.

"Mom?" I speak softly, even though I know she won't answer. "I brought breakfast for you."

There's no response from her, so I enter the room and find her lying in bed, enveloped by darkness.

"Mom." I hold out the tray. "Please eat something."

She just turns away.

"How about we go for a walk, then?" I suggest. "It's really nice and warm outside and the fresh air will do us both good."

She doesn't move, and I wonder if she even heard me. Then she speaks. "Not today, Isobel."

"Mom," I plead, "you haven't left the house since you came home from the hospital. Please, let's go outside just for a moment. Do it for me?"

"I'm not ready yet," she whispers. That's always her reply, every single day.

I want to shake her out of this despair, but all I can do is nod.

"Okay," I give in. "But we should really try later, okay?"

"Later," she repeats, still gazing away from me.

Feeling defeated, I leave the room and head to the bathroom. When I look in the mirror, a sigh escapes me as I take in my pale skin and the deep shadows under my eyes.

Just then, my phone pings inside my pocket. I pull it out with trembling hands and see a message from Joe.

It's been months since I thought I saw him outside our house, a sight that made my skin crawl with fear. The next day, I did receive a message from him, asking to get back together, saying that he made a mistake, that he would be better, more understanding. I immediately blocked his number.

Two days after that, I received another text from a different number. Since then, he's been sending me at least one text every day. Too busy with Mom and thinking he will eventually give up and stop, I ignored all of them. But this latest message gives me pause.

Don't make me live without you, Izzy. I don't know what I would do without you. I'm going crazy here. I miss us.

Taking a breath, I respond:

There is no us. If you don't leave me alone, I will call the police.

I shove the phone back into my pocket and, before I know it, I'm breaking down into tears. Then I'm leaning over the toilet, purging all the emotional turmoil inside me along with my breakfast. Afterwards, feeling a little better and relieved, I return to Mom, my priority.

I try to get her to eat again, but she won't even look at me. I feel so helpless.

"Mom," I beg, "come on."

I wish Tom was here, but he hasn't been doing great himself.

He's out for his morning jog now, running away from his own pain. I hear his struggles every day, bottles clinking late at night, the front door slamming before dawn as he leaves the house to go for a run before work.

When he leaves for work, dressed in his suit and tie, he's always the picture of normalcy, as if the late night drinks have no impact on him. But I know better. I've seen the subtle changes—the emptiness in his eyes, the scent of alcohol on his breath that he tries to mask with excessive mints, the way his hands tremble slightly when he thinks no one is watching.

Fifteen minutes later, as I leave Mom behind and step into the hallway, I see him coming up the stairs, but he doesn't see me at first, lost in his thoughts.

"Morning, Tom," I say, stopping at the top of the stairs.

He startles and then forces an empty smile. "Morning, Izzy." His voice is rougher than usual.

"Mom's not doing well." The words taste bitter on my tongue. "I tried to get her to eat, but she won't. I'm really worried."

Tom's gaze drifts past me toward their bedroom door. "I'm off today, so I'll spend some time with her."

"That's good because I have to go to campus today. There's a paper I need to hand in and other things I need to take care of." The summer break is approaching quickly, and I have a lot of tasks and projects to do before then.

"You go ahead. We'll manage."

I hate leaving Mom on her own when I go to Amberfield, but on those days, since the high school where he works is not far from our house, Tom is often able to pop in between his meetings. Since they lost the baby, he also took a few days off work.

I've also called in sick several times, but I know I cannot

keep doing that without putting my scholarship at risk. At least I don't have much of a social life to maintain. Between my studies and managing things at home, I have little time left for anything else, including waitressing, which I have put on hold for now.

Either way, as much as I hate to think it, it's a good thing Joe and I have broken up and I don't have to feel guilty for not spending time with him. Whenever I have the time to be there for my mom, I am. It's not always possible, but we try our best to make sure someone is always home with her.

"Thanks," I say and turn away from the man who seems to be fading away more each day. "Keep an eye on her, please."

"I will." He reaches out to squeeze my shoulder. "You don't have to worry, Izzy. Focus on your studies."

Even as I seek peace and calm in the library after a lecture, not even the familiar scent of books can soothe the tightness in my chest.

My gaze keeps drifting to the clock, counting the minutes until I can return home, until I can be sure that Tom kept his word and isn't downstairs drinking and watching his comedies while Mom is alone in the bedroom staring into space.

It's early afternoon when I finally allow myself the luxury of leaving the campus, glancing over my shoulder every few minutes, expecting to find Joe standing there, but I don't see him. Maybe my last text was enough to scare him off.

There's a bakery called Baker's Bountiful just around the corner from the apartment I used to share with Lauren, my apartment. I decide to make a quick stop there because they sell some pastries Mom used to love and I would take some home with me on weekends.

As I enter, I imagine her face lighting up at the sight of her favorite donuts, with a filling of rich, tart raspberry jam and a delicate dusting of powdered sugar on top. I pick a dozen of those, each carefully selected, and the owner, Mrs. Garfield, wraps them up in her signature brown paper stamped with a playful image of a frosted doughnut and the name of the bakery in a whimsical cursive script.

"I don't see you around here much anymore, young lady," she comments.

"I know. I've been busy with college and other things."

"Life has a way of sweeping us up in its current, doesn't it?" Mrs. Garfield gives me a knowing smile. "But remember, dear, everyone needs to give themselves a break from time to time."

"I'll remember that." With a fragile smile, I tuck the brown bag under my arm and pay for the donuts.

Just as I'm about to turn away, I catch the familiar gait of a man outside the bakery's window and I freeze in place.

It can't be. But as he moves closer, there's no denying the set of his shoulders, the weary tilt to his head.

It's Tom. What is he doing here?

"Mom," I whisper to myself, my pulse quickening. He was supposed to be with her. Anger and fear bubble within me as I push through the door.

"Tom!" I call out, my voice sharper than I intend.

He stiffens and turns, surprise flashing across his face, quickly replaced by guilt. "Isobel, what are you doing here?"

"Me? You know I had to go to lectures. What about you?" I step forward to bridge the gap between us. "You said you'd stay with Mom. Why are you here?"

"The apartment has a leak. I had to check on it to prevent flooding." His words tumble out, rushed and rough around the edges. "Your mom was sleeping. I didn't want to wake her."

"But you said you'd stay with her. She needs you even when she's sleeping, Tom. We shouldn't leave her alone right now."

Tom glances at the watch on his wrist, then up the street. "I didn't mean to stay away long."

"Well, no need for you to hurry back now. Take your time, I'm done for the day. I'm on my way to Mom. See you." I don't wait for him to respond before turning on my heel and storming off.

Inside my car, I take a deep breath and lean my forehead against the steering wheel, not yet ready to start the car. I feel so angry and betrayed that I could cry.

I know he has responsibilities as a landlord, but Tom abandoned Mom when she is in a state of crisis. He could have paid for someone else to go and fix the leak. But he chose to help Lauren in her time of need. He put Mom in danger. And once again, it was all because of Lauren.

FORTY-FOUR

I clench up inside as I grasp the front doorknob. I really hate that Tom left Mom alone yesterday, but in the end, she seemed to have managed okay, which made me feel confident enough to go to college today even though Tom was tied up at the school.

Mom insisted that she would be fine without us and I made sure to call several times to make sure she was.

Now, with a breath drawn deep into my lungs, I open the door. As soon as I step inside, I notice the basket on the floor near the coat rack. There is a baby blanket inside and a bottle.

My mother hasn't had any visitors since Danielle died. And she definitely wouldn't invite anyone with a baby right now. Lowering my backpack to the floor, I take hesitant steps toward the murmurs drifting from the living room; cheerful voices.

As I swing open the door to the living room, I see Mom sitting on the couch with Tom standing beside her. She's cradling a tiny bundle in her arms. Her usually somber expression has been replaced by a gentle smile.

"Mom, wha... What's going on?" I ask, my tone confused.

"Hey, honey," Mom says, her voice and demeanor

completely transformed. "Look who we found on our doorstep. Someone left her there."

My gaze meets Tom's and he avoids my eyes for just a moment too long. In a split second, I understand everything. Why he was in Amberfield yesterday when he should have been with Mom.

The baby in my mother's arms has to be Lauren's. She must have given it to him in the end and he hasn't told Mom the truth. But there is so much happiness in this room, so much joy in my mother's gaze. It's heady and intoxicating.

Without thinking, I find myself asking to hold the baby, the tiny bundle that has brought back the light in my mother's eyes.

After dinner, while my mom is upstairs with Daisy, I find Tom in the kitchen washing dishes. As soon as I enter the room, he stiffens and stops scrubbing.

"You know," he murmurs.

"Yes. You lied to me yesterday about why you were in Amberfield. There was no leak at the apartment, was there?"

He turns to face me with a heavy sigh, clearly exhausted. "I'm sorry, I couldn't tell you. I didn't think you would understand. Lauren called me yesterday and said she was having contractions."

He reaches for me, but I step away, waiting for him to continue. "I tried to convince her to go to the hospital. I wanted to drive her, but she refused." His eyes beg for understanding. "She said she'd call a friend instead, so I left. I couldn't stay, Isobel. I didn't feel like it was right and I was way out of my depth. I left. She must have delivered the baby successfully and then left it for us to find on our doorstep." He reaches out again, a soft urgency in his tone. "Please, you can't tell your mom about this. Not yet."

My gaze hardens as I look up at him. "Why?"

"Because..." He hesitates, his jaw clenching. "She's barely hanging on. If she finds out that this is Lauren's baby, if she goes and talks to her, and hears those lies about me being the father..."

"Tom, no. I can't do this. You're asking me to lie to my own mother... again."

"Only for a little while," he insists desperately. "She needs this time to bond with the baby, to find some strength again, to regain her sense of self."

"You really think it's wise to keep her in the dark?"

"We will tell her whose baby it is eventually. But when the time is right, when she's stronger. For now, please just let her have this happiness."

My mind drifts to the image of my mother's radiant smile and I let out a sigh. It's been so long since I've seen her happy; how could I even consider taking that away from her?

"And what happens when she finds out? It could be even more damaging then."

"We'll deal with it when the time comes. Right now, we need to buy her time to heal."

I struggle to swallow as the betrayal lingers in my mouth. "Fine," I reluctantly agree. "For Mom's sake."

Tom lets out a small sigh of relief and his shoulders visibly relax. He takes hold of my hands with a firm, yet gentle, grip. "Thank you, Isobel. We'll find a solution together, I promise."

I withdraw my hands. "I don't understand. You told me Lauren had decided she wanted to keep her baby."

"Well, clearly she changed her mind, again."

Without saying another word, I step out of the kitchen. Standing at the bottom of the stairs, I hear my mother's laughter as she chatters to the baby, and I can't help but smile.

But the secret between Tom and me feels like a living thing now. A serpent, coiled and waiting to strike.

FORTY-FIVE

The metal gate slams shut behind me and I'm snapped out of my thoughts as I enter the Furry Hope animal shelter where the sharp smell of cleaning solution blends with the natural scents of fur and hay. Mom literally pushed me out of the house to do something I love, something that brings me peace.

Although I miss helping out at the shelter in Amberfield, this smaller, quieter local place is close to my heart. The rows of cages are filled with dogs of all sizes and a chorus of barks and whines greet me as I walk past them.

"I'm so glad you could join us today, Izzy." I look up to see Matt, one of the regulars, standing over me with a grin. He's a man in his thirties, tall with broad shoulders, and his forehead is partially covered by blond waves of hair.

"Me too," I respond with a smile.

"That's good to hear. We've got a bunch of new rescues that could use some attention today."

"Hey, Isobel!" Evelyn, another volunteer, beckons me over. "Can you assist me with this little guy?" Evelyn is a whirlwind of energy with small braids she wears piled up on top of her head. Today, she's cradling a frightened terrier mix. "Found him by the side of the road. Hit and run, maybe. He's scared stiff, but he's gotta learn that not all humans are bad news."

"Hey there, buddy," I whisper, letting the dog sniff my hand. "We're going to take good care of you." In response, he gives my hand a lick and his tail wags as I give him my attention.

Afterwards, I find myself refilling shelves with heavy bags of dog food, feeling the strain on my muscles. When I take a pause to wipe the sweat off my face, I hear a discussion going on from the next aisle between Evelyn, Matt, and a few other people.

"Did you hear about that poor woman?" It's Evelyn, her usually cheerful voice heavy as she speaks.

"Yeah, she was found on Gray Peak Beach," Sarah, another volunteer joins in. "It's quite the mystery."

"Not anymore," Matt adds. "I heard on the radio earlier that they have identified the body. Lauren something."

The world drops away. The name, like a bolt of lightning, sears through the fog in my head. Moving away from my own station, I stumble toward them, my knees feeling suddenly weak. "Lauren who?"

Matt shrugs. "Don't remember the last name. It's starts with an M, I think."

I swallow hard, my breath hitching as I part my lips to speak again. "Mont... Lauren Montgomery?"

"Yes, that's it. Lauren Montgomery," Sarah repeats. "That's her. She wasn't much older than you, Isobel."

Each word feels like a physical blow.

Lauren Montgomery. My best friend. Or my former best friend.

The shelter walls close in around me, the space suddenly suffocating. I need air.

"Excuse me." I turn to walk away, but even though my legs are moving, they don't feel like mine. The concrete floor beneath my sneakers might as well be shifting sand.

Panic is setting in, and all I can think about is getting out of here. Unable to breathe, I stumble toward the exit, grasping on to a metal cage for support.

"Isobel? You okay?" Matt's concerned voice reaches my ears, but it sounds distant and muffled. I can't answer him because the air feels thick, suffocating, and my words won't come.

I just keep moving. My vision blurs as tears well up. Every step I take is mechanical, robotic. I'm aware of the alarmed faces of the other volunteers, their whispers. But I can't find it in me to care.

Outside, sunlight stabs my eyes forcing me to blink away the sudden brightness.

The moment I get behind the wheel of my car, a message pops up on my screen.

> *I heard what happened to Lauren and I'm wondering if I should go to the cops. I may know a thing or two they might be interested to hear. Unless we meet up and talk. How about a date? I'll call you later and if you don't answer, you'll leave me with no choice.*

I drop the phone on the passenger seat and clutch my chest, suddenly gasping for air. I haven't heard from Joe since my last response to his text. I thought he had given up on me, scared of me going to the cops. But this... this is a warning, a threat, right after my best friend's body has been found.

Joe is blackmailing me. If the police knew what Lauren said about Tom it would make him a suspect. Now he is using this information, and Lauren's death, to try to get me back. How sickening. Tom didn't do this to Lauren. He wouldn't. I just need to prove it.

As I drive, my mind races back to my last conversation with

Lauren on campus, when she begged to speak to me and I walked away.

I turned against her, so caught up in my anger, and now, guilt grips me. I could have done something to help her. No matter what she did, no matter how appalling her actions were, she was my friend, and I loved her.

I should have been there for her, I should never have let her go through the whole pregnancy and childbirth and then giving up her child, all alone. The thought of her in those moments—struggling, scared—rips me apart. But now it's too late. I'll never have the chance to fix it, to wrap my arms around her and tell her she wasn't alone. She was so upset the last time I saw her.

Oh God. What if she was so hurt that she took her own life?

The weight of that thought crushes me, and a sob escapes my lips, raw and desperate. I grip the steering wheel, fighting back tears, as the reality of it sinks in. The image of her—my vibrant, beautiful friend—slipping into such despair, thinking that ending her life was the only way out, is unbearable and yet I know it's a possibility. But if there's any chance that she didn't do this to herself, then I'm going to find out who did. And I'm going to get justice.

FORTY-SIX

Lauren's death feels like a terrible nightmare that I can't seem to wake up from. I spent the past hours in an almost catatonic state, grappling with the reality of her being gone.

As soon as Mom and I enter the house after the vigil, I excuse myself, desperate to be alone. All I can think about is going to my room, to climb under the covers, to grieve my friend in peace.

"Goodnight, Izzy." Mom comes to draw me into her arms. She, too, looks devastated and her eyes are rimmed with red.

Before Tom can hug me as well, I hurry out of the living room and up the stairs.

In my room, I sit on the edge of my bed, the fabric of my black dress crinkling beneath me, and the dam inside my chest threatening to break.

Lauren's face swims before me. I see her smile from happier times. I hear her laughter. She was too full of life, too bright to have just been snuffed out like a candle.

Did she really take her own life?

If not, then someone killed her.

Someone stole her life from her, made it impossible that I could ever have my best friend back.

The room is suddenly too small, too confining. I can't breathe.

Getting to my feet, I move to the desk where a picture of me and Lauren stares back at me, a memento from our last summer vacation together. I put it up again the day I found out she died. We're both grinning, sunburned and radiant.

A thought slithers into my mind. When I spoke to Mark at the vigil, he was devastated not only about her death but also the fact that Lauren was pregnant, and she never told him. He assured me that the baby couldn't be his because they never once slept together without protection. Was he lying, and he actually found out about her pregnancy before she died? Would he kill Lauren and leave the baby on our doorstep, out of rage at her betrayal?

Or, what if it's Joe who killed her? But what would he have to gain? We broke up after Lauren and I were no longer friends. He no longer had a reason to be jealous of her. No, Joe is just a crazy ex-boyfriend and, when I get the chance, I'll go to the cops to get a restraining order, something I should have done a long time ago.

And Tom... could Joe be right in thinking of him as a suspect? Could he have done this?

I don't want to believe that either. But I feel sick as I remember seeing him in Amberfield when he was supposed to be home with Mom. The way he had looked so flustered when he saw me. The way his hands trembled just slightly when he tried to explain his presence there. I remember how nervous he looked when I came home to find Lauren's baby there.

Things that seemed unimportant at the time now haunt my thoughts, begging to be examined closer.

"Stop it," I whisper.

But Tom must have been one of the last people to see Lauren alive. He was there the day she gave birth.

I slump to the floor.

What if the man I call my father is a stone-cold killer? What if he killed my best friend, and then stole her baby?

"Please, no," I plead to the empty room.

I need to uncover the truth.

Before I know it, I'm walking out of my room headed for the master bedroom. Mom, Tom, and Daisy are still downstairs and I can hear the gentle hum of the evening news from the living room. I tread softly, hoping they won't hear me. I need to hurry before they come to bed.

As soon as I enter, I go straight to the closet, my gaze sweeping over Tom's clothes, which are neatly hung in color-coded order. I run my fingers over the material and then plunge my hand into one pocket and then another, hoping and dreading to find something, anything.

Nothing.

The emptiness of the pockets mirrors the feeling in my chest, but I can't stop now. Not when every instinct screams that there's more to uncover. I move on, combing through drawers and shelves, my fingers brushing against cold metal, soft cotton, and—

Paper?

The texture is out of place among Tom's socks, and I draw it out with a sharp intake of breath.

As I unfold the crisp, cream-colored paper, I see the bold strokes of Tom's handwriting. It's a letter addressed to Lauren that he probably didn't get a chance to send. My pulse quickens as I smooth it out against my thigh, then begin to read.

Lauren, I want to ask you to reconsider keeping the baby. Nora recently lost another baby, and it has broken her heart. We both know you're not prepared to be a mother at such a young age.

As your child's father, I have a say in this too. Nora and I can offer a loving and supportive home for our baby. It would be the best thing for all of us. Please take some time to think about it.

"God, no." I squeeze my eyes shut, but the darkness doesn't stop the swirling chaos of blurred words.

Seeing in black and white that my stepfather is the biological father of my former best friend's baby is too horrifying to bear. What if he wanted to keep the baby and feared that his secret would come out, that Lauren would eventually tell Mom the truth?

Mom needs to know and I'm the one who has to tell her. But I can't bear to see the look on her face when she hears the truth.

An idea forming in my head, I sneak out of the room again with the folded letter. With every step I take down the stairs, the reality of what I'm about to do presses down heavier on me. But it has to be done. Mom has been kept in the dark for far too long.

At the bottom, I pause to listen for Mom and Tom, but they are still watching TV in the living room. When we got home Daisy was asleep in her baby basket, but now I can hear her crying softly.

Acting fast before they call it a night, I dart to the entrance. Mom's purse is on top of the old cherrywood console table. I reach inside, my fingers searching, but they don't come in contact with the memorial envelope. It must be with her in the living room.

But I find something in a hidden pocket, a folded article. I only read the heading that tells me it's about Lauren and her death.

Without thinking, I pocket it and put the bag back where I found it.

Then I walk past the kitchen and notice the unopened envelope on the table.

Perfect.

The letter slides into the envelope easily for Mom to find and decide what to do with it. I take a deep breath and walk back to the stairs. There's no turning back now. I'm about to shatter our family's facade. I brace myself for the fallout, knowing that once the truth is out, nothing will ever be the same.

FORTY-SEVEN

NORA

Two Weeks Ago

It's after five in the evening, and the ceiling is staring back at me. The dim light seeps through the partially closed blinds, stretching across the room. It's just me at home as Tom and Isobel are still out.

Isobel has been busy all day in Amberfield with lectures and a group project, and Tom had an emergency to attend to at the school. I know they don't like to leave me alone if they can help it, even though I sometimes wish they would.

Part of me wants to get up to prove to them that I'm still functioning. Maybe I could make a simple dinner, do a load of laundry, or just take a shower. I want to get out of bed, do something, anything, but I remain anchored to my bed by some invisible force.

Then my phone rings. I expect it to be Tom or Isobel, but it's someone I haven't spoken to in months.

"Lauren?" I'm surprised to hear from her. She hasn't called me since before she and Isobel stopped being friends. She used to come to me for advice often; we even went out for coffee sometimes just the two of us. I have missed her, but I didn't feel comfortable reaching out to her knowing that she and Isobel had fallen out.

"Nora!" Her breaths are quick and erratic, laced with panic. "I'm pregnant and—"

"What?" Her confession hits me hard and her words reverberate through me like a shockwave. Pregnant? The word resonates in my skull. Isobel never said a word to me about Lauren's pregnancy. Is this what drove them apart?

"I think I'm in labor," she continues, each word punctuated by a sharp intake of air. "I... I'm alone. I don't know what to do."

Alone. Memories from my past resurface, of me in labor as a teenage girl: the terror, the pain, the desperate wish for someone to hold my hand. I gave birth to Isobel alone in an abandoned building. I remember the trauma all too well.

"Stay calm, Lauren," I find myself saying. "Are you at the apartment? I'll call 911."

"No, please don't... I... please just come and help me. I can't go to the hospital. I don't have any money. And I can't take care of a child. I'm scared, Nora."

Her words seep into my consciousness, heavy with desperation and fear. A secret pregnancy, a hidden life growing inside her—how did she bear such a burden alone?

"But Lauren, you can't do this alone. You need medical attention."

"Please, Nora, I need you. If I go to the hospital, they'll take my baby away from me. I don't have anything to give her... I—"

"Lauren," I say, taking a deep breath, "you're not alone. Do you hear me? I'm on my way now."

"Thank you," she whispers. "You're like the mom I never had. Thank you so much."

"Just keep breathing," I urge her, trying to project a calm I don't feel myself. "Just focus on your breaths until I get there. I won't let anything happen to you or the baby."

The line goes dead then, and I force myself to move.

There's no room for hesitation. No space for the crushing depression that has held me captive. Adrenaline surges through my veins.

The moment my feet touch the floor, I spring into action, throwing on the nearest clothes.

Leaving the house hurriedly, my energy suddenly renewed, I don't leave a note for Isobel or Tom. There's no time; two lives hang in the balance. As I dash to the car, my keys clutched tight enough to imprint on my palm, it strikes me that I haven't been out of the house since Danielle died and the ground feels a little foreign beneath my feet, as if the earth has shifted.

I hop into the car and quickly reverse out of the driveway, causing my tires to screech in protest.

Even though I know Lauren and Isobel don't speak anymore, Isobel is the nearest person to her right now and could get there before me. Not sure what else to do, I pick up the phone and dial her number, but it goes to voicemail.

After driving for forty-five minutes, I park my car in front of the apartment building. As I get out, I take a deep breath but it does nothing to calm my shaking hands.

I have a spare key but I find the door unlocked, so I step inside.

I just hope I'm not too late.

Lauren is lying on a makeshift bed of sheets and blankets strewn across the living room floor. Sweat sheens her forehead, and her short hair clings to her skin.

"Lauren," I breathe out, rushing to her side. My hands find hers, gripping tightly enough to offer strength but gently enough not to hurt.

"Help me," she whispers, and it's all the permission I need.

Pushing my own fears aside, I guide her through each push and strangled breath.

"Focus on your baby," I coach. "Your beautiful baby needs you."

Pain twists Lauren's features, her knuckles white as they clutch at the sheets. Her breaths come in ragged gasps and in a calm tone, I continue to encourage her without revealing my own fears. "Keep pushing, Lauren. You're almost there."

Time seems to stretch past its usual boundaries, each second a minute, each minute an hour. Her cries are raw with urgency and fear, and I remain by her side, providing what little comfort I can.

Then just as I think of breaking my promise and calling 911, with a final, monumental effort, Lauren brings her child into the world. As her cries reach their peak, they suddenly stop, replaced by the piercing shrieks of a newborn baby, a little girl.

"Perfect," I whisper tearfully as I cradle the tiny life in bloodied towels. "Absolutely perfect."

But as I turn to Lauren, pride and joy ready to spill from my lips, I catch the paleness of her face and the lack of focus in her eyes. An icy fear begins to creep into my body.

"Lauren?" The newborn's cries are now a distant sound as I reach for her hand. "Stay with me, sweetie."

She mouths words without making a sound. She doesn't look like she's here at all. And there's blood, so much blood.

In a moment of utter terror, I realize that something is very wrong and she's slipping away fast.

My mind races as I lower the newborn into the makeshift crib hastily set up at the corner of the room. It's a poor substitute for a professional maternity ward, but it's all we have right now. The baby girl wails, oblivious to the danger her mother is in.

"Fight, Lauren! Please!" But even as I plead, I know it's too late. My hands, slick with blood, are useless right now. I was able to help bring life into this world and now there's a possibility that I may not be able to stop one from being taken away. "I need to call 911, Lauren."

"No," she chokes out, her fingers barely grazing mine. "No authorities. Promise me. Take care of my baby. Be her mother." She blinks, struggling to keep her eyes open. "Her name is Daisy."

"I promise," I say even as I reach into my bag for the phone.

But before I can lift it to my ear, Lauren goes still, leaving behind only the fragile wail of her baby girl.

FORTY-EIGHT

My hand shakes as I hold the phone, my other arm cradling the newborn. I know I should still make the call to 911, but I can't bring myself to do it. The baby's cries break through the numbness, pulling me back to reality.

As I feel her tiny body against mine, a surge of protectiveness rushes through me, heating up my skin and awakening something in my heart.

Gazing into the tiny face, an idea unfolds slowly in my mind.

Lauren wanted me to have her.

It was her final wish.

"Sweet girl," I murmur, brushing a kiss on top of her head. Suddenly, I feel a strong determination growing within me. Lauren's last request will be fulfilled. This child will always have love and protection in her life. And I'm the one to give it to her. I was chosen for this.

No one needs to know Daisy is not really mine, except Isobel and Tom, of course. I will have to make them understand. I'll find a way.

But the guilt is there, gnawing at the edges of my

conscience. If I had called for help sooner... But no, she begged me not to. I had to honor her request. But what if I end up being blamed for her death? When the authorities come for her body, won't they take Daisy away? With my history of mental illness, they'll never let me keep her.

It's terrible, unconscionable, but as I cradle Daisy to my chest, I come up with a plan. A plan to honor Lauren's last request. A plan to ensure Daisy is never taken away.

I need to do something about Lauren's body.

Her estrangement from her family and her isolation means that no immediate alarms will be raised if she disappears. I'm sure she will have taken time off from college classes to get ready for the birth. Time is on my side, if only for a moment.

I bring my attention back to the baby and the umbilical cord that still connects her to the life that just left us. I carefully unwrap the cord from around Daisy's tiny waist and with trembling hands, I gently snip it, careful not to hurt the baby.

As I work, I notice a bottle of pre-made formula on the coffee table. Lauren had been prepared for this moment, and I can't help but feel a fresh wave of sorrow wash over me. How could she have known? It's heartbreaking to think of her meticulous planning, all for a baby that she wouldn't be there to nurture.

It breaks my heart to realize that she'll never get to experience the joy of watching her baby grow. The weight of that loss feels like an anchor dragging me down.

As tears burn my eyes, I wrap the cord in a cloth to dispose of it somewhere on my way home.

"Shh," I whisper to Daisy, but it's more for myself than for her. "It's going to be okay."

As I clean her and dress her in a pink onesie, my mind races through scenarios, each more desperate than the last.

I need to erase all evidence of my presence in this apartment.

Then I'll think of what to do with Lauren.

Struggling to hold back tears, I lower Daisy into the green and white car seat I found in the living room next to a pristine white Moses basket, then I decide to dress Lauren as well to avoid leaving evidence that she gave birth.

After wiping her down with a towel dipped in warm water, I go to Lauren's room and rummage through the closet, finding a soft blue dress that she had loved.

I gently slip it over her lifeless body, smoothing the fabric as if it were a fragile treasure. The contrast of the vibrant dress against her pale skin breaks my heart. I wish more than anything that she were still here, sharing these moments with her baby.

When both Lauren and Daisy are cleaned and dressed, I get started on wiping down surfaces and collecting anything that might betray my involvement or suggest that a baby was born here. Bundling up the soiled linens with unsteady hands, my movements are mechanical, but I keep going. This has to be done. For me, for Daisy, and for Lauren.

With each step I take to cover my tracks, I feel the pull of an invisible thread, tugging me toward a path I can't return from.

"Nobody will know," I keep telling myself. "Nobody will ever know."

When I'm done, I cradle baby Daisy, her breaths shallow whispers against the stillness of the room. I'm so desperate to keep her. She has been pulled into my world by a twist of fate, and now I feel sick to my stomach at the thought of losing her, of surrendering her to a system that can leave children traumatized and abandoned.

Am I being too rash? Maybe adopting Daisy wouldn't be too hard if I told them the truth.

I could explain that Lauren wanted me to have her, that she asked me not to call anyone, even in her final moments. Maybe they would understand.

But the recent loss of my own baby and subsequent depression will count against me, won't it? They'll think I could be unfit.

They'll think I could be a dangerous mother. They'll snatch this baby from my arms and I'll be powerless to stop them.

"Your mommy loved you so much," I murmur, stroking Daisy's soft cheek with a finger. "She wants you to be safe, with me. Nobody will take you away. I won't let them."

She stirs, her hand curling around my finger, and something primal within me awakens, confirming that I'm doing the right thing.

I wipe away the trace of tears that had managed to escape, resolve hardening in my heart. I will keep Daisy safe, come hell or high water.

Lauren trusted me, chose me for this role, and I can't let her down. I won't.

I need to hurry because soon Isobel and Tom will come home and find me gone.

I grab a pen and paper and write. I'm holding my breath as I fold it, the note with a hasty scrawl across it masquerading as a final message from Lauren.

"Forgive me," I whisper, and it's not clear whom I'm asking for forgiveness—God, or myself.

I tuck the note in my pocket along with Lauren's phone. Then I steel myself for what comes next, what needs to be done.

First, I put the baby in the car, making sure she's safely strapped in and comfortable in her car seat, before putting the Moses basket into the car as well.

Finally, I go back and get Lauren, feeling uncomfortable at having to leave Daisy in the car even for a moment. My legs feel heavy with dread as I approach her, my pulse thundering in my ears. Before I do what I know needs to be done, I drop down next to her, pressing my lips to her forehead for what feels like an eternity. Her face, once full of life and laughter, is now slack, her skin pale and cool to the touch. A sob rises up my throat, but I swallow it down. There's no time for tears. If I break down now, I won't be able to stop.

I gently lift her limp body into my arms, and it takes all my strength not to collapse under the weight—not just of her lifeless form, but of the crushing reality that she's gone. This girl I've known for years, loved like my own, is dead.

Since she's not easy to carry and I have to keep checking the surroundings to make sure I'm not being watched, it takes me a while to move Lauren to the car. Luckily, the doors in this apartment complex open out onto the street rather than into a common hallway, giving us a clear and direct route to my car, which I parked as close to the building as possible, which also makes it easy for me to keep an eye on the baby.

I shift my weight, cradling Lauren in my arms as if she were only sleeping, her head lolling against my shoulder. I struggle to hold onto her, trying desperately not to think about the fact that she will never move, breathe, or laugh again.

I blink away tears threatening to spill from my eyes, focusing on the task at hand. But a deep, guttural sob escapes from my lips despite my best efforts, causing me to shake so uncontrollably that I almost drop her. Still, I refuse to let her go. Adjusting my grip with determination, I take a deep breath and continue on.

Each time I check over my shoulder, I tell myself that if anyone sees us, they'll think she's just passed out, drunk or sick. Not dead. Please, God, not dead. But she *is*, and she's not coming back.

I finally manage to place her in the back seat of the car next to her baby girl's car seat before collapsing into the driver's seat, taking a moment to catch my breath and gulp down the tears and bile lingering inside my throat.

My sweaty hands shake on the hard plastic of the steering wheel, their tremors echoing my pounding heart. I force down another sob, glancing at Lauren's pale face in the rearview mirror.

The car seems to vibrate with my pain, with the emotion pouring from every inch of me. My chest heaves, tears blurring the haunting image of Lauren's unmoving reflection.

The sight of her feels like a punch to the stomach, but I grit my teeth and turn the key in the ignition.

The drive to a clifftop above a nearby deserted beach is a blur of streetlights and, when I arrive, the sea churns below, foam-crested waves thrashing and roaring.

"Goodbye, Lauren," I say, though the wind snatches away my words. With tears heating up my eyes, I kiss her forehead, allowing my lips to linger on her cool skin for a moment longer. "Sweet girl, I promise to take care of your baby... no matter what," I gasp, then just as I catch my breath, a painful hiccup pushes past my lips and I start to cry so hard that my knees grow weak, my legs threatening to give way.

The cliff edge looms, and then, biting hard on my bottom lip until it throbs with pain, I muster every ounce of resolve to tip Lauren over the side.

She doesn't land in the water as I'd hoped but on a part of the beach that's slightly hidden from sight, a small cove obscured by rocky outcrops. Hopefully, there will be a tide and it will carry her away, erasing the evidence of this day and what I have done.

I leave the note on the cliff, tucked under a stone to keep it from being blown away by the wind.

Guilt and relief wrestle inside me as I return to the car, my hands clawing at my chest as I sob, my fingers gripping onto the fabric of my shirt as if to tear it open.

I've crossed a line from which there is no return.

It's close to seven when I get home. I bring Daisy in with me and when Tom arrives home, I go into our downstairs bathroom with her and feed her to keep her quiet. I listen as Tom heads upstairs to change, and then I sneak out and lower Daisy into the baby basket before placing it on the front porch. I make sure she is wrapped snugly in a baby blanket I found in the car seat and tuck a note I wrote earlier next to her.

"Be brave, little one. I'll be back soon," I whisper, pressing a kiss to her forehead. Then I ring the doorbell before hurrying back into the house and climbing under the blanket on the sofa.

FORTY-NINE

Two Weeks Later

Long after midnight, I'm still sitting at the kitchen table. Memories of the night I pushed Lauren over the cliff flood my mind as I clutch on to the letter I discovered in the envelope Isobel gave me. My fingers trace the words, as though they might rearrange themselves into something else. But they don't. They can't.

It's all here in black and white. Lauren slept with Tom and they had a baby together. A baby I have been raising for two weeks, pretending she's mine. A baby I have fallen in love with.

My mind takes me back to that day I read Isobel's diary and it all falls into place. The secret she was talking about wasn't mine. It was Lauren's.

Tom, my husband and the man I love and trust so deeply, is just one flight of stairs away, sleeping peacefully next to his baby daughter. How can he have done this? With Lauren, of all people, our daughter's best friend since childhood. Lauren, the girl I treated like my own daughter. How could she do this to me?

All of a sudden, anger pushes me forward, a livid force that seizes my limbs and hurls me toward the kitchen door and toward the staircase. The letter crumples in my palm as I climb the steps. By the time I get to the top, it hits me why Larry didn't turn us in. Tom must have told him the truth, that the baby is actually his.

In the moonlight streaming through the bedroom window, Tom is a picture of innocence as he lies in our bed, fast asleep, a soft snore escaping his lips.

Before I do anything else, I pick up the baby and take her to Isobel's room because things are about to get ugly.

When I return to the room, and continue to watch Tom sleep, a bitter laugh claws at my throat. Does he dream of her?

My fingers flick the switch and harsh light floods the room. He stirs with a groan, then his eyes flutter open—eyes that soon widen in horror as they register my expression.

I throw the crumpled letter at him, he opens it and scans over the words. Then his eyes meet mine and I see it. Guilt. It's written all over his face. He doesn't need to say a word because it's all true. Every damning word.

"Daisy..." I swallow hard. "She's your daughter. You had an affair? With Lauren?"

He swallows, the silence between us stretching out to an unbearable length as he looks down at the letter, then back at me. "Nora, I... I can explain."

"Explain?" I scoff, and the words feel like acid on my tongue. "You slept with our daughter's best friend. Your lover's child is sleeping in the other room... and you want to explain?" I feel like a volcano threatening to erupt, the fury flowing, hot and unstoppable within me. "Go on, Tom, explain! I'm listening."

"No!" The vehemence in his denial startles me. "I didn't have an affair with Lauren. You have to believe me."

"You're kidding me, right?" I choke back a laugh, a sound so hollow it scares even me. "How can I possibly believe anything you say now?"

"Please, Nora..." Tom's Adam's apple bobs. "Look at me, baby." He gets out of bed and takes a tentative step forward. "I did what I thought was necessary—for us."

"Us?" The word is poison on my tongue. "You think betraying our marriage was for us?"

As I stand there shaking, he pours it all out there, every sordid detail of what was going on behind my back while I wrestled with depression.

He makes it sound so simple.

He wanted a baby for us, so he came up with the brilliantly twisted idea of using Lauren as a surrogate. She needed the money, and she cared about us. She accepted, and they slept together when Isobel brought Lauren to stay with us in July.

It's so ridiculous. Unbelievable. Unbearable.

"Every choice I made," he pleads as I stumble to the bed and sink down, "was to give us what we lost. You wanted a baby so badly that I thought—"

I stare at him in disbelief. "How could you play God with our lives, Tom? How did you even come up with such a terrible idea? Lauren was our daughter's best friend, for God's sake!"

He looks so ashamed, his shoulders sinking. "I know. It just happened, it's hard to explain. One weekend, when Lauren visited with Isobel, they were talking about surrogacy. Lauren told Izzy that she'd consider it," he continues, "if the price was right. That's when the idea came to me."

The room spins as a nauseating mix of betrayal and horror washes over me.

"So, you paid her. You paid our daughter's friend to have your baby? Without telling me? And you expected me to just accept that? Or were you never going to tell me? Does Isobel know?"

He shakes his head. "She doesn't know the truth. Please,

baby, try to understand." He drops to his knees in front of the bed, in front of me.

I stare at him, my chest heaving. "There's nothing to understand, Tom. This is beyond belief."

He's babbling now, tears in his eyes. "Lauren was strapped for cash, Nora. And you know I... I've always wanted a child with my DNA, my blood."

"With your *DNA*? Is that what this is to you? Just some kind of... genetic vanity?"

"No, Nora, it's not like that—I—"

"Isn't it?" I interject sharply. "You do realize there are ways to do this officially, right?"

"I couldn't go through official channels, not without involving you. Not without your consent. I didn't tell you because you were going through a lot. I planned to, once the baby was born."

"Tom," I manage, "how could you? You slept with her. You cheated on me."

In my mind, I see images of Lauren—so young, so vulnerable. He took advantage of her, I see that so clearly. And now, she's gone, leaving behind a child born from desperation and deceit. If Tom didn't get her pregnant, she would still be alive.

"Nora, it wasn't like that. It was only once." He's crying too, tears trailing down his cheeks. "Lauren had an app to check... that she was fertile. We had sex then. Once. It was so clinical. A necessity. There was no chemistry between us."

It's sickening, but I can almost visualize the scene he is describing, a twisted business deal.

Tom continues, his words laced with shame. "I drank a lot first. I hated the idea, Nora. Sleeping with anyone but you"—he drags his palms down his face—"let alone Lauren. She agreed to keep it secret, and the plan was that once the baby was born, she'd offer it to us for adoption. But then she decided she wanted to keep it." He rubs the back of his neck. "Nora, I know how this looks, but I didn't kill her, I promise. When she went into labor, okay, I—I was there. But I couldn't do anything. I had no idea what I was doing, and my panic was just making her even more stressed, so I left when she asked me to. She said she'd call a friend to be with her instead." He pauses and rakes a hand through his hair. "She didn't want to go to the hospital."

Before he can say anything else, before I can confront him further, I hear a muffled sob behind me.

I turn and see Isobel standing in the doorway with Daisy.

I've never seen my daughter so angry. Her skin is pale and her eyes are at first wide and round, then they narrow into thin slits.

"Isobel—" Her name comes out as a strangled plea from my lips, but it's too late. She knows. She heard everything.

I hurry to her and take the baby from her arms because she looks like she's about to faint.

Saying nothing to either of us, Isobel stumbles back, turns and runs off. By the time we get downstairs, she's out the front door and getting into her car.

Then she's driving off in the middle of the night.

"I'm going after her," I say to Tom. "She's upset, she could get into an accident."

Tom nods, then without thinking, I hurry to the car and secure Daisy into the car seat. I slip behind the wheel and turn the key. The engine roars to life but before I can drive off, Tom is beside me, the passenger door slamming shut.

I soon realize Isobel is heading to the cliff and we follow her. Less than thirty minutes later, our car skids to a halt at the top, gravel crunching under tires, and I scramble out and get Daisy from the backseat, wrapping her in a blanket.

The sky above is inky-black, with only the faint glimmer of stars overhead, and the world below is swallowed by darkness.

As I hold on to the squirming baby, a gust of wind rushes in from the sea, cool and biting at my skin.

Around us, there's still evidence of the vigil. A ring of half-melted candles sits at the cliff edge surrounded by floral wreaths. A framed picture of Lauren rests in the center of it all, her face smiling back at us in the glow of Isobel's car headlights. The flowers, picture, and melted candles appear ghostly in the glow, witnesses to the grief that lingers here.

I shiver, suddenly aware that I'm standing on the edge of the cliff in just my satin pajamas. The thin fabric does little to protect me from the chill that creeps into my bones. But I can't think of me right now. Isobel, who's now getting out of her car, needs me.

"Isobel!" Tom stumbles after my daughter, who has parked a little too close to the edge. But she turns on him, her eyes wild with fury.

"You made me doubt my best friend," she hisses. "You made me think she was a liar. Maybe Lauren wouldn't be dead now if I'd known the truth. What you did was terrible, but she was never trying to destroy our family on purpose. She wasn't obsessed with you. She did it because she cared, and because she was vulnerable, and it was all your idea. You used her."

"Isobel, please—" Tom starts, but there's nothing he can say.

"I would have been there for her," Isobel continues then her eyes grow wider. "After all your lies, what if... what if Lauren didn't jump? What if you..." She chokes on the words, and I can see her mind grappling with a darkness too terrible to put into words. "What if you killed her?"

"I did not," Tom answers back, tears streaming down his face. "I promise you, Isobel. I did not do that."

"I don't believe you." Isobel edges closer to the cliff edge. "I don't... I don't want to live with this."

"Isobel, no!" The cry tears from my throat as I wrap my arms tighter around Daisy.

"It's all my fault," she says, gazing down at the water below. "I should have believed her, been there for her."

"Isobel," I scream, "don't do this. Please, baby. Look at me, look at your mother, I'm here. Please stop."

My every muscle is taut, yet I'm rooted to this spot, petrified. My mind screams for me to move, to act, but my body refuses to listen.

Then Tom moves past me and edges closer to Isobel. "Izzy, please. I'm so sorry, sweetie. None of this is your fault. It's all mine. I'm to blame for Lauren's death, not you."

"Sorry?" Isobel sobs. "For which part, Tom? For lying? For sleeping with my best friend? Or for killing her?"

"Izzy," he gets closer until he's standing next to her on the cliff edge, "I should have told you the truth. But I was scared. Scared of hurting you and your mom. Your mother was fragile and then there's your eating disorder. I didn't want you to lose both me and your best friend. I didn't want to trigger—I thought..."

"Thought what?" Her voice rises with the wind that whips around us.

"That protecting you meant keeping it a secret." His words are laden with regret. "But I was wrong. I am so, so sorry. I made a big mistake."

"Sorry doesn't bring her back, Tom!" Isobel's shout slices through the night air. Then before I can process what is happening, her flat palms are on Tom's chest and she shoves him so hard that he falls, disappearing over the edge.

FIFTY

"Tom!" I scream, my heart pounding in my chest, a raw mix of fear and desperation choking my throat.

The cliff is sharp and dangerous, with steep edges that drop off into darkness. The sound of the ocean waves crashing below is muffled by the cool night air.

At first, it all looks hopeless, but then I see something, a movement.

Tom's arms stretch desperately over the edge, his fingers clawing at the rocky ledge, trying to find a grip. His trembling hands barely manage to hold on to the loose dirt and stone that crumbles beneath his weight. Thank God. If I hurry, maybe I can save him.

Daisy whimpers softly as I hand her to Isobel. "Watch the baby," I instruct, then I'm sprinting forward over the loose stones and grass.

Déjà vu crashes over me, a memory from years ago.

I cannot let it happen. I won't let my daughter make the same mistake I did when I was sixteen.

I won't allow Isobel to carry the same guilt I've been carrying all these years.

Isobel is frozen in shock, her face a mask of horror as she watches Tom's desperate struggle to hold on.

As I reach the edge of the cliff, the wind whipping around my hair, I throw myself down onto the ground and grab Tom's wrists, pulling him with all my strength.

"Tom, hold on!" I brace against his weight. His eyes lock on to mine, wide with shock and fear. He's dragging me back with him now, but I can't let go.

With a grunt, I pull, muscles burning, heart screaming, until miraculously he finds a way to pull his torso up over the rocky face of the cliff.

Finally, with one last heave, he collapses fully onto solid ground.

"Thank you," he says, gasping.

The world tilts as I hold him. Then I think of Isobel, and of Daisy, and I crawl toward them. Isobel is sitting, rocking Daisy who is somehow slumbering peacefully. They are safe. Both my daughters are alive. We'll all be okay now.

Because however Daisy came into this world, I love her with all my heart, and that will never change.

I turn back and watch as Tom slowly pulls himself up into a crouch. I don't know how I can ever forgive him for sleeping with Lauren, even if it was just to give us a baby.

But whose sin is greater, mine or his?

I did not kill Lauren, but I hid the truth about her death from her parents, from her friends, from everyone who loved her.

I led them to believe she took her own life. I could try to explain, but they will not understand, no one will. And the police certainly won't believe me.

So, I swallow my confession, yet again. I let it sit like a stone deep in my mind, alongside the other secret I carry.

Because long before Lauren died, I watched another person

fall from this very cliff. And that time, I did nothing to save them.

FIFTY-ONE

ISOBEL

At first, a surge of relief washes over me when Tom rolls onto solid ground, gasping for air. But the longer I watch him, my relief curdles into something darker.

I shoved him. It was an accident—a reflex fueled by anger and disgust—but for a fleeting, monstrous moment, I wished... I wished he would plummet into the sea below, be swallowed by the churning waters, to pay for what he did to Lauren, to my mother, to me, to our family.

"Isobel, are you all right?" Mom's voice cuts through my tangled thoughts.

I turn away, my eyes stinging. "I'm fine."

Mom has taken Daisy back from me and is holding her close, tears sliding down her cheeks. The sight should soften me, but it doesn't. Not now. Not after everything.

"I need to go home." I wrap my arms around my body and start walking in the direction of my car.

"Isobel, please," Mom begs. "Don't go off alone. You're too upset. Let's drive back together."

The idea of being trapped in a car with Mom and Tom feels

suffocating. I need space. I need to process what just happened —what I nearly did.

"Tom can take your car and you can drive with me," she insists. "Please, Isobel."

I look at Tom, still crouched on the ground, his head in his hands, and then back to my mother. Her face is etched with worry, and her wispy blonde hair tousled by the wind.

"Okay," I finally say, and I slip into the passenger seat of her car while Mom puts Daisy in her car seat.

The road unwinds before us, a ribbon in the night. I keep my focus out the window, watching the blur of scenery rush by.

"Isobel," Mom continues softly, "we'll get through this."

I nod but say nothing. There are too many thoughts crowding my mind, leaving no room for empty words. Tom's betrayal, Lauren's death, what I just did—all form a knot inside me so tight it feels like it might never come undone.

When we're fifteen minutes from the house, the car lurches as we hit a bump in the road. Something slides across the floor and nudges against my shoe. In the fading light, I lean down to pick it up and when I lift it into view, I inhale sharply.

The phone is encased in a distinctive cover—a vibrant medley of blues and purples swirled into a galaxy pattern, dotted with tiny specks of glittering stars.

It's the same one Lauren had excitedly shown off after winning it at the Amberfield Outdoor Movie Night Festival last spring. The festival we went to together—back when things were simple.

My mouth feels suddenly dry. How did Lauren's phone get into my mother's car?

"Isobel, do you want to talk?" Mom asks. "I know what happened is—"

"No." I tuck the phone out of sight. "No talking."

She doesn't push further, her focus returning to the winding road ahead.

Panic claws at my insides as I slip Lauren's phone into my coat pocket.

As Mom's car rolls into the driveway, the familiar sight of my home doesn't offer me any comfort. Tom isn't here yet; we've arrived before him.

As soon as the car comes to a stop, I jump out and quickly make my way up the porch steps while Mom fumbles with Daisy's car seat and calls for me.

"Isobel, wait! We need to—"

But I'm already through the front door, then I'm taking the stairs two at a time. Every nerve in my body screams that something is terribly wrong.

Once inside my bedroom, I lock the door, something I rarely do, and collapse onto the bed, the phone now a burning weight in my hand.

Why was it in Mom's car?

I power the device on, and soon the screen illuminates the shadowed corners of my room. It's not hard to unlock it since I know Lauren's password like she knew mine.

As the screen comes to life, I'm greeted by a wallpaper of us —Lauren and me, arms draped over each other's shoulders, grinning carelessly into the camera.

Fresh tears fill my eyes. Even when we were no longer friends, she didn't change her wallpaper.

"Sweetie, please talk to me!" Mom is outside the door, but I can't face her, not now. I push her words away, focusing on the phone.

"Isobel, open the door!"

"Not now, Mom," I say through gritted teeth.

"Isobel, you're scaring me..." The sound of her voice—so raw and vulnerable—almost breaks me.

"Later," I promise, though the word tastes like ash in my mouth.

"Please..."

"Later," I repeat, firmer this time, and she seems to get the message because I can hear her walking away.

Alone again, I turn back to Lauren's phone.

As I navigate through the digital remnants of my friend's life, I steel myself for the truths that will change everything. Because deep down, I know. I know that I'm about to discover something terrible, and nothing will ever be the same again.

My fingers tremble as I scroll through Lauren's call history. There it is—Tom's name, a call from that day I saw him in Amberfield. But it's not the sight of his name that makes me feel queasy; it's another name, one right at the top. The last call she ever made.

To Nora, my mom. My vision blurs, and a cold sweat breaks across my skin. Why didn't Mom mention that she spoke to Lauren before she died? If she did, she must have known that Lauren was pregnant. She must have known Daisy was her baby all along. Did she know the truth about Tom and Lauren too? Maybe Lauren confessed to her on that call.

Dizziness overtakes me as I switch on the light and yank open the bedside drawer, pulling out the article about Lauren's death that I found in Mom's purse when I was looking for the memorial envelope.

Until now, I avoided reading about Lauren's death because it was too painful. But now, I need to know the ugly truth.

Sweat forms on my forehead as I smooth it against my thigh.

Then I notice that it's very old actually, the ink almost faded. It must be from years ago.

A Tragic Fall from Gray Peak Cliffs Leaves Community Reeling.

The headline talks about a woman who fell to her death on Gray Peak Beach.

At the bottom of the article is a grainy photo of another woman, an older woman named Amber Stevens.

My mother's maiden name was Stevens.

Mom told me her mother died of a heart attack. But this article, dated twenty years ago, says the woman fell and left behind a sixteen-year-old daughter.

"Last week," the article begins, "the sleepy town of Ellery Creek was shaken by the tragic loss of one of its own. Amber Stevens, beloved local chef and single mother, fell to her death from the scenic clifftop at Gray Peak Beach. Forty-one-year-old Stevens left behind a sixteen-year-old daughter, Nora, who friends say was the light of her life."

The words splinter inside me as I read on.

"The circumstances surrounding her death remain unclear, but authorities have ruled it as a tragic accident. Amber Stevens was well-known in the community for her charitable work and her dedication to her family. Her sudden death has left the community in mourning and her daughter devastated."

"Mom..." I whisper as I skim the lines again, faster.

Everything aligns with a sickening click. Both Lauren and my grandmother fell from the same cliff.

When I realize what happened, my entire body goes cold.

It was Mom. She did it. She killed Lauren.

And maybe she killed her own mother too.

FIFTY-TWO

The door to Tom and Mom's room creaks open, and I find her there. My mother, curled up on the edge of her bed, her shoulders quivering.

I take a step forward. "Mom?"

She doesn't startle; it's as if she knew I would come. Without looking at me, she takes a shaky breath. "I told Tom to leave for a while." Her words are feather-light but laden with a depth of sorrow. "I needed to think."

I step into the room, the air thick with tension, every nerve in my body pulled taut. The only thing that matters now is the truth.

"I found this." My hand trembles as I thrust the crumpled article toward her.

Immediate panic flits across her face, her blue eyes darting from my face to the paper clutched in my hand.

"Tell me about her," I say, pointing to the grainy photograph. "Your mother. How did she really die, Mom?"

Her lips quiver. Her complexion is completely drained of color. If I've ever seen a guilty person, it's now.

"You said she had a heart attack," I force out, then before

she can recover and come up with lies, I ask the next question. "Did you push your mother down the cliff, like you pushed Lauren?" I pause to let her digest the accusations. "I know you were the last person to speak to Lauren on the phone before she died."

I watch as a single tear escapes her eye and trails down her cheek.

The room suddenly feels chilly, and the silence between us grows wider with each second that ticks by. My mother seems to have shrunk somehow.

"Isobel, you have to understand—"

"Understand what, Mom?" I glance at Daisy, knowing she's not safe here with her. My mother, the killer.

Mom wraps her arms around herself as if to hold herself together. "Your grandmother... she never wanted you. She told me to get rid of you, to—to abort you or give you up for adoption."

The confession slices through the air.

"Is that supposed to justify anything?" I demand. "Does it make it right? To kill?"

"Never!" The word explodes from her lips. "But the pain, Isobel, the fear of losing you—it twisted everything inside me."

"Twisted enough to make you a murderer?" I spit as tears attempt to drown my words. "And what about Lauren? You killed her too, didn't you? You killed my friend because she was pregnant with Tom's baby. Don't even think about lying."

Her silence is deafening.

As if she has shoved me hard, I stumble backward toward the door.

My mother is a murderer. It's unthinkable, unfathomable. Yet, here it is, the bitter truth sprawled out between us, stark and undeniable.

"Isobel... that's not how it happened, how it looks. I only—"

"Save it! You pushed her down that cliff. You killed my

grandmother and my best friend. You stole her baby." I cover my mouth with a trembling hand as another realization hits me. "Did you... Did you kill my father too? You admitted that he's dead."

"To me," she murmurs. "Dead to me. I didn't do anything to him. He left me... you. He didn't want you, Izzy. But I didn't kill him."

"But you did kill two other people. You are a murderer, Mom."

When she says nothing, I cross the room and lift Daisy from the attached bed, then hurry with her to my room. Behind me, I hear her calling, wanting to explain as she runs after me, but I make it inside and lock the door, pushing earplugs into my ears so I can't hear her lies anymore.

Still holding Daisy, I rock back and forth on my bed, needing her comfort more than anything, the last piece of my friend I have left.

I feel like I'm drowning, and in this moment, I am completely isolated. My mother, the woman I trusted and loved the most, is a monster.

"Lauren, I'm so sorry," I whimper between gasps for air. "I promise, I will make it right."

FIFTY-THREE

NORA

Twenty Years Ago

The chalky edge of the clifftop crumbles slightly under my sneakers as I look down at the vast expanse of the ocean that sprawls below us.

"Watch your step, Nora," Mom warns without looking at me, staring at the horizon where sky and sea melt into one. "Beautiful, isn't it?" she continues, a rare smile touching her lips.

My mother is a strict woman. I can only remember the one time she smiled genuinely: when we moved from New York to her hometown of Ellery Creek, after my father passed away. She had always talked about the beach and how as a child she used to spend countless hours exploring the rocky coves or pretending she was a mermaid, diving into the ocean to explore her underwater kingdom.

Now that we live here, I understand why she loves it so much.

Since we don't live very far, every evening after dinner, my mom and I drive up here to this clifftop, where she used to come as a child, in order to get the best view of the ocean. It has become our ritual, but today is different. Today, I am going to tell her my secret, and it may very well be the last time she joins me on this cliff.

She doesn't know yet. She doesn't know how everything is about to change.

"Mom..." I start, secretly crossing my fingers inside my jeans pockets.

She turns to face me, her moss-green eyes searching mine. "What is it, Nora?"

A raven caws overhead as if warning me to keep my mouth shut. "I... I have to tell you something."

"What?" She stops walking and her brows furrow. "What is it, girl? Speak up."

That's my mom, never the kind to beat around the bush. Always wanting to face things head on. But I'm not sure how she will take this. Maybe I should listen to that raven.

"Last night, I took a test," I say, my words trembling.

"A test? At night?" She plants her hands on her hips. "What are you trying to say, Nora? Get to the point."

The wind whistles through the tall grass on the cliff, and the waves crash against the rocks below us.

"I'm pregnant, Mom."

There it is, the truth. My mother's mouth falls open and the look of disappointment, anger, and confusion she gives me is one I'll never forget.

Then, without saying a word to me, she starts walking again.

"Mom. We need to talk about this."

I struggle to keep pace with her brisk steps, but she doesn't slow down or look at me, just keeps marching forward, her jaw set in a hard line.

"About what you're going to do?" she asks coldly, startling me with the venom in her tone. "There is nothing to talk about. Abortion is the only option here."

I stumble, nearly losing my footing on the uneven ground. "No," I blurt out, the single word heavy with all the defiance I can muster. But inside, I'm crumbling.

"Then give it up for adoption," she retorts without missing a beat, as if she's been mulling over these options long before I told her about my pregnancy.

"Give it up? Like it's just some... some *thing*?"

"Exactly." She finally turns to face me and I see the tears rolling down her cheeks. "Right now, that's what it is—a thing. A thing that will ruin your life."

Tears start to pool in my eyes too and, taking a deep breath, I tilt up my chin and push my shoulders back. "No, I won't do it. This is my baby."

"You don't have a choice, Nora," she says, her tone final. "You're sixteen, far too young to be a mother. And if you won't listen to reason, there are other ways."

"Other ways?" Panic flutters in my chest.

"Yes, places you can go. Homes for girls like you."

I stumble back. She must be talking about shelters for young expecting mothers, where they are hidden away in secrecy until they give birth and their babies are given to couples desperate for children.

"Mom, please... you can't do that." Fresh tears start and I feel them stream down my face.

"Please won't change anything, Nora. This is for your own good. I'll do whatever it takes to protect you. Even from yourself."

"Mom, please," I choke out. "I can't—"

"You have no choice, baby," she murmurs, stepping forward with arms wide open.

But instead of walking into them, I take a step back. "Don't touch me!" The words erupt from me and, when she refuses to keep her distance, I shove hard at her.

She staggers, a gasp escaping her lips, her body swaying

close to the edge. As she tries to catch herself, her foot slips and she tumbles backward, her arms flailing wildly.

Shock freezes me as she falls. But somehow, she manages to hold on, grasping on to a protruding root from the cliffside. Her fingers clutch it with a desperate strength.

"Help me," she gasps.

Her grip on the root is slipping, and I'm frozen in place, unable or unwilling to do anything.

Her wide eyes lock with mine. "Help me and I'll... you can have the baby!"

She continues to plead and makes endless promises, but I can barely hear her. All I see is her surviving this and forcing me to kill my child or give it to a stranger.

How can I rescue her without putting my child in danger?

"Mom..." I trail off, unable to form words. There's a hidden part of me that whispers terrible things. That tells me I will find freedom only in letting her fall.

As I watch, her grasp gives way, her fingers slipping. A cry wrenches from her chest, a sound so raw it makes my skin crawl.

Then she falls and I hear her brief and terrified scream before it's cut off.

A shudder courses through me, a mixture of fear and twisted relief.

I feel my knees weaken, and I sink to the ground, trembling.

Moments pass, or maybe hours. The wind howls in my ears, cold and biting, but all I can hear is the faint echo of her scream.

In the eerie stillness that follows, I isolate a single strand of hair between my trembling fingers, just like Mom used to do to me when I was bad. I tug, the sharp sting of the pluck sending a tiny ripple of pain through my scalp.

FIFTY-FOUR

ISOBEL

Now

Hours after confronting my mother, I wait until I'm certain she's asleep before pulling a duffel bag from under my bed and starting to pack.

The house is quiet, suffocatingly so, as I slip into the hallway, holding Daisy, and head to the nursery, where I switch off the baby monitor so Mom won't hear us. Then I pack Daisy's belongings as well.

When I'm done, I gather Daisy in my arms again and look down at her sweet face, her small features relaxed as she sleeps, her tiny fingers gripping the edge of her blanket. The innocence and faith she exudes fill me with the courage I need. As I lean down to softly kiss her forehead, I whisper, "It's just us now, sweet girl."

Her lashes drift open for a brief second, and I smile as warmth spreads through my chest.

Cradling her with one arm and careful not to wake her, I zip up the diaper bag. I'm very much aware that this is a huge responsibility, but as she snuggles into me, a sigh escaping her lips, I promise to protect her with everything in me.

I have no clue where we'll end up, but anywhere is safer than here, living with twisted murderers and liars, not to mention a stalker ex-boyfriend somewhere nearby.

I will raise Lauren's stolen baby on my own. It will be hard, yes, but if Mom could do it, so can I.

The only thing I leave behind is a note.

If you ever loved us, Mom, let us go.

A LETTER FROM L.G. DAVIS

Dear reader,

Thank you for diving into *Stolen Baby*, set in the charming, fictional town of Ellery Creek. I hope you enjoyed exploring this captivating community and following the lives of Nora, Isobel, Lauren, Tom, and little Daisy. I truly relished writing about Daisy and watching her discover the world during those precious first days of life.

Ellery Creek, with its beloved Ellery Oak and heart-warming traditions, was a joy to bring to life. I hope you experienced a touch of the oak's legendary good luck as you read.

If the story left you feeling chilled to the core, I hope you found comfort at the annual Warm Up Fest with a steaming mug of hot chocolate and one of Mrs. Donahue's delicious pastries, while staying cozy in a pair of warm socks from Mrs. Henderson's Knitting Booth.

If you enjoyed *Stolen Baby* and want to stay updated on my future books, I invite you to join my email list. You'll be among the first to hear about new releases, exclusive content, and exciting updates.

www.bookouture.com/l-g-davis

Hearing your thoughts and feelings about my books is one of the greatest joys of being an author. Your insights and support help me continue creating stories that connect with readers like you. So, if you enjoyed *Stolen Baby*, please consider sharing your experience by leaving a review.

I genuinely love hearing from my readers. Whether you want to share your thoughts on the book or just say hello, please don't hesitate to reach out. Your messages bring a smile to my face and inspire me to keep writing.

Thank you for reading my books. I'm already looking forward to sharing new stories with you.

Yours always,

Liz

www.lgdavis.com

 facebook.com/LGDavisBooks

 x.com/lgdavisauthor

 instagram.com/lgdavisauthor

ACKNOWLEDGMENTS

Writing *Stolen Baby* has been an extraordinary experience, and I am filled with gratitude for the amazing people who have supported me along the way.

To the wonderful team at Bookouture—thank you for your dedication and hard work in bringing this story to life. You've helped transform a manuscript into a book, and there are countless people behind the scenes whose tireless efforts have made this possible. From the first round of edits to the final touches, your commitment has been truly inspiring, and I am humbled by each and every contribution.

To my editor, Rhianna Louise—what can I say? I couldn't imagine being on this journey with anyone else. Our brainstorming sessions are some of the most cherished moments in my writing process. Your thoughtful insights and belief in me, even during the toughest moments, were key in shaping *Stolen Baby* into what it is today. Thank you for pushing me beyond my comfort zone and for your unwavering faith in this story—and in me.

To my family—Toye and our wonderful children—thank you for being my rock and my constant source of strength. Your love, encouragement and understanding have seen me through every late night, every moment of frustration and joy. You've shared in the highs and lows, and I couldn't be more grateful. I love you all deeply.

And to my readers, old and new—knowing that this story has resonated with you is the greatest reward. Your reviews and feedback mean the world to me, and I'm so thankful for every one of you. Thank you for embracing *Stolen Baby*, and I'm excited to share many more stories with you in the future.

With all my gratitude,

Liz

PUBLISHING TEAM

Turning a manuscript into a book requires the efforts of many people. The publishing team at Bookouture would like to acknowledge everyone who contributed to this publication.

Commercial
Lauren Morrissette
Hannah Richmond
Imogen Allport

Data and analysis
Mark Alder
Mohamed Bussuri

Editorial
Rhianna Louise
Lizzie Brien

Copyeditor
Donna Hillyer

Proofreader
Emily Boyce

Marketing

Alex Crow

Melanie Price

Occy Carr

Cíara Rosney

Martyna Młynarska

Operations and distribution

Marina Valles

Stephanie Straub

Joe Morris

Production

Hannah Snetsinger

Mandy Kullar

Jen Shannon

Ria Clare

Publicity

Kim Nash

Noelle Holten

Jess Readett

Sarah Hardy

Rights and contracts

Peta Nightingale

Richard King

Saidah Graham

Made in United States
Orlando, FL
26 January 2025

57854272R00168